SPRINGBROOKVILLE

SPRINGBROOKVILLE

AN LT NICHOLS MYSTERY

ALBERT WAITT

LEVEL
BEST BOOKS

First published by Level Best Books 2025

First edition

ISBN: 978-1-68512-938-5

Cover art by Level Best Designs

This book was professionally typeset on Reedsy.
Find out more at reedsy.com

To Kim, Sydney, Aaron, Betty, Elvis, and Presley.

Praise for Springbrookville

"As usual with any of Waitt's LT Nichols books, there's humor, pathos, and an ending that surprises."—Sarah Bewley, Author of The Eden County Mysteries

"Well-drawn characters and small-town intrigue fuel a twisty plot in this mystery featuring intrepid police chief LT Nichols. An excellent, entertaining read!"—Alan Orloff, Anthony, Agatha, Derringer, and Thriller Award-Winning author of *Late Checkout*

Chapter One

If my eyes had been on the road, I wouldn't have hit the kid on the bike. It didn't happen because I was daydreaming, envisioning Suzanne Anderson smiling at me from across a candlelit table. I had no idea why she'd invited me to dinner, and the event was still a day away. I'd managed to drive our relationship off a cliff years earlier just by being myself, so my hopes there were modest. Nor was I distracted by the oaks and maples lining Providence Hill, a billboard of red and orange, and the kind of foliage people drove hours to see. It was the clear-cut construction site at the top that got me. I couldn't help staring into the mounds of dirt, piles of desiccated limbs, and stacks of chipped, gray logs. I must have passed it ten times a day, and it pulled me in every time. Something was there for me, and I kept missing it.

The boy could barely reach the pedals of his ten-speed, and the football uniform he sported—pants, practice jersey, shoulder pads, and helmet—probably wasn't helping. He was wobbling like crazy. I told myself to watch for him. But he and I arrived at the cut at the same time. The moment he swerved into my lane, I was locked on a tangle of unearthed stumps, roots twisting from it like tentacles. When I finally realized what was happening, I whipped the wheel. It was too late. He careened off my right fender and toppled.

I jumped out of the Bronco. He was already picking up the bike when I reached him. We were lucky. I'd been crawling, looking for who-knows-what in that scorched earth, and his fall had been cushioned by the blanket of leaves that covered the roadside. His gear had also protected him. He inspected the Schwinn like it was made of gold.

"Are you hurt?" I said, my heart barreling in my chest.

"I'm okay," he said. He looked up and noticed the uniform. "Oh, shit."

"You're sure?"

"Chipped some paint," he said through his facemask.

"Who cares about that? Are *you* hurt?" He was small and thin, no lineman.

"I'm okay until my brother sees I messed up his bike." He took off his helmet and checked the navy blue with the yellow double Ls. "Sorry for the accident."

"Not your fault," I said. There was no excuse for an officer, never mind a police chief, to nail a kid on a bicycle. He appeared fine. My pulse started returning to normal.

"I came out into the road," he said.

Though true, it didn't matter.

"What're you in? Sixth grade? Play for the Lighthouses?"

He nodded. His brown hair had been compressed by the helmet and sweat. Other than that, he looked okay.

"What position?" I asked.

"Receiver."

"You live in Cape Laurel?"

He nodded. "Beachtree Street."

"You one of the Paquins?"

He nodded again. "Mikey."

"Is that bike too big for you? You seemed to be having a hard time," I said, expecting a denial.

"I can handle it. It's the boneyard. It freaks me out."

"The what?"

"There's a bunch of bones in there." He aimed his head toward the gutted land, the future site of the Lost Woods Resort, a project that, when completed, promised to bring ungodly amounts of commerce to town, as if we weren't already choked with tourists all summer. "It's creepy as anything."

"Bones?" I said, my heart rate again spiking. When I considered that I may have sensed something disturbing there, I shook it off. I'd never put stock in such things. "Real bones?"

2

"Yeah," he said, nodding.

"Show me."

It was likely that what he'd found were animal remains. Laurel, Maine was not littered with missing or unaccounted-for persons. We did have plenty of hunting, however, in and out of season.

"Do I have to? I'm going to be late for practice." I had a feeling he just didn't want to go back in there.

"Yes, you have to."

"Coach will make me run."

"If you're a receiver, you should like running."

He grunted, an indication that he wasn't buying it. I hadn't either when I caught passes for the same team twenty-five years earlier.

"Lead on," I said, pointing. "We can throw the bike in the truck, and I'll drive you down afterward." The Laurel Lighthouses practiced at the elementary school at the bottom of the hill, a mile away.

"I don't like it in there," he said, stepping into one of the tracks made by a logging truck. Apparently, I wasn't the only one unsettled by the site. I kept that to myself. The cleared space was as wide as a football field and twice as long.

"How'd you find these bones?" I said, following as he skirted a stack of pruned limbs as thin as his arms.

"We were messing around making jumps out of the dirt piles," he said. "Gary—one of the guys—wiped out and almost landed in them. I'm glad it wasn't me."

"Who is we?"

"I don't want to squeal."

"You're not getting anyone in trouble. Unless you're the ones who put the bones here."

"No, we didn't. The only thing I did was wreck my bike, which is why I've got Alfred's."

"How long ago did you find them?"

"A couple days." He wouldn't look at me. "But we didn't touch them."

"Did you tell anyone?"

"No."

I understood this, too. "No Trespassing" signs plastered the entrance road and the property's frontage. They'd have had to admit that they'd been somewhere they weren't supposed to be. Kids.

We were fifty yards in when he stopped and pointed to the back left, where a second, more roughed-out road went further into the woods. We headed over. While the clean, crisp air of fall never failed to vanquish the humidity of summer, the atmosphere in the pocket of the cut was thick and heavy. A few bulldozers and land movers patched with rust were parked in a line to our right. Ten-foot-high mounds of dirt loomed throughout like gigantic ski moguls. The ground was lined with knobby-wheeled bike tracks. It was easy to picture kids channeling their inner Evel Knievels. We were lucky none of them had gotten hurt. The project was supposed to encompass three hundred of the five hundred undeveloped acres that comprised the geographic center of town. The site work had stalled two hundred and ninety-something short. I hadn't noticed anything going on here in over a week.

When we reached the back of the cut, Mikey Paquin stopped walking. He raised an arm and pointed to the edge of the woods thirty yards beyond the base of the last mound. I stepped toward it. Mikey didn't move.

A dugout the size of a kiddie pool was cut into the ground at the edge of the trail. It was less than a foot deep. If I'd been hiking by and glanced, what was there would have registered as birch twigs. But, sure enough, among the dead leaves was a bed of bones. Before my heart started banging again, I spotted a ribcage. Thankfully, it was horizontal and thin, that of a young deer. I took a breath. We wouldn't be moving into serial killer territory. I knelt at the edge of the hole, which must have been uncovered by a bulldozer. Small footprints, likely Mikey and his friends, were evident in the dirt surrounding it. They'd been brave enough to take a good look.

"I think they're deer," I told the kid. I was not an expert but could tell animal remains from human. The straight bones were long and slender. The skulls were nearly oval, and two had been busted up, likely bucks that had their antlers pulled. There probably had been a tree nearby where they'd hung and butchered the carcasses. One couldn't dress a deer in an open garage or from an oak on the front lawn when it was taken out of season. That's what I guessed happened here.

Of course, a pile of deer bones would be a good place to hide the human variety, should one be extremely cunning and aware of this boneyard's existence. It would be wise to have them looked at by someone whose last science class wasn't in high school. I remember when I didn't use to think like this. It was before I had this job.

I'd have to shut down the site work until I verified that these were, in fact, deer bones. This would be less of a problem in that I hadn't seen much recent activity. I doubted the bones were the reason. Nevertheless, it would likely piss off Adam Springbrook, the entrepreneur behind the project, time being money and all that. And if the kids had seen them, it was safe to assume that someone running the site also had. Yet, no one had notified us. Even if the contractor had thought they were deer bones, they still should have let us know. Paquin and his buddies had probably figured it out, too, though to a kid, any bone not on a plate with steak attached to it was probably scary enough.

I turned to Mikey and told him that we would hustle him to practice and that I'd talk to the coach to see if I could get him out of running. Then I'd return, collect the bones, and bring them to the state police lab to confirm they weren't human. When I pivoted back to the cut, a splash of purple along the tree line caught my eye. It was not a color found in these woods, even this time of year. I told the kid to stay where he was. He looked up at me and started to say something, then stopped. He put his helmet back on.

Once I moved, I lost the color but aimed for the last tree at the edge of the clearing, twenty-five yards away. What I'd seen was the upturned collar of a long-sleeved Izod with an alligator on the chest. The rest of the sweater wasn't purple. It was the black of dried blood. While the fabric reptile had survived the gut shot, Adam Springbrook had not.

I didn't need to check for a pulse, but did anyway. His skin was cold, stiff, and starting to gray. Blue eyes were open and lost. The mouth was twisted as if in disbelief. He hadn't seen this coming. The ground beneath him did not seem stained like the shirt. Maybe he'd been dumped. I'd let the state police forensic team determine that.

Springbrook's project was the largest commercial development to hit the town in years. There were plans for solitary cabins and A-frame chalets to be spread around the property, with a grand hotel in the center. Two separate restaurants would flank a swimming pool in the shape of a hemlock. I only knew these details because I'd been asked to speak on the impact of it on my department at the Planning Board meeting. I'd mentioned that a few hundred more people weren't going to make much difference to us. That was the case even if the guests were paying the outrageous sums I'd heard it was going to cost to stay there. I didn't understand why someone would come to Laurel to inhabit a mosquito and black fly-infested forest when the ocean and beaches lay just a few miles away, but that was something I hadn't felt the need to share. Nor had I anticipated the project's owner getting shot before it was barely off the ground.

Springbrook was regarded by locals as a newcomer. He'd only been here ten years. His first move had been to buy an old Captain's house and turn it into a restaurant, having it designed by a hotshot decorator from New York and run by a chef imported from Boston. That the Reef House sat on a hill offering views of our most famous estate and the mouth of the Laurel River didn't hurt business. While I tended not to eat there, as it ran a car payment for a party of two, plenty of well-heeled summer people and tourists packed the place. Those folks didn't know they were eating frozen seafood, but they did enjoy the view, as well as being seen doing so. Springbrook had been able to get the place featured in several magazines catering to professionals living along the northeast corridor. After his initial success there, Springbrook purchased two inns and gave them similar makeovers. They catered to the people who could afford his food. I'd been told that he was a marketing genius. I had no reason to doubt it. No Vacancy signs perpetually hung in front of his inns, and in season the Reef House was booked out weeks in advance.

I hadn't had much interaction with him in either a professional or personal capacity. He seemed a nice enough guy, but not without quirks. He spoke very particularly, with a precise enunciation of every word. It was always "cannot" or "must have," never "can't" or "must've." He was forty but wore the look of a college student, favoring khakis, Topsiders, Alligator shirts, and blue blazers, with a propensity to flip up his shirt collars. Anytime I talked to him in public, I had the feeling that as he smiled and nodded, he was glancing over my shoulder to see if there was someone more important he should be speaking to. I did know, however, that when the town asked for donations for the Fourth of July festivities every year, Springbrook didn't hesitate to write a healthy check.

Other business owners in Laurel loved him. Around town, he usually traveled with an entourage of Chamber of Commerce types. They were only challenged for his attention by our local politicians. The Selectmen and Planning Board had granted him multiple waivers for this very project. If Lost Woods had paid off like he promised, it wouldn't have surprised me if they'd carried him down Main Street in a litter. Earl Goodwin, Laurel's leading Realtor, told me that if I was smart, I'd start buying up land myself because things were happening, and I should be ready to cash in. He was presuming that Springbrook's undertakings had the potential to line all our pockets, and also that I had money lying around to drop into speculation. If Earl was forgetting that we had seen some dark moments in Laurel brought about by this type of pursuit, I was not. I couldn't ignore how easily things could go wrong and how often they did. While that kind of thinking may have been another result of my career choice, evidence of its validity lay at my feet.

I stood and sighed. That we couldn't get through the first year of the Nineties without a dead body was just wrong. Once we'd made it past summer, when anything could happen in a tourist town, it should have been nothing but peace and quiet. I had a choice: Stand there and complain, as if that ever did anything, or get to work.

It had been warm for October, and the ground was soft. While the body lay amongst the leaves, the main section of the site was floored with dirt. I'd seen no signs of a path that indicated Springbrook had been dragged here. He could have walked in and been shot where I'd found him, or killed somewhere else and dumped. The hundreds of footprints marking the site were potential evidence. They couldn't be disturbed.

"Did you forget I need to go to practice?" the kid said. "Wednesdays, the coach goes over the game plan. It's important."

"Don't you move," I said. I was fairly certain he had no idea there was a body twenty yards from him, or he would've sprinted all the way to the field, no matter what I told him.

"What's the matter?" He whipped his helmeted head around as if a linebacker was about to flatten him.

"Nothing," I said, stepping backward, trying to keep my feet where I had placed them on the way in.

Mikey Paquin was not making it to practice on time, and Adam Springbrook wouldn't be building his deluxe resort.

Chapter Two

O nce I reached Mikey at the boneyard, I told him to follow me. It was another ten paces to the floor of the work site. We stopped there. Footprints covered the dirt, sinking in a quarter of an inch. I could see my own covering some of them. Other than another full-sized pair heading in the same direction as mine, which could be Springbrook's, the rest were small and pointed in every direction. Those had to be from the kids.

"I'm going to pick you up and carry you out of here," I told Paquin.

He looked at me like I was a dope. "I can walk," he said. "I wasn't hurt, I told you."

"I don't want you messing up these footprints," I said.

"What's the big deal? I thought you said we weren't getting in trouble."

"You're not."

"Then what's going on?" I wasn't about to tell the kid he was arm's length from a dead body.

"Do you want me to talk to the coach and get you out of running or not?"

"Okay."

I picked him up and threw him over my shoulder until we got halfway across the pit.

We reached the road, the kid trailing me after I'd put him down, mumbling to himself. I radioed the station and had Estelle Maynard, our dispatcher, contact the state police detective in charge of York County, Rick Pettibone. We needed him, his forensics crew, and the medical examiner here. I also had her roust my regular officers, Gwyneth Robinson and Ted Solinski, and direct them to Providence Hill. They'd served as summer seasonal cops, and I'd hired them to replace officers who'd retired. It was Gwyneth's first year and Ted's second. The good news was that they were hard-working and enthusiastic. I could count on them, and though they'd make mistakes, none were different than those I'd made at their age. I often reminded myself that they were learning. At times I felt more like a teacher than a cop, but it gave me the opportunity to work on my patience, something I wasn't known for. On the plus side, I'd mastered calming breathing techniques.

While we waited for my officers, I grilled Paquin for ten minutes. He'd been in there with three other kids from Cape Laurel on Sunday, as they'd had a game Saturday and practiced every other day. I had him specify where they'd been playing and jumping their bikes—he naturally pointed to the mound closest to the boneyard and a larger one further away. He was oblivious to Springbrook's body.

Although I hadn't given Adam a close inspection, I suspected that Springbrook hadn't been there longer than a day or two. There was little discoloration, just a gray sheen like the skinned trees he'd taken down. He hadn't been nibbled by raccoons or gouged by a coyote. Mercifully for Mikey Paquin, the unmistakable toxicity of a body in decay hadn't yet poisoned the air. That was something that might have stayed with the kid.

As soon as Solinski pulled up in a town cruiser, I had him take a picture of the soles of the kid's sneakers. Then I had Ted throw the kid's bike in the trunk and take him to practice, with instructions to talk to the coach to get him out of punishment running. At least, I'd managed to remove Mikey from the scene before he realized what was going on. As they drove off, I wondered if he and I had felt the same strange voodoo coming from the site. I then reminded myself that I didn't give credence to such cosmic awareness.

By the time Ted returned, Gwyneth was pulling up in her Crown Victoria, a used police car that she'd bought at auction. The girl was all in. My rookies gazed at me, wondering why we were here and why I kept looking at my watch. As we waited for the state police, I formed a mental checklist of what we'd need to get from the crime scene. I could see them dying to ask what was going on. That they were waiting on me showed discipline.

"Adam Springbrook is in there," I said, finally, nodding behind us. I didn't have to tell them that he owned the land. The coming resort had been news for the past year, starting when it was first proposed to the Planning Board. There'd been multiple articles trumpeting it in the County Star and the Portland Press Herald. They'd read like they were written by Springbrook himself. That's how positive the reporting had been. "He's dead. Someone shot him."

My young officers' jaws dropped in unison. I was fairly certain that they'd seen as many dead bodies as Mikey Paquin.

"Are you sure?" Gwyneth asked.

"The bullet hole in his stomach is a pretty good indication," I said.

"What do you want us to do?" Ted asked.

I refrained from saying that I'd like them to hang onto the contents of their stomachs when we examined the body, remembering how queasy I'd been seeing my first in the line of duty, and how hard I had to concentrate not to lose it in front of Chief Dederian. Instead, I told them that I'd contacted Pettibone and asked for the state police lab to come out. I related how we'd come to find the body and let them know what the lab crew would examine and catalog: measurements and pictures of footprints, starting with the area approaching the two-track that went further in the woods, blood loss, position of the body, possible shooting angles, and they'd canvass the area for physical evidence like shells and casings. We'd been lucky that the site work had stopped. But that also made me wonder if there was something to that. I doubted an entire crew would take vacation all at once, especially as it was not yet deer season. The equipment remained, but it wouldn't be moving anytime soon.

I told Gwyneth and Ted that I'd be taking them in to see the body, as it was something that they needed for their professional development. I also made it clear that our prime directive was to not compromise any physical evidence. That would keep us from getting shot ourselves by the lab team, who preferred that their crime scenes were not trampled.

Chapter Three

I had them follow me to the boneyard in my footsteps, walking in a line. I pointed out the kids' bike tracks. Then I showed them the bed of what I hoped were deer bones.

"We're going to get those checked, right?" Gwyneth said. She got down on her haunches and looked them over. I told her she was correct. She nodded. She had a wide, pretty face with soft features. She was the same five-seven that I was, but a bit wider. She was a powerlifter and took it seriously enough to enter regional competitions. It had only taken one clown giving her shit in the Port Tavern's parking lot after last call to get everyone "Yes, Officer"-ing her. She'd tied the guy into a knot in seconds. Ted, a six-two former defensive end at Plymouth State, occasionally worked out with her at a gym in Milltowne and admitted that she could handle the weights as well as any guy he knew. If nothing else, our department was fit.

I pointed out where Mikey Paquin had been standing and how I'd spotted Springbrook's purple, which didn't fit in with its surroundings. That was a point I wanted to make, to be always watching for something out of place. Then I took them to the body. We kept to the side of the trail and on the leaves, careful not to disturb anything.

I knelt down and looked up at them. Gwyneth had on her game face as if she were about to hit a challenging deadlift. Ted, on the other hand, looked seasick. So, I asked. Neither had seen a dead body in the line of duty, and it was Ted's first, period. I told them that though I hoped otherwise, it would likely not be their last.

"The first thing you want to do," I said, beginning another lecture, "is to make sure the body is actually a body, meaning not alive." We put on our exam room gloves, and I had them check the carotid artery that had stopped pumping hours earlier. I told them how they could check for breath by holding a hand to someone's mouth as a second way to verify. I didn't reiterate that someone whose gut had a hole in it and a coating of dried blood were pretty good indications of death, as well.

The cause of death had to be that gunshot to the midsection. Given the width of the bullet hole, it appeared the killer had used a large-caliber weapon. We'd be combing the area for a cartridge. Where it happened, I wasn't sure. He was on his back, so he hadn't crawled there. Of course, he could have staggered and then fallen. I checked the tree behind Springbrook, but as the light was fading, it was hard to see if there was blood splatter on it. The state police lab crew and medical examiner would tell us more. That didn't mean I couldn't point out the anomalies I saw to the two rookies and walk them through my thought process.

If someone were going to dump a body, why wouldn't they have taken him further into the woods, where it would not be so easily discovered? If brought far from the trail, it could have decomposed undetected unless a stray hunter stumbled across it. Or it could have been buried. There was plenty of equipment around for that. This led me to believe that whoever did this was either in a hurry or didn't think things through. Ted suggested that perhaps the killer couldn't physically carry a body over a rough trail any deeper than they had. Not everyone was built like my officers. Gwyneth floated that whoever shot him might have wanted it found in this specific spot. The looks on their faces indicated that they were discovering their profession was more complicated than they'd originally thought.

With the rookies looking over my shoulder, I examined the body more closely. There were no contusions on the face. His hands were clean and uncut. Nothing on his arms, either. I went through Springbrook's pockets. His front pockets were empty. His wallet was buttoned in a back pocket. It held three one-hundred-dollar bills, two fifties, a ten, and assorted credit and business cards. That ruled out robbery, as did the gold watch on his wrist. One of the cards was for Eddie Mancini, Excavation and Sitework, whose name was stenciled on the equipment on the other side of the cut. I slipped that one into my notebook.

We checked the soles of Springbrook's dress shoes, flat-soled loafers, and kept to the leaf-strewn side of the trail so as not to disturb existing footprints as we checked for a match. None of them near where we'd found him appeared to be his. There were smaller sneaker prints heading in every direction in front of the boneyard, and they were all different. When I was a kid, practically every boy wore the same model of Adidas. It appeared that wasn't a thing anymore. Several sets of boot prints went to the back of the cut. Those could have been from site workers. The other thing missing from this scene was Springbrook's car. He'd come here with someone. Whether he'd been dead or alive at the time would need to be determined.

Once we'd covered the basics, I had my officers tape off a thirty-by-thirty-yard perimeter around the body, as well as the entrance to the site. Then I asked them to wait for the state police. Until they arrived, no one was to get through. Once the staties were on the scene, I would have Gwyneth and Ted canvas the neighbors to see if they'd heard gunshots over the past few days. While the nearest houses were a quarter mile away on all sides, sound carried in the quiet of fall. Of course, this was also the time of year when people started sighting in their deer rifles. Though today was a Wednesday, the previous weekend could have sounded like the Fourth of July. Folks here would be used to it and might not have noticed. Nothing was simple.

"What about the bones, Chief?" Gwyneth asked. Her attention to detail was a magnificent thing. She kept both Ted and me alert.

"The least of our problems," I said. "But I'll ask the staties to take them."

Pettibone showed up in his state-issued cruiser with the lab van following him. They pulled in behind our cars. In the state of Maine, most capital cases are handled by the State Police. I'd worked most of ours with Rick, the lead detective for York County. Others, I'd had to handle on my own, for one reason or another. Pettibone was good, however, and we worked well together when we got the chance.

"You got a body?" he asked me as he waited for his crew to get their equipment.

"In the woods. Adam Springbrook."

"The guy building the resort?"

"That's him. Shot. Not exactly left out in the open, but not well hidden. One could have done a much better job had they wanted to hide the body."

"You know anyone who would want to shoot him?" He looked into the cut where we'd taped it off.

"I've heard the hunters who are losing these woods are red-assed over it, but I can't imagine enough to shoot the man. He's pretty popular around here. Supposed to create all sorts of business and jobs and make people money. Also, he paid out well to a few different families for the land, from what I understand."

Pettibone nodded. "Who found him?"

"I did. A kid led me in to show me a deer bone graveyard. Not connected to this, I think, but you should have your guys check it out anyway. I caught a glimpse of Springbrook's purple shirt further up the trail."

"A kid?"

"Sixth-grader. He and his buddies were jumping their bikes off the dirt piles and found the deer bones. Springbrook's been there maybe a day or two. The kid had no idea."

"What've you done so far?"

"Shut down the site. I'm hoping your guys can determine if he was shot here or dumped. There are plenty of footprints in there. We tried not to disturb them, mostly work boots, kids' sneakers, and mine, and bike tire tracks on the dirt. It's not exactly a place where people would go hiking. Work stopped a week ago, but I don't know why. I'll be looking into it." I handed over what we'd found on the body.

"You notify the family yet?"

"He's not married, and there's no family up here, to my knowledge. I'm going to his restaurant now to see what they know."

"There's no shortage of reasons to kill someone," Pettibone said. "But if you break it down, it's usually either money or love gone bad. I hate to limit things from the start, of course. Though you might want to see if Springbrook was porking some other asshole's wife."

"I haven't ruled anything out," I said, suppressing a sigh. While Pettibone was often right, he was more often carelessly blunt and a fan of stating the obvious.

"I've eaten at that damn Reef House," Pettibone said. "Had to take out a second mortgage because my wife saw an article about it somewhere. The food wasn't great, and you can look out a window and see water from a lot of places around here."

I laughed.

He nodded to Gwyneth and Ted, who were working as a team on the footprints in front of the gate.

"I'll babysit these two for a while," Pettibone said.

"They'll be okay," I said, giving him a look. I wasn't too happy about that crack. It was okay for me to recognize their greenness, but I didn't appreciate it from outside. I thanked him and climbed back into the Bronco. I hoped not to hit any kids on my way to the Reef House. I didn't even glance at football practice when I passed the school. Eyes on the road the whole way.

Chapter Four

The Reef House wasn't busy at five o'clock on a Wednesday in the middle of October. But at least it was open. Ten years ago, Laurel turned into a ghost town on Labor Day. Now, there was enough traffic on weekends to keep places open through Halloween. That was a result of the state tourism board and the Laurel Chamber of Commerce convincing people that our fall colors were as desirable as the summer sun.

Five cars were lined up at the end of the parking lot. They were domestic, so that meant employees. Louie Williams, the manager, was stationed at the host desk. I told him that I needed to talk to him in the office. He didn't question the request and told Nancy Norton, a waitress who was polishing water glasses and looked like the task was the only thing keeping her awake, to watch the door. She smirked, not fearing a stampede.

The office was on the second floor, opposite a loft that functioned as a private dining room with a long oak table the size of a boat. A chandelier hovered over it. As Williams led me into the office, I felt a letdown. Three beat-up tables retired from the dining room served as desks. They were strewn with phones and adding machines, register tapes, and stacks of paper. Two of them had Heineken coasters under their legs for balance. A woman worked at a third. She frowned when we came in. Her neat, ordered desk was an exception. Her fingers scurried like spiders over the keys of a calculator. She didn't stop working when Williams introduced me to her, Tricia Lombard.

"What can I do for you, LT?" Williams asked. His lips closed, and a sheen appeared on a forehead that reached back to his crown. He seemed to always be expecting bad news. In this instance, he was going to be right.

"Well," I said, pausing and taking a breath. Lombard's fingers stopped working the keys. "It's Adam Springbrook. He's dead."

"Excuse me?" Williams said, lowering himself into one of the desk chairs.

"I'm sorry. We found him this afternoon at the Lost Woods worksite."

"He had a heart attack or something?" Williams said.

"He'd been shot," I said.

Lombard gasped.

"I don't believe it," Williams said, reaching for the desktop to steady himself. "Who would do something like that?"

"That's a great question," I said. "Would you know anyone who was upset or had an issue with him? Threatened him?"

"Not in this restaurant," Williams said. "If you did your job here, you were treated quite well."

"What about outside of here?"

"I'm sure I wouldn't know about that," Williams said, shaking his head and looking to Lombard. She said nothing.

"Is there anyone then who doesn't do their job well?" I said.

"Of course not," Williams said. "They wouldn't work here if that were the case. We have fairly high standards."

I did not respond that they would need to if they wanted service to match their prices. But I did ask if anyone was recently let go. That got a no. Williams explained how the place ran: He handled operations, which Springbrook didn't get directly involved with. When Adam was here, he mingled with guests, greeted people at the bar, and had a presence. He just liked to see what was going on. If he was unhappy with anything, he would tell Williams, and then Louie would handle it. Springbrook rarely addressed the staff, so an employee likely wouldn't even know if the owner had a complaint. Though Williams was sure of that, I had my doubts.

"There were no problems here, at all?" I asked.

"No, Chief," Williams said.

I'd seen Maureen DiGiovanni setting up the bar. I could ask her and perhaps get a less sanitized response.

18

"How is the Lost Woods project going?" I said. "Any problems there?"

"I wouldn't know about that," Williams said, now repeatedly clicking and unclicking a pen. "I mean, I focus on this restaurant. Just what I hear in passing."

"What would that be?"

"They might be a little behind schedule, but that's not unusual. When we opened here, we were three months late. That's just the way it goes."

"What about you?" I asked Lombard.

"I just do the books and payroll for here," Lombard said. "We pay our bills. I can tell you that."

"You don't hear anything?" I asked. That she had to tell me they paid their bills, like every other business on the planet was supposed to, made me think that maybe they didn't. I had become less trusting and more cynical every year I spent on this job.

"I have lunch with Sally Cooper, the controller for the Springbrook Coastal Group, once a week. And with Lila Dalton, who does the books for the Captain Fairweather and Seagrass Inns. As far as I know, we're all doing great. All the properties in the Group, I mean. Financially. I don't know about Adam, personally." Her face flushed as she stumbled, trying to explain herself.

"What's this Springbrook Group?" I asked, wondering why basic questions never seemed to have straight answers.

"It's the corporate umbrella that all of Mr. Springbrook's properties fall under. It's technically one business, with different components, you could say."

"When did this happen?" It sounded like something that could complicate one's life, though the kind of thing that only accountants worried about.

"When the Lost Woods project first got underway," she said. She looked to Williams for confirmation. "We all run our own locations, but now we have a corporate headquarters that we report to. I think Adam was waiting for Lost Woods to get close to completion before announcing it publicly. He thought there would be PR and marketing opportunities when that happened, from what I understand."

"There's a main office somewhere?" I asked.

"The professional building on Route One in West Laurel."

I knew the place. I'd sent away a lawyer who'd had an office there.

"Does he still have his house at Bishop's Beach? Is that where he lives?" While Springbrook had one of the more modest homes there, the yard of his white New Englander with purple shutters was legendary, clearly sculpted by more skilled landscapers than his neighbors, who also had their grounds professionally done. His shrubs had sharp, artistic angles. The trees were trimmed to linear perfection. Rock walls and stones were configured in ways that did not recall that of nineteenth-century farmers.

"That's correct," Williams said. He stopped with the pen.

"When's the last time that you saw him?"

"Here?"

"Or anywhere." It wasn't a difficult question.

"He had dinner here early Monday night," Williams said.

"Alone?"

"No, with Ed Mancini, one of the construction people he's using for Lost Woods."

"How would you describe the dinner?"

"They had three courses, both had the yellowfin tuna. They had a nice bottle of Montrachet with it."

"I'm sure it was lovely," I said, my voice rising. "But that's not what I was asking. Did he seem bothered or upset? How were he and Mancini getting along? Were they arguing?"

"I did not see them arguing," Williams said. "They were having a grand time. That's a hundred-dollar bottle of wine they washed down their dinner with."

"Springbrook was buying?"

"So to speak. We just write it off as a comp."

"Did you hear from him yesterday or earlier today?"

"No, but he had dinner here Sunday night, too."

If I owned restaurants, I guess I'd never cook, either.

"With anyone?" I asked, wondering why one always had to pull information out of people.

"Yes, his ex-wife."

This was a complication. I didn't know he'd been married. He'd arrived in town single and had managed to stay that way. Though we didn't often travel in the same social circles, I'd heard that he was a very eligible bachelor among his cohort. That he'd remained one was a disappointment to many, I'm sure.

"This ex-wife's not from Laurel, I take it."

"No, I think she's based in Connecticut somewhere, just outside of New York City."

"Her name?"

"Talia."

"Re-married?"

"I don't think so. She goes by Springbrook."

"Any kids?"

"No. She's been here a few times this year, more frequently than in the past, I'd say."

"Do you know why?"

"I'm not sure. She may have been helping with Lost Woods."

"Does she stay with him or somewhere else?"

"I believe she's usually with him at the beach."

I wasn't aware of this. But I couldn't be expected to know everyone who steps foot in town, especially during tourist season.

"How was that dinner, not the food so much as the tenor?" I assumed that clarifying might eliminate some aggravation on my part.

"Well, now that you mention it, there was some uneasiness."

"What do you mean?"

"I passed by the table once, and she was wiping her eyes."

"As if she'd been crying?"

He nodded. "I don't know if it was serious. Or if it had anything to do with Adam."

"Was it just the two of them at the table?"

"Yes."

"When was the last time she was here prior to this week?"

"Labor Day, and then once more in September."

An ex-wife shows up, and then a few days later, a man's dead. Coincidences were like ghosts. They may exist, but I didn't believe in them. After fifteen years on the job, that seemed like a foundation on which to form a religion. I stopped short of asking Louie if this Talia Springbrook could operate a forty-five.

"You think she could be at his place?"

"I don't know. Maybe she went back to Connecticut."

"He didn't mention these things to you?"

"Adam kept his private affairs just that, private. She could also be at one of the inns, perhaps. They seemed to be on good terms. But I only spoke with her briefly. She had a glass of wine at the bar before he arrived. I kept her company. When I first met her years ago, I thought she was his sister. Until, you know, it came out otherwise. That's how they seemed anyway. Not at all romantic. Adam came from the office in West Laurel to meet her."

"Does he have any other relatives?"

"I don't believe so. His mother passed away several years ago. He never mentioned his father."

I nodded. Job one was finding Talia Springbrook. I asked Tricia Lombard if she could call the inns and see if she was staying at any of them. She nodded and picked up the phone.

"I'm going to need any contact information you have for her. Does he have a Rolodex?"

"He might at the main office, but not here," Williams said. "I know he's been spending time at the new restaurant he just bought, Dante's. It's closed now, but we were hoping to get it open by spring. It's getting a complete makeover this winter. He may only stop in here but Adam stayed on top of his construction and renovation projects. He wasn't an operator so much as a visionary."

"Could you explain that?" I said. I thought he was just a guy who owned a restaurant and a few inns.

"He has great ideas. We're making more money than ever here, and Dante's would have been a gold mine next summer. It made money even before Adam put his stamp on it, and that would certainly have increased its net by a good margin. He had a unique skill in imagining spaces. Once he builds it, he lets others like me do the work. Of course, I don't mean it like that. It's just different. He wanted things a certain way, with an atmosphere of distinction. I don't think he could seat a dining room, mix a martini, or boil a lobster. But he was brilliant in creating environments where people wanted to experience those things."

"Did he ever piss anyone off in the process?" I asked, getting to what mattered.

"I wouldn't know anything about that." Williams looked down into his lap.

"Did you like working for him?"

"I am treated very well here. Though you didn't want him to walk in while the place was slammed. He didn't really understand how it worked when things went into the weeds as they do in this business. He could be dismissive in moments like that, but if you met expectations, he was extremely grateful."

"And if you didn't?"

"You'd hear it. Or I would hear it. But he wasn't one to hang onto something. All his properties are very successful, as I'm sure you're aware. And it put wind in his sails, so to speak. Take Lost Woods, for example. He wanted to turn this fishing village into the next Newport, Rhode Island. Laurel was on its way. I'm sure you can see a difference in the type of people who are coming here now compared to just a few years ago."

I nodded. Those who stayed at his inns, the Captain Fairweather and the Seagrass, enjoyed the most expensive rooms in Laurel. As I'd never been in one, I couldn't say if it was worth it. But the town had yet to be overrun with limousines, nor had our marinas been swamped with luxury yachts. Home prices had risen, and summer rentals were creeping up. I wouldn't have called it a tidal wave, however. Nor was I sure it could be attributed to Springbrook chasing this vision of Laurel.

"I think he was in talks with the America's Cup people," Williams added.

"He wanted to bring those races here?"

"He was exploring it," Williams said.

"How was he going to swing that?"

"I have no idea," Williams said, waving at the desk. "This place keeps my hands full. But he was excited about the prospect."

Whether the town could handle those sailboats and ESPN and the crowds was a matter of debate. We didn't have a line of cliffside mansions. No Vanderbilts or Rockefellers. The one Hinckley sailboat docked here, I don't think made it out more than once this past summer. But that was another story. As a department, with our three officers and college-age summer help, we were far from ready for what the America's Cup would bring. We'd barely made it through the state Little League championships this year. If nothing else, Adam Springbrook had big plans that few could have imagined. While that could have made him a visionary, it could also be a sign of someone with a very loose grip on reality. Both seemed dangerous.

"Who do I talk to, to learn more?" I asked.

"His associates. He has silent partners in these ventures, I believe. Certain people in town were very excited, from what he said. Just about every shop owner was thrilled. Of course, transforming the town wasn't going to happen overnight."

"Is there something wrong with how Laurel is now?" I asked. I was a person in town, and I wasn't excited. I hadn't heard these grand plans, other than Lost Woods, of course. Maybe spending the summer doing my job instead of socializing had left me out of the loop. The Laurel, Maine makeover had yet to cross my desk in any official way.

"Oh no," Williams said. "Who doesn't love it here?

"You said just about every shop owner was excited. Were there some opposed to this?"

"I wasn't aware of any. I'm sure someone could have been upset. There always are those who are opposed to change. Of course, they're usually the ones who end up thrilled after the fact."

This discussion of business philosophy wasn't getting me anywhere.

"Can I get a list of those silent partners and current employees, please?"

"We don't have much of that here," Lombard said. "You might try the office at the professional building. His lawyer's in the same space. Marv Fitzgerald. You'll need to talk to those people anyway, I imagine."

"Fitzgerald handled the restaurant's legal issues," Williams said. "If he's not his personal lawyer, I'm sure he'd know who is."

"What would the Reef's legal issues be?" I said, wondering if I'd missed something.

"Nothing that would get your attention, I assure you," Williams said. "Licensing and permits, those are the things he helped with."

"You can talk to Sally Cooper there, as well," Tricia Lombard said, "the controller. She makes sure the bills are paid."

There it was again. She was going out of her way to tell me that they didn't owe anyone money. I'd be finding out if it were true soon enough. I looked at my watch. It was nearly six.

"I assume that they work normal business hours over there?" I said.

"For the most part," Lombard said.

"Can you see if you can catch them for me?" I asked.

She picked up the phone and started dialing. When she got Cooper, she told her the chief of police wanted to talk to her and handed me the phone as if it was on fire. I gave her the news. Her voice retreated from authoritative to choked up in a matter of a few words. I would have liked to head right over there, but my first step would be to find Talia Springbrook, whether she was still in town or not. I asked Mrs. Cooper if she and Mr. Fitzgerald could meet me at their office at eight that next morning. She replied that they usually came in at nine, but under the circumstances, she'd see to it that they were there. I thanked her and replaced the phone in its cradle.

"Chief Nichols?" Williams asked as I was returning my notebook to my pocket. "What do I do with the restaurant?"

"What do you mean?"

"Should I close?"

"That's not up to me," I said. "Out of respect, you might. Or you might not. I can't advise you on that. There must be someone you can check with."

"Should I call Sally back?" Lombard asked.

"Until I can find and notify Adam's ex-wife," I said, "I'd like you to keep this quiet. No talking about this to anyone other than Cooper and this lawyer, Fitzgerald. I'll let you know as soon as I find her."

"Is this because someone killed him?" Williams looked like he might be heading straight to a bottle downstairs after I left.

"Exactly. It wasn't an accident." If this is what I had to say to gain some time, it was okay. I needed to find Talia Springbrook, as she seemed to be the next of kin, as well as an obvious suspect. Should it be the second shoe that fit, I didn't want her getting a head start.

"If we don't open, what do I tell people if we aren't allowed to say?"

"You can tell everyone the kitchen hoods are broken or that a pipe burst."

"I can't believe this." Williams sat at the desk and put his head in his hands. I'm sure it wouldn't be an easy decision for him, what to do. But I wondered if his worry over the restaurant eclipsing his sorrow for Springbrook told me more about him or his former boss. I left the office with a list of Reef House employees, their addresses, and phone numbers. But my first stop was going to be the bar, and I wasn't going for a drink.

Chapter Five

I 'd known Maureen DiGiovanni for years. She'd come to Laurel from Boston, taking a summer job at the Port Tavern, where she became known as Mary Queen of Shots, as she had recipes for hundreds of them. After a few years, she hopped over to the more civilized atmosphere of the Sea Squall, where her martini and people skills took over. This spring, she moved to the Reef House. While I saw her far less than I did in my younger days when I carried less responsibility, I could count on her to talk honestly. She wasn't known for keeping opinions to herself.

She was lining up cocktail shakers over the service well of her white marble bar when I pulled up in front of her. She looked surprised when I told her that, no, I didn't want a drink.

"What I'd like," I said, "is for you to tell me how things are going over here."

"Good." She stopped moving and looked at me, her lips together, trying to figure out what I was asking her.

"Are the employees happy?"

"Sure, LT, there's a lot of traffic here, even this time of year, and the people who come aren't shy about spending money. That's a good thing."

"Anyone have a problem with Adam?"

"No, why do you ask?"

"Louie told me that was the case, but I've worked in restaurants. I didn't believe it. Someone always has something to bitch about."

"He comes in, watches for a little while, then leaves. He barely says anything to anyone."

"He never approaches employees, even if he sees something he doesn't like?"

"No, he'd talk to Louie, who'd pull you aside later. Louie might be freaking out, but Adam stayed clear of it."

"Do you like it here?"

"Sure. Adam's paying me ridiculously well. And the tips are about the same, as a lot of folks followed me. You know I am fantastic."

"There's no denying that," I said.

"Adam talked my ear off at the Sea Squall as a guest, but over here, he barely looks at me other than to order his usual cosmopolitan. I've been seduced and dumped worse, believe me. Maybe if I were twenty years younger, he might have more interest, but that's life."

"You don't look a day over thirty," I said, knowing she was in her forties.

"As long as the paychecks don't bounce," she said.

"Any customers have a problem with him?"

"The only problem he may have is his ass getting chapped from people kissing it. People love to know the owner, and he is a handsome man with a presence. He's like Laurel's prom king, and everyone wants a dance. It's funny as hell to watch."

"No one was mad at him?"

"Not that I know of. What's with all the questions, LT?"

"He was found dead earlier today in Lost Woods. He'd been shot."

"Come on," she said. She put down the strainer she held and stepped back to lean against the back bar, made from the same marble.

"I wish I were joking. Can you think of anyone who'd want to harm him?"

"Jesus Christ." An entire summer's worth of tan seemed to drain from her face. She folded her arms in front of her chest. "As I said, everyone liked him. At least everyone here."

"If something comes to you, you'll call me?" I said.

"I can do that, LT," she said.

"Louie will be down with instructions in a few minutes," I said. "I'm sorry."

"My God," she said, heaving a deep breath. Her eyebrows came in over her nose as she tried to process what I'd told her. She could have been wondering about her job security or who in this quiet little town would have been psychotic enough to shoot her boss. This kind of thing shouldn't happen here, where excitement was supposed to come from leaves turning color. She looked at me for an explanation. I didn't have one.

Chapter Six

I drove downtown toward Adam's place at Bishop's Beach. I hoped to find Talia Springbrook there. An ex-wife showing up out of nowhere and a dead man with a lot of money dictated urgency. That she was potentially next of kin was a convenient technicality for tracking her down.

Springbrook's house, a New Englander, fit in with the Cape Codders and salt boxes that lined Bishop's Beach. It was longer front to back than wide, which limited the amount of house overlooking the ocean. However, he'd compensated by making the side facing the Atlantic a wall of windows. The driveway was empty, but his antique Triumph convertible, top up, was parked in the garage. I looked it over, found nothing of interest, and made a note to have Pettibone dust it for prints. A slate walkway led from the garage through manicured shrubs to the house.

The Adirondack chairs on the small, covered porch were painted white and, unlike the ones on my own, looked unused. I rang the bell and waited. There was no answer. The door was locked.

I went around back. A ten-foot lawn reached a rock wall where a five-step wooden staircase led down to the beach. A square deck ran the slim width of the house. The cedar chaise lounges arranged on it were faded. A hot tub was sunk in the far end, covered by a fitted black canvas. I had no desire to be in the same state as my ex-wife, never mind the same Jacuzzi. The coffee table between the lounges was empty. Then again, beach season had passed. It wasn't one of those places that could sleep a dozen people, but with that wall of dark glass, the five or six that could fit would enjoy the view.

The sliding door to the kitchen was also locked. From what I could see, there was no blood in sight. I took a minute to think. With the owner dead and his ex-wife unaccounted for, the argument could be made that there was probable cause to enter the dwelling. That the lock on the slider could be opened with the blade on my Swiss Army knife made the decision that much easier.

The house looked as if no one lived there. Maybe my experience as a bachelor with infrequent company colored that impression. If my place were described as looking lived-in, it would be a compliment to the point of exaggeration. Springbrook's kitchen was neat and clean. The wicker chair backs of the stools at the center island sat parallel to the edge. The flower arrangement on it was fresh. The three dirty wine glasses in the sink surprised me, each with crimson remnants crusting the bottom. Different shades of lipstick marked two of the rims. Maybe it was the maid's day off.

The living room in front was just as ordered. The couch, taut black leather, looked like it had never been sat on. Instead of the newspapers and *Sports Illustrateds* that blanketed my coffee table, a sculpture of an elephant and cat o'nine tails in an orange glass vase stood there. I noticed a stereo receiver, tape deck, and turntable, but didn't see a television.

I went upstairs. There were three bedrooms. The master, Springbrook's, was at the beach end of the house, naturally. Its view was spectacular. The bed was made. The bathroom was clean and orderly, an army of cologne neatly arranged across the top of the vanity. The folds on the shelved bath towels would have made a military man proud.

A hall ran along the right side of the upstairs. Two other bedrooms were stacked on the left of the house. The first hadn't been touched. Talia must have been staying in the other. A suitcase had been thrown onto an easy chair, and a makeup bag rested at the foot of the bed. Clothes were strewn across the rest of it, an indication that she was still in town. Hopefully, she was upright and unharmed.

Chapter Seven

I returned to the Bronco and headed to the station. If Talia Springbrook was here from Connecticut, I doubted she'd taken a Greyhound. Thankfully, Laurel Police Headquarters finally received a computer. It would make tracking down the make and model of her car easy enough. But, as I drove through downtown, I spotted a black BMW with Connecticut plates parked in the trapezoid of the square, steps away from the Port Tavern. In summer, the car would have been camouflaged among others of its kind, and I may have missed it. But in October, there were only thirty-five hundred of us, and anything that wasn't a pickup, Ford, Chevy, or Dodge stood out. I pulled over and went in. The Tavern was one of the few places that stayed open year-round. It was not owned by Adam Springbrook.

Rosemary Fecteau was bartending. She twirled the end of the red ponytail resting on her shoulder and gave me a little wave. Ed Pickey, Cranky Fisher, and six other workmen stretched in a row across the bar: flannel shirt, Budweiser, flannel shirt, Budweiser, all down the line. At the end, however, I found a martini glass and a thirty-ish-looking brunette with dark eyes and red lips, sitting at an angle, talking to Chet Tibbets. She wore a loose-fitting black blouse and a long houndstooth skirt. A silver chain with a cross hung into the chasm of her cleavage. It, or she, seemed to have grasped Chet's full attention. The two upside-down shot glasses in front of her indicated that she was backed up. A few of the men turned and sighed, shaking their heads when they saw me, like teenagers whose parents had returned earlier than expected. It was rare that I entered one of these establishments in uniform bearing good news. The woman who I assumed was Talia Springbrook and

Chet kept talking. One was mesmerized, and the other probably didn't care who I was.

"Excuse me," I said, standing just off her shoulder. She glanced in the mirror behind the bar to see who had spoken, then turned. While I was wearing jeans, which I did this time of year unless I planned on spending the day in the office, she wouldn't miss the uniform shirt and badge. "Are you Talia Springbrook?"

"I am," she said. She let those words hang in the air. Her eyes were big and gray. If I hadn't been focused, the eyeliner surrounding them could have made me forget I was there on business. "Let me guess. I managed to find the only no-parking zone in town?"

"Can I talk to you in private?" I indicated a space amongst the empty tables on the other side of the room.

"You could, but I have another drink on the way."

"You can get it after. You might need it."

Her lips came together, and she breathed in through her nose, as she tried to determine if I was joking. That didn't stop the eyelashes from fluttering.

"It sounds serious," she said. She looked back at Chet. "Do you know any good lawyers up here?"

"I didn't know there was such a thing," he said.

"You'll bail me out, though, right?" She winked at him. He probably hadn't been flirted with in forty years.

"Course I would," he said, grinning like a fool, his teeth pale yellow. "But, LT, he's a damn cupcake. You don't need to worry about him."

"Very well then," she said. She slid off her seat and followed me into the dining area. She certainly wasn't acting like a killer, if there was a way one would expect a killer to act.

"You're the lieutenant?" she said when we got there five seconds later. "Impressive."

"No. It's a nickname, short for Little Timmy." I'd broken a kid's nose for calling me Tiny Tim in fifth grade, so the geniuses at my elementary school switched to Little Timmy, hoping it would lead to less aggression on my part. It managed to stick. I'd been explaining it ever since and had tired of doing so. Talia was nearly my height.

"This town is full of color, isn't it?" she said, smiling widely and insincerely. Her shirt was the hue of her ex-husband's dried blood, but I thought it better not to start there.

"I need to talk to you about Adam."

"Has he filed a complaint because I'm not drinking at that awful Reef House? Completely boring and so cliche. I told him that he should have let me do the design. He certainly learned his lesson on that one." Her smile motored down to normal levels.

"No," I said, lowering my voice. "I'm sorry to say that we found him this afternoon. He's been killed."

"You're kidding, of course." Her grin lessened but didn't vanish as she folded her arms. "Did he put you up to this?"

"No, Mrs. Springbrook. I'm sorry. We found Adam earlier today on the Lost Woods property. He'd been shot."

"It can't be," she shouted. Her hand went to her heart as her voice carried across the room. I could feel every head turn.

She took a step back and sank into one of the worn wooden chairs at the table behind her. She looked over to the bar, then up at me.

"You're not kidding," she said. Her eyes got watery. She shuddered. A sob escaped as she tried to compose herself.

"I'm sorry, no."

"What happened?" Her hands gripped the arms of her chair. I gave the Tavern crew a "turn around" gesture with my hand. We didn't need them gawking at us. "I mean, why? Who would do that?"

"We haven't been able to make any determinations yet," I said.

"You have no idea?"

"No, Mrs. Springbrook, we just found him a few hours ago."

"This place is tiny. Shouldn't it be obvious?"

"Things aren't that simple, even here. We'll be investigating fully, of course. That goes without saying."

"You're equipped to handle something like this?"

"The state police have already been called in. We're quite capable."

"So, there's a killer out there somewhere?"

"I'm afraid that's true. Your cooperation could be very helpful," I said. "When was the last time you saw him?" I hoped answering questions might head her off on the road to hysteria, as well as provide us with information.

"We had dinner Sunday night at the Reef. I came up that morning."

"Are you staying at his house or one of his inns?" I knew the answer, but wanted to hear it from her. If she skirted the truth, that would tell me something.

"I am at his beach house."

"What brought you here?"

"I can't see my ex-husband?" she said, her head angling to the right. "Must I explain that we managed to stay friends, unlike so many of those dreadful, bitter people who are surprised when a relationship runs its course?"

I was one of those people. A decade earlier, I had come home to a missing wife, emptied closets, and a note on the kitchen table.

"How were you getting along?" I said, remembering that she'd been crying during the dinner she'd just told me about.

"Fine," she said. "Why would you even ask that?"

I took a deep breath. She hadn't realized that an ex-wife showing up and an ex-husband dying would warrant suspicion. I could have told her that everyone was a suspect until I knew otherwise. That was the only way to operate. Though I would have liked to see her reaction to my pointing that out, I needed to be practical. If I were patient, I would get what I was after.

"One of the first things we need to do is establish a timeline, Mrs. Springbrook. I need to know where he was and what he was doing these past few days, right up until the last minute."

"My name is Talia Murphy. I no longer go by Springbrook."

"You were getting along?"

"We were just fine if you must know. We've often worked together. I'm going to be—or was—part of the Lost Woods project."

"Nature of your involvement?"

She sighed. "Consultant."

"Officially? In what area?"

"Yes, officially. I do design work of all kinds. I work with photographers, architects, and retail developers. There's an art to establishing a continuity of aesthetic, from the hotel decor to the landscape to the window displays in the retail spots, and magazine ads, too. I see that it happens."

"You were going to do this for Lost Woods?"

"That's right. I was going to be the liaison for the creatives. I understood what Adam wanted and could communicate it more effectively than he."

"This was all settled? You had a contract or something?"

"We had outlined responsibilities and compensation, but we've never needed a contract to work together. With the scope of this endeavour, it took us a day or two to iron out the details. We finalized it over lunch on Monday."

"I thought you last saw him on Sunday."

"I guess I was mistaken," she said, her hand going to her mouth. Her eyes blinked rapidly. "This is so unsettling, getting the news and then being interrogated like this."

I felt my eyebrows shoot up on reflex—before I could quell the reaction and respond.

"Excuse me," she said, "if I'm not composed enough to have every fact instantly correct." Her eyes narrowed, and her lips clamped shut after she said it.

"I understand. But you're staying and working with him. I imagine it would be odd for you not to see him over the course of a twenty-four-hour period. You didn't see him at all yesterday?"

"I did not."

"The last time you saw him was Monday, then?"

"That's right, at lunch."

"Just the two of you."

"Yes."

"What did you do?"

"We talked."

"About?"

"The project, of course. He wanted the different elements to come

36

together, while each area maintained a certain uniqueness. It's somewhat complicated."

Her cheeks remained cool and white through a layer of make-up.

"Were you drinking?"

"We had wine. What does that have to do with anything?"

"Just trying to see the state of mind he may have been in." That also meant that if she were telling the truth, the wine glasses in the sink must have been there for a few days, which could explain why the remnants had dried and crusted. That also left a glass unaccounted for, marked by different lipstick.

"He was doing very well, from my understanding, Tim, or Officer, or whatever it is I'm supposed to call you."

"Most people who've known me call me LT. That will work, or Chief."

She looked put out by that answer.

"Everything was good between you?" I asked. "No points of contention?"

"Not one, personally. Professionally, of course, with something like this of significant vision, there's tension between what we'd like to do and what we can do. There are many factors in a business venture. Risk and reward. Who would be responsible for what. We'd come to an understanding of how that would function. You know how it is; good fences make good neighbors."

"The neighbors had an issue with the project?"

She took a breath and smiled slightly. "No. Adam and I work better if we have a clear delineation of vision, that's all. We were all on the same page Monday."

"All?"

"Yes, really, he and I. But also others involved in backing the project. The investors, I guess. It's a figure of speech."

"Were you going to move here?"

"God, no," she said. "Maybe for a time during certain points of construction, I would stay with him, but blueprints and mockups can be shipped and delivered. I'd be surprised if any of the specialists we're looking at using will be from within two hundred miles of here."

I suppressed a sigh. I must have done it poorly.

"I don't mean to be disrespecting Laurel. My family used to come here

37

when I was a child. In fact, I was the one who first brought Adam here when we were just married. He liked it more, obviously, than I did."

"You didn't see him at all on Monday night or Tuesday?"

"No. Monday after lunch I went to Portland to see a friend I know from Greenwich. She owns a gallery in the Old Port. It's not exactly beach weather, and what else is there to do here? We were at her gallery, then went out for dinner."

"When did you return?"

"I stayed with her. I came back Tuesday morning."

"Was Adam home when you returned?"

"No. I assumed he'd gone for the day."

"Was his car there?"

"It wasn't in the driveway."

"Did you check the garage?"

"Why would I? I thought he'd gone to work."

"Did you talk to him yesterday?"

"No."

"That seems odd. You're staying there, you're potentially working with him, yet you don't touch base all day or night?"

"He is an adult man. I knew that he was going to be busy yesterday. He's also rather popular, from what I understand, and he and I are not in any way romantic. Nor are we each other's parents, so don't feel the need to check in. His life didn't stop when I came to town, so to speak."

Yet, technically, it did.

She sighed. "We did have plans for tonight, however. We'd made them on Monday. So, I really didn't expect to see him yesterday or need to talk to him."

"Did he mention what he was going to be doing on Monday evening? Or yesterday?"

"No, he was rather vague. I assume he was with a friend at night, which is no longer my business, and not something we discussed with each other."

"Was the last time you were in contact with him Monday at lunch? That's when you made these plans?"

"No. I called him Monday afternoon as soon as I saw the paintings." She stopped to sniffle, taking a napkin from the table and wiping her nose. "I was very excited and thought they'd be perfect for the hotel in Lost Woods. I wanted him to see them. And, as I mentioned, he had told me that he was busy on Tuesday, so we scheduled for tonight to check them out and have dinner in Portland."

"When you didn't see him yesterday, you assumed that he was either working or shacked up with someone?"

"That's rather a crass way to put it," she said. "We just hadn't crossed paths. I do leave the house on occasion. I visited some outlets in Kittery and the galleries in Ogunquit that were open. What he was up to was what he was up to."

"Did you look in the garage today?"

"No."

"You weren't curious to see if his car was there?"

"I assumed that it wasn't. He wasn't there, why would his car be?"

"It is there, that's the thing."

"He came back at some point?"

"Yes. Has anyone been at the house other than you and him?"

"Not that I know of."

The three wine glasses that I shouldn't have seen came back to me.

"Did he, by chance, take you to the worksite?"

"Yes, Sunday afternoon, before we went to dinner. He wanted me to get a visual so I could capture the naturalness of the area in design. That was to be a vital component of the project."

"Did you go into the woods?"

"We drove into the center of the space. I didn't think his car was going to make it. But we got out and walked around. To be honest, I found it somewhat eerie, everything stripped and torn up like that."

It appeared that Mikey Paquin and I weren't the only ones picking up on it.

"They haven't worked on it in a week," I said. "Do you know why?"

She shrugged. "No idea."

"Do you have a name, address, and contact number for your gallery friend in Portland?"

"You're serious," she said, stamping a small, heeled foot on the hardwood floor. Her face reddened. "I'm a suspect? The tawdry ex-wife shot him? That's right where you go?"

"Please don't be offended. I wouldn't be doing my job if I didn't follow the most obvious lines of investigation."

"Here's my alibi." She sighed and dug into the small pocketbook slung over her shoulder. She handed me a business card for Amy Randall, owner of the Fore Street, Five Arts Gallery. "Now maybe you can get on with finding out who killed Adam."

I could do that. Halted construction: "We pay our bills," echoed in my head.

"As you were involved in this project, were finances a problem?"

"Now it's follow the money?" she said, shaking her head. "The ex-wife, the money trail, I see where this is going. You're a very suspicious person, but in a very basic way."

"I find that a pretty good approach." I tapped my fingers on the table. "Just so you know, where we found Adam in Lost Woods is being analyzed as a crime scene. As soon as the body is taken to the morgue, you'll be granted access if that's something you want to do. But I have a few more questions if you don't mind."

"Do I have a choice?" she said, wiping eyes that had shed few tears. "I'm in shock trying to process this. I've lost someone I've known my entire adult life, and once loved very deeply. I'm sure you can understand why I might find it difficult, especially when you're considering that I may have had something to do with it. Which is unfathomable to me."

I tried to nod solemnly. She hadn't broken down. She remained calm. These things themselves didn't necessarily mean anything. People handled bad news in different ways. But I had yet to see anyone breaking down and sobbing over the man's death, and I'd only talked to people close to him. I didn't know what to make of that.

"Were there any personal points of contention between you two?" I asked.

"You're like a dog with a bone. I'm sure you think I have some sort of nefarious reason for being here. But there isn't one. We enjoy working together. Our collaborations have been very successful."

"While you were spending time with him, did he mention having difficulties with anyone?"

"Not at all. Everyone loves him. That's the kind of charisma he had."

"As far as you know, everything was fine in his life?"

"As far as I know, yes."

"You don't know if he was seeing anyone, other than you?"

"No. I wouldn't say he was seeing me, either. Strictly business."

"Does Adam have any other relatives that should be notified? Would you like me to do that?"

"My parents. They're in Connecticut. They're in their seventies and are not going to take this well. He's still like a son to them. It's better coming from me. I don't know how I'm going to tell them."

"Very well. Other than on this project, were you in contact regularly?"

"Sure. We got married while I was in college. Adam was older, swept me off my feet. It lasted a few years. He stayed the same. But I was young and still developing as a person. Sometimes people become closer the longer they're together. But my growth led me in a different direction. Luckily, we realized it before we…." She stopped and frowned. "It wouldn't have been healthy for us to stay together as a couple. However, as friends, we were fine, and as work colleagues, we were great. You've seen his inns, correct? We did those together and as products of our collaboration, they are fabulous in design and aesthetic."

"I wasn't aware of that." Why would I have been? I'd never been in one. But I'd heard and read about them and seen the No Vacancy signs. "When were you divorced?"

"Fifteen years ago? I won't bore you with the details, and that is certainly not relevant now."

"Were you receiving alimony?"

"I sure was."

I nodded. She must have seen my mind at work.

41

"There you go: I would have no reason to kill him. That's a loss of steady income if you want to enjoy the black humor of it all, which you seem to revel in."

I'd never found such things to be that simple of an equation. But I decided not to bite.

"Do you have plans to stay here for the time being?"

"I didn't, but now I suppose I'll have to, what with arrangements and all. I don't know that there's anyone else. His parents are gone. He lost his brother a few years ago."

"I was going to ask you to stay until we find out more about who did this."

"Because I'm a suspect or for my protection?"

"Let's just say it's the most prudent course of action. Is there a reason you would fear for your safety?"

"There wasn't, but now I'm not so sure. Because who would want to hurt Adam?"

"How long have you been here at the Tavern?"

"Maybe an hour."

"You came straight from the beach house?"

"Yes."

If that were the case, she was either lying or I'd just missed her. She was wearing dark red lipstick now, but the shade on one of the glasses had been much lighter. Of course, she could have changed it for an appearance in Laurel's off-season high society of carpenters and fishermen. I wasn't going to ask just yet, however. I wanted to see in what direction she might try to point me.

"Would you like me to drive you back to the beach house?"

"Oh, no. I'm going to need one of those drinks that were offered me, in light of the news you've so awfully shared."

I ignored the barb.

"If you can't drive safely afterward, please let me know. We'll get you home." I handed her a card. She didn't bother looking at it and seemed to be stopping herself from telling me to get lost. "Call me if you need anything or think of something that might be relevant to Adam, please."

She gave a quick nod as I stood up. She continued to sit. I waited until she was ready and returned her to her seat at the bar. "Sympathy for the Devil" played softly on the stereo. No one spoke. I left, passing the front window on the way to my car. Chet had one hand on her shoulder and the other beckoning Rosemary for a drink.

I could have used one myself. Instead, I headed for the station.

Chapter Eight

The three of us went into my office and sat down. Ted ran a hand through his short hair. Gwyneth was straight-backed, but pushing forward on her chair, her eyes bright. A homicide investigation was something I don't think they'd expected. Gwyneth looked like she saw it as a bonus.

They'd completed their canvass but had little to report. Two folks had mentioned that they hadn't minded not having to listen to land-clearing machinery for the past week. Henry Jones, south of the site, had heard several shots on Saturday, which preceded Springbrook's death, and was possibly someone sighting in their deer rifle. The Parkers, who lived west of the cut and had sold Springbrook some of their land, hadn't heard a thing. No one heard a solitary shot in the last two days. It seemed odd that one ringing out on a weekday wouldn't have grabbed someone's attention. It also could be that Springbrook hadn't been killed where we'd found him. That had me calling the lab and asking them to fast-track their inquiry. They told me they were working on it. Springbrook had been last seen Monday night, and if that's when he died, that was information we could start working off of.

I sent each officer on a mission. I wanted Ted to follow Talia Springbrook. I imagined that she was still at the Tavern and that eventually she'd go back to the beach house. Unless she made a run for it. That was something we'd need to be ready for. I told him to ditch the cruiser for his own car, dress warm, park across from the Tavern, and wait for her to leave. If she went back to the beach house, I instructed him to park at one of the empty summer houses up the street from Adam's and watch her until morning. Gwyneth, I sent to the gallery in Portland to check Talia's story. They left with serious expressions and quick steps.

I drove to Portland to see what the Medical Examiner had learned. Fritz Bannon would no doubt file a detailed report, but I didn't want to wait for it. Even if he hadn't completed his autopsy, he'd at least have something that would prove useful as we got this investigation rolling. By the time I got there, he'd finished and was having a scotch in his office. He poured me one, then showed me the mangled sixteen-gauge deer slug that he had pulled out of Adam Springbrook's midsection. It had done a splendid job splintering a series of ribs before shredding his organs. He assured me the shooter hadn't been more than fifteen feet away. That told me that Adam had likely known his killer. But then, it was a small town, and as they say, everyone knew everyone.

Chapter Nine

First thing in the morning, I brought Ted coffee and a breakfast sandwich from Bartley's. He was sitting in the driveway of a mammoth Cape on Bishop's Beach Drive. Talia Springbrook hadn't stepped outside the house. I sent him home to grab a shower and a nap. I sat in the Bronco for an hour watching, waiting for Gwyneth to relieve me. If Talia didn't run today, I thought we'd be safe, but a few more hours of surveillance wouldn't hurt.

Of course, Gwyneth was early, and thirty minutes later I climbed the stairs to the headquarters of this new Springbrook Group. There were formerly two offices there, and it looked like they'd been combined. I didn't bother to knock. I introduced myself to Sally Cooper, and she picked up the phone to summon Marv Fitzgerald from across the hall. He came in and shook my hand. I asked if he was Springbrook's personal lawyer, as well as that of the business.

"That's correct," he said. He appeared younger than me, with blond hair in a musician's haircut, short over the ears but long enough that it crested his collar in the back. I'm sure he and Springbrook would have made a positive impression on the professional women in Portland had they chosen to socialize together. It also didn't look like he bought his suit at Sears, a gray pinstripe that moved with him and fit as if tailored. While that might not be unusual in Boston and New York, it was a rare sight here out of season. I surprised myself by noticing. This time of year, I never wore anything other than flannels or sweatshirts, if not in uniform.

"What can you tell us?" he asked. His left eye seemed poised to twitch.

I told them that we'd found Adam Springbrook's body in the woods and that he'd been shot. And that it was no hunting accident. Cooper's hands pressed to her face. They looked at each other as if to confirm what I'd just said could be true. Cooper took off her tortoiseshell glasses and rubbed her eyes. Fitzgerald looked down at his shoes and shook his head. He suggested that the three of us go into the conference room and sit down. He opened the door for Cooper and put his hand on her shoulder to steady her. He took the head of the table. We sat on either side of him.

"Do you know who did it?" he said. "Have you made an arrest?"

"We've just started investigating." Maybe it was television that gave people the impression that these things were solved in sixty minutes.

"I hope this will be a top priority," Fitzgerald said. A sheen of sweat appeared on his forehead.

"Of course." I restrained myself from saying that we'd be pulling manpower from pumpkin-smashing details and putting it on this case.

Fitzgerald nodded, assuming he'd assisted us in prioritizing appropriately.

"I didn't know this office existed," I said, "so my first stop was the Reef House, where I called you from yesterday. Louie Williams let me know that Adam's ex-wife, Talia Murphy, was in town. I was able to find her, and she's been notified. If you could answer some questions, I'd appreciate it."

"Certainly," Fitzgerald said. The two of them looked at each other again.

"When was the last time you saw him?"

"We have a standing meeting on Monday afternoon at two o'clock, the three of us," Fitzgerald said. "To go over the previous week's sales from our existing properties and to update business in the works."

"Did Lost Woods come up?"

"Of course," Cooper said. "You don't think that the project has something to do with Adam getting killed, do you?"

"I'm not sure of anything at this point. That's why I'm asking." It could be that he was left there to send a message. "I noticed that construction stopped a week ago. What was the reason for that?"

"It's nothing unusual," Fitzgerald said. "Some of these contractors have several jobs going on simultaneously. They get pulled from one to the other depending on scheduling urgencies that arise."

"There weren't any issues with the Lost Woods project, then?"

"There are always issues with a job that size."

"Such as?"

"There's permitting, which really hasn't been a problem."

"If it's not a problem, why would you bring it up?"

"I guess I was looking at things from a legal standpoint. The town has been very cooperative on that level."

"What about from Adam Springbrook's perspective? What would have stopped the work?"

"I guess you're not overly familiar with how these things go," he said.

"You would be correct. We don't do land clearing and resort construction in law enforcement."

He started to sigh, then tried to reel it in before I noticed.

"In general, work is done in phases based on funding. We have investors. Sometimes, cash flow isn't steady. It's not like Adam wrote a check out of his personal account, like you pay for your mortgage. These projects often run in fits and starts at this stage. There's not a pile of money at the beginning, and we just draw on it until the project is completed."

He was right. That was exactly how I thought things worked.

"Were there money problems then?" I asked.

"No," he said.

"I assure you," Cooper said, adjusting the barrette that held the hair over her right ear in place, "that everything is as it should be."

Other than their boss being gutted by a bullet.

"It wasn't a lack of money that halted the site work, then?" I said.

"I highly doubt it," Fitzgerald said. "We have several projects underway. And so does the contractor. Most likely a scheduling issue."

This sounded like bullshit, especially with the Reef's bookkeeper repeatedly going out of her way to mention that they paid their bills.

"How many investors are there?" I asked.

"Ten or so."

"Is this public knowledge?"

"No. We are a privately held company, so that information isn't shared."

"I'd like a list of those investors, please."

"Of course," Fitzgerald said.

"There can't be problems coming from that area," Cooper said.

"Your many years of law enforcement experience with similar cases would tell you that?" I said it as pleasantly as I could manage, not being good with condescension. Their eyes widened in tandem. They probably had little experience with getting talked back to.

"Well, there's a certain level of people that aren't likely to become involved in a shooting. Unlike some others around here." Cooper rose and went to a file cabinet.

"With our other properties so successful," Fitzgerald said, "people were falling all over each other to invest. I'm sure that no one is upset about their prospects. The more you're successful, the easier it is to get funding. We're in fine shape in that regard. I'm sure no one had a problem with where we are in the process."

"Who is the bank? I assume there's one involved." Even I knew that much.

"Of course," she said, "it's the Southern Maine Bank and Trust."

"Are there also investors for the Reef and the two inns?"

"There are. They're being paid ahead of schedule, in fact. Those properties have been hugely profitable."

"But you don't know exactly why work stopped in Lost Woods? Whether it was cash flow or some kind of scheduling urgency for the outfit doing the work?"

"I'm not sure," Fitzgerald said, "but I assume it wasn't anything serious. That's something that Adam would have been aware of."

I was glad Fitzgerald didn't have my job. His attention to detail seemed to be lacking. Of course, he could be giving me that impression for a reason.

"That didn't come up in your meeting on Monday?" I asked.

"No. Adam must have thought it wasn't worth mentioning, which leads to my supposition that it wasn't anything important."

"All your information came from Adam?"

"And the books," Cooper said. "We monitor the cash flow of all our locations. There is nothing lacking in our financial reporting and oversight."

"Glad to hear it," I said. "It might make my job easier. Is there a general contractor involved here or does Adam run the project?"

"Larry Scott, out of Portland. He'll assume construction management once the site work is completed."

"Eddie Mancini is clearing the land?"

"That's correct."

"And everyone involved is happy?"

"Well, I wouldn't say that," Fitzgerald said. Sally Cooper's mouth opened, then closed. "I can tell you where to start. It's with that idiot Bill Tatum."

"He sold Springbrook some of the land for Lost Woods," I said. His family home bordered the project. I know he owned a shotgun or two.

"Yes, and he was well paid for it," Fitzgerald said. He tapped the table with his fingers. "Above market price. But he was in here not two weeks ago, accusing Adam of swindling him."

"Why would he think that?"

"He saw the article in the Press Herald that called Lost Woods a multi-million-dollar hospitality project. You've seen what Adam's done with his restaurant and the inns. There were big expectations."

"Why was Tatum upset about that?" Bill Tatum was a cabinet maker who had his workshop on his property. His family had owned quite a few acres, some of which he sold to Springbrook. I'd heard he'd received a fair price, nearly six figures, but, like him, I hadn't suspected we were talking about a multi-million-dollar enterprise.

Fitzgerald started spitting out cost-per-acre numbers at me, offering comps from properties around the state, and telling me that Springbrook had paid as much for the land alone as others were paying for land with houses on them. Tatum, who'd been happy when he'd sold the land, once he heard "multi-million," believed he'd been shortchanged.

"What did he want Springbrook to do?" I asked.

"He said that another twenty-five thousand would make things right. Mind you, he could have bought waterfront with what Adam paid him. We are talking about undeveloped woodland. He was very well compensated."

"You told him that?"

"Adam did. I pointed out that at the time he signed six months ago, he was thrilled, pumping our hands like we'd donated a kidney. It wasn't until he read that article and learned what we were trying to accomplish here that he got upset. When he showed up last week, at first, he was polite and civil. But when we told him, no, he wasn't getting any more money, he lost it. He started claiming that we'd taken advantage of him and that he wasn't going to stand for it. If we didn't make things right, he was putting up no trespassing signs and if any of our guests wandered onto his property, they were going to get an ass full of buckshot."

"Did he threaten Adam?"

"Not exactly. Though he was so worked up that he was spraying us with spit with every word. But he wasn't getting another cent."

I'd only known Tatum to be easygoing. The extent of his criminality had peaked with a ten-dollar parking ticket.

"And now that I'm thinking about it," Fitzgerald said, "there was a man who Adam said accosted him at Bartley's store last week. This one was upset because we posted the land for no hunting." He paused. "Mancini told us that he'd have a hard time getting people to show up for work if hunters were tramping through with buck fever."

It was hard to argue with that logic.

"Do you know who that was?"

"Adam mentioned him, went by a nickname. Slimy or something like that."

That had to be Cranky Fisher, not happy about prime land getting posted. Hard to believe, however, that he'd shoot him over it. It was more likely that he'd ignore the posting and pull his deer just to prove a point. Cranky would also know better places to stash a body than where we found it. Still, like Tatum, he'd need to be followed up with.

"I guess I can talk to Mancini directly," I said. "Anyone else I should be aware of?"

Fitzgerald took a deep breath. "Of course, I don't know much about Adam's personal life. He and Talia seem to work well together, and she is here, as you noted. She is involved in the project. She's going to handle some of the design work, and she's an investor, as well. They seem to get along great for a divorced couple."

"An investor, as in contributing money?" I asked. She'd failed to mention that. When people hide the truth from the beginning, it usually isn't a good sign.

"Yes, Chief Nichols, that's what that means."

I looked up at Fitzgerald and counted to ten in my head. It amazed me that more lawyers weren't assaulted on a regular basis.

"Who would know the most about this project, other than you and him?"

"Well, Talia may know quite a bit. Mancini would know about what is currently going on. I don't know if Larry Scott would be up to date, but he could tell you what was coming. It's my understanding that actual construction plans are far from finalized, however. The first step, of course, is clearing the land, then preparing it for construction, and as you can see, we still have a way to go there."

I asked for copies of those contracts, too. I would have assumed that everything right down to the last screw and nail would be lined up before they started knocking down trees. But what did I know?

"Do you think this is somehow connected to that project because that's where you found the body?" Fitzgerald asked.

"I haven't come to any conclusions. I'm two hours into this." 'If you don't get an answer, keep asking the question' was quite a legal strategy.

"Talia might know more," he said.

This was an interesting choice of words. Neither of them showed concern as to how she took the news or worried that she could be heartbroken. I'd made three stops reporting and investigating Springbrook's death and had yet to see a flood of tears. Unusual, to say the least.

"How long have you been working with Adam?"

"I came in six months before he purchased the last two restaurants, Dante's and the Clam Shed. It's quite a story. Adam had gone on a trip to India, a spiritual quest, when he was younger. His guru told him that a time would come to grow his empire and to do so, he would need to centralize. I think bringing me in was the first step. We were able to tie all the single entities, the now three restaurants and two inns, together under one roof. Of course, it makes complete sense with the vision he had for Laurel. Adam was putting this town on the map as a destination in the Northeast. He would have enriched everyone here. That's why I can't fathom that anyone other than those crazy hunters would want to kill him. Lost Woods was a major step in achieving that."

That Adam actually had a guru might be a crazy enough reason for him to think he could accomplish this.

"Now, without him, will it go forward?" I asked.

"Adam was running things by himself. But that was soon changing. He was starting to put an operational team together to take care of the day-to-day. That would give him time to move forward and focus on expansion."

"Was that a yes or a no?"

"I don't really know at this point."

"Does anyone benefit from this not happening?"

"Other than those hicks who were upset about not being able to blast every deer in town, no. Lost Woods would bring money to be spent in every store and restaurant, not just those owned by Adam. Everyone liked Adam. Even when we went into places that passed for competition, like the Sea Squall, people were patting Adam on the back and buying him drinks. He was the tide that was going to raise all boats."

"Until now, he oversaw all this himself?"

"He hired good people at each location, gave them a directive of what he wanted, then expected them to execute it. With Sally looking at the numbers, and him maintaining a presence, he'd been very successful. But with two new restaurants and Lost Woods starting, we were going to need help. We were planning a talent search this winter to have people in place by spring so Adam could focus on getting Lost Woods on track."

"Who will step in now to run things for the places that are already going?"

"I'm not sure. There's the matter of the will."

"And if a decision needs to be made today?"

"I am the Vice President of the Springbrook Coastal Group. I guess it would fall to me to make decisions for the time being, but eventually, we'll need someone to run the company as Adam would have. My operational knowledge of the hospitality industry is limited, other than I like my vodka martinis shaken and with a twist. Though much of it seems like common sense."

"Are you also an investor?" I guessed that Fitzgerald had never spent time as a waiter or bartender. Six months had been enough for me to know better.

"I am. In a small way."

"Did Adam owe anyone money?"

"Technically, he owed a lot of people money, but only in the due course of business. Very few of these projects are privately financed by a single individual. One gathers investors to share the financial risk and stake in the enterprise. Things are well planned out regarding Lost Woods, and revenue projections were fantastic. Admittedly, we have a few years and some work to do before we get to the part of the program where money is returned. But everyone knows that coming in. The investors don't have an official voice in the operation of the company. There's no board like Ford Motors or IBM. Of course, it was in Adam's best interest to keep them happy."

"And they're all content at the moment?"

"Concerning the Springbrook Coastal Group, they'd have no reason not to be. Everything is as it should be. In fact, we have no shortage of investors. Anyone can drive by a Springbrook enterprise and see a full parking lot. Now, if someone wasn't happy with the way their lobster was prepared at the Reef or they weren't served with sufficient reverence, they could have a problem with that, but not with their investment."

"No one had demanded their money back?"

"They would have no reason to. Everyone understood that these are long-term investments. They might not see their return for up to ten years in Lost Woods, for instance. It was that massive of an undertaking. I believe you're barking up the wrong tree here."

"I'll hold off on making that determination if you don't mind." I'd review the financial documents myself. My father had been a businessman. He'd hoped I would follow in his footsteps, but it wasn't for me. He believed that if something wouldn't be paid off in five years, it shouldn't be touched. But he also hadn't been thinking on the grand scale of Adam Springbrook.

"To clarify," I said, "you're in charge now, Mr. Fitzgerald?"

"Until we look at the will and see what that dictates."

"Did you write it? Are you in possession of it?"

"It preceded me. I assume it would be in Adam's safe, and I presume his previous personal attorney, Ben Ramsey, from Hingham, Massachusetts, would have a copy."

"You'll be contacting him?"

"Shortly," Fitzgerald said.

"I'd like to be notified as soon as it surfaces. I'm sure you can understand why. Are you also presuming that whoever is inheriting Mr. Springbrook's investments would take possession of the properties and have the responsibility of running the restaurants and inns?"

"That would be correct."

"They wouldn't close them, would they?"

"I would think not. They are profitable. But I wouldn't hazard a guess as to what someone I don't know as of yet might or might not do. Expansion plans could be put on hold. For how long is anyone's guess. Plans weren't limited to the Lost Woods property. Adam had made proposals to purchase several other establishments, as well."

"Such as?"

"If there's a restaurant in Laurel, I'm sure Adam has talked to them."

"About selling to him?"

"That's correct. Adam saw practically unlimited potential here."

"He did all this himself?"

"The planning and purchasing, yes. The running of them, no. That's where the search for operational help was coming in. That was another of Adam's philosophies. Put good people in place and let them do their jobs. You've seen the results."

"Why not just promote someone who ran one of the existing places?" My thoughts went to a potentially passed-over Louie Williams. My cynicism was one more October frost.

"That would have been up to Mr. Springbrook."

"Everything was proceeding as planned?"

"Nothing is without challenges, but yes. I'm sure that you've heard the Clam Shed is going to need its pilings sunk deeper into the riverbed. There are always unexpected hurdles cropping up. But nothing insurmountable. That was Adam's talent: imagining what could be and making it happen. Laurel was really starting to thrive."

"It's been busy here in the summer since the 1920s, Mr. Fitzgerald," I said.

"Not quite on the scale that Adam was reaching, if I may correct you. The per caps—the spends per person—at Adam's places are far over what people have traditionally spent at other establishments. It's not just steamers, fried clams, and ice cream. This is becoming a different type of town, more resort than fishing village, with more upscale offerings."

Yet, instead of nominating Springbrook for sainthood, someone shot him.

"So, there's a happy ex-wife," I said, "a happy group of investors, and happy employees. And other than Cranky Fisher and Bill Tatum, no one had an ax to grind with Adam?"

Fitzgerald shrugged. "From what I understand, everyone was satisfied."

"You're in a position to know that?"

"I wouldn't say exhaustively so. I am only aware of what I'm aware of. Plans were proceeding as conceived. Adam's personal life was his own, if you know what I mean."

"Can I have a look at Adam's office, please?"

"Certainly."

The door to Adam's office at the end of the hall was unlocked. He had a huge glass-topped desk covered by a neatly arranged day planner, Rolodex, traditional green blotter, and gold pen and pencil set. A computer and monitor sat at one end. There were two file cabinets made of dark wood to the side. It looked like the kind of office that you'd see in a museum of what a modern office should look like, rather than one that had actual work done in it. Of course, there was an exception. On the interior wall, a four-by-six-foot line map of Laurel stretched across it. Names of existing businesses were written in place by pen; magic marker circles in black, blue, green, and red surrounded them. I moved in for a closer look.

Every restaurant, hotel, inn, and store that sold food was circled in black. Most were also circled in blue, outside the black. Some had either red or green rings around the blue. I scratched my head. The Reef's lot was outlined in black, then blue, then green, as were the Captain Fairweather and Seagrass inns. Wink's General Store, I noticed, had black, blue, and red. There were green outer circles around Dante's and the Clam Shed, which he'd recently purchased. Babe's Marina also had a green circle, and I hadn't heard anything about that. The Lost Woods footprint was marked by an outer green circle that snaked around the new property line. It cut a lopsided rectangle through the middle of the map. The key wasn't difficult to figure out. The green and red stoplight code seemed obvious enough.

"Adam recently bought Babe's Marina?" I asked, testing my theory.

"Yes," Fitzgerald said. "We haven't closed yet, but we are under agreement."

"Will that go through now?"

"That remains to be seen, to be honest. It depends on who is going to wind up with the company and what they'd like to do. But if it didn't make sense to purchase it, Adam wouldn't have gone after it."

"What does the blue mean?" I asked, referring to the second circle around each business.

"That Adam had approached the owner."

"Approached as in made an offer or chatted about the possibilities?" Those were two different things.

"I'm not sure. I only presented when Adam needed a legal document, such as a formal offer sheet or purchase and sale agreement. He kept much of the behind-the-scenes in his head, until something progressed, of course, one way or another."

There was only one place I could see on the map that he'd missed.

"There's no interest in the Rusty Bullet?" It was the town dive. I liked it just the way it was: out of the way, rundown, and surprisingly peaceful.

"I don't know that we could clean it up enough to ever open as a Springbrook spot, to be honest," Fitzgerald said.

I nodded. I would have been surprised had Springbrook stepped foot in it. A few minutes on a bar stool there would have ruined one of his linen suits.

57

At least that made it safe from a makeover. I stepped back and took a long look at the map. Ambitious was an understatement.

"Was he planning on renaming the town Springbrookville when he was done?" I tried to say it lightly, but failed. I didn't like what I'd seen, and there were a lot of folks here less reasonable than myself.

"Really, Chief?"

"It's a lot," I said.

"He was a visionary," Fitzgerald said.

"That's what I've been hearing."

He watched as I went behind the desk and sat in Adam's chair. No files had been left out. Nothing was written on the notepad next to the phone. The top page was smooth, so even shading it wasn't going to reveal a last phone number. The Rolodex was closed. The desk had no drawers, so it wasn't like I was going to be able to slide something open and find a clue. The cabinets were no help, either. All files were in alphabetical order, and none were askew. I'd have to come back and go through them one by one. My own desk had never been this organized, even with Estelle straightening it up for me daily, which I'd asked her not to do.

"Is there a safe?" I asked.

"Yes."

"Do you have the combination?"

"I do."

"Do you mind if I take a look?"

"I do. You'll need a warrant for that. There could be company business in there that may need to remain private. Our investors could potentially have a problem with that."

"Do you think your investors may have a problem with their visionary getting gunned down?"

"We don't know that the killing was related to this company."

"That would be a way to find out."

"Why don't I check later and see if there's anything in there that might be of importance? Then I can contact you."

"You're trained and qualified to judge that?"

"I believe I am. I want to know who killed Adam just as much as you do."

"I guess I'll return with a warrant."

"That's your prerogative."

"I'm going to need that list of investors with contact information. Financial documents for the businesses, as well. And employees of all establishments owned by Springbrook."

"Of course," he said. He didn't move.

"Could I get that now?" I asked.

He tried to stifle a sigh. "I'm sorry I'm a little off. This is a lot to take in, hearing about something like this. And then getting showered with questions. Can I trust that what you see will remain confidential? There are potentially sensitive materials that may be handed over."

"I would only share information that I need based on investigating the case, and that would only go to law enforcement. We aren't in the habit of sharing gossip, business or personal."

"This will take us a little while, maybe even a full day for all the financials."

"That's okay. I'll study this map while you work on compiling the items you can get now, if you don't mind." I got out my notebook and started lists of red, green, and blue-circled establishments.

Thanks to Mrs. Cooper's use of the computer, I was leaving a few minutes later with pages worth of documents. But it was the lead that Fitzgerald had provided that sent me back across town.

Chapter Ten

Bill Tatum lived at the end of a serpentine gravel driveway, his lawn a sea of leaves in the middle of the woods. Across from the house were a garage and a workshop in separate buildings, where he made top-end cabinets that went all over the state. I didn't hear a saw running, so went to the house. His wife, Millie, answered the door and led me to the kitchen, where he was enjoying a coffee break. He sat straight up when he saw me following his wife into the room. I turned down her offer of a cup. I was jittery enough.

Millie invited me to sit down and joined us at the table. She picked up a crossword puzzle book but didn't open it.

"What do you want, LT?" Tatum said. "If that asshole Springbrook and his pretty boy lawyer sent you over here, I've got a message for them. They can kiss my ass." He nodded and slurped his coffee.

"Did you threaten Adam?" I asked.

"I wouldn't call it that," he said, his head bobbing from side to side. "I'd say I made a strong request."

"Which was?"

"I wanted more money for the land he bought off me. He took advantage."

"That's a nice new Whaler you've got sitting next to your garage. I heard you were pretty happy when you sold."

"Yeah, for getting rid of some lumber. I had no idea that there was a gigantic, fancy resort coming in. If I had known that was what Springbrook had up his sleeve, I would have held out for more. Which he should have offered in the first place instead of trying to put one past me."

"They told you no when you went to confront them about this, correct?"

"He and that lawyer wouldn't even discuss it, the bastards. Springbrook was lucky I didn't lay him out right there."

"You said that if any of their guests came onto your land, you'd shoot them?"

"Jesus Christ, Bill," Millie said before he could answer.

"What I said was that they'd get their ass shot. I didn't say with what." He grinned, thinking he'd dodged some sort of liability.

"You own a shotgun, Bill?"

"Of course. Got a Remington twelve gauge, and a thirty-thirty, and a couple of twenty-twos." He pushed his empty mug to the center of the table. "You know, I'm surprised at you running over here like Springbrook's errand boy just because I talked a little rough. Taking his side over someone who's lived here their whole life. Like you."

"Bill, you came to an agreement, signed a contract, got paid, were happy about it, read some shit in the paper, and only then decided that you wanted a do-over. Don't try taking the high ground with me. I'm doing my job."

He started to say something but thought better of it. Millie looked ready to cuff him.

"Have you been doing any shooting lately?" I said.

"Why are you asking?" His eyebrows rose. "You aren't thinking of confiscating my guns over some silly shit talk, are you? Deer season's just a few weeks off."

"I guess you haven't heard. Someone put a bullet in Adam Springbrook a few days ago. He was found in the Lost Woods property, not that far from here."

Tatum slumped in his chair.

"You stupid bastard," Millie said. The crossword puzzles flew across the table. He managed to deflect the book and sent it skidding across the floor.

"I didn't shoot him, Millie, for Christ's sake," he yelled, more frightened of her than me.

"I know that, moron." She shook her head violently. "I told you to take what we got and shut up about it, as if he was going to give you anything

61

else, no matter how big a stink you made. Now we got the chief of police here, and he thinks you did it because you couldn't keep your big mouth shut. If you were half as smart as you thought you were, you'd still be short of the cat on brains."

"But I didn't do it," he said, in the voice of a kid who'd spilled grape soda on a white rug.

"Where were you Monday night?" I asked.

"I watched some of the game at the VFW with the boys. Came home at halftime. Wasn't much of a contest." He held his hands up like I had a gun on him.

"Who else was there?"

"The usual crew. Ed Pickey, Blockhead Roger, Derek Anderson, Vinnie Pasqualla. Maybe a couple other guys."

"What time did he get home, Millie?"

"He came busting through the door at ten-thirty. He stomps around like Frankenstein. Woke me up, so I'm sure of it." She rapidly tapped her fingers on the table.

"Did you go anywhere between there and here?"

"Where the hell would I go?" Exasperated, his hands flew up again.

"Look, LT," Millie said. "If he shot Springbrook, you would've been here five minutes after it happened. He's not smart enough to get away with something like that for a goddamn hour."

"Now, Millie," he said.

"If you want to lock him up for a few days while you look into it," Millie said, "I could use the break."

"Don't go joking about that," Tatum said.

"Who's kidding?" she said.

"You know who you should be talking to?" Tatum said, turning to me. "George Paquin. There's someone who had a major problem with Springbrook."

"About what?"

"It ain't my place to say. But he had good reason to put one in him."

"Isn't he one of your best friends, Billy?" Millie said.

"Yeah," he said.

"You don't think he'd really shoot anyone, do you?" she asked. I sat back and watched.

"Of course not," he said, sounding unsure as he looked back and forth between us. Pick your poison.

"Then why ain't your mouth shut?"

"I didn't say he shot him. I said he had reason to. I don't want Chief Nichols to think I had anything to do with it."

"He knows you didn't do it, numb nuts."

"What would that reason be?" I asked, deciding to jump into the fray.

Bill looked over at Millie to see if he should share it. She raised her hands, giving up.

"You might as well now, dumbass," she said.

"I don't think it's right of me to say. But I wouldn't blame him one bit."

"See what I mean?" Millie said, sighing and looking at me.

I shrugged.

"I'm going to need to look at those guns," I said. I wanted to make sure that he hadn't left a sixteen out of his accounting.

"I ain't worried," Tatum said. "I might have yelled at those assholes, but I know I didn't shoot them."

"Thank God for small miracles," Millie said.

I confirmed that Tatum owned a twelve-gauge and several rifles. He was clear on the sixteen. I added the Paquin household to my itinerary. They had more going on than their youngest bouncing off my fender. Not to mention that both Alfred, owner of the dinged-up ten-speed, and Lucy, his sister, were on the list of Reef House employees.

Chapter Eleven

With Paquin likely out on the water working, I thought I'd next hit Eddie Mancini, who was clearing the land for Lost Woods and had dinner with Springbrook on Monday night. The way there took me past Wink's General Store. If anyone knew what was going on in town, it was the three-hundred-pound owner and father of my childhood best friend. I decided to stop. Wink wasn't at his usual station behind the front register, but Suzanne Anderson was stepping out from behind her food service counter. I said hello. She looked surprised to see me, as we were having dinner that night. It was then that I thought bringing her flowers might have been a good idea, another indication as to why I had been a lousy boyfriend. I hadn't frequented the store as much since we'd broken up, but would occasionally swing by late on days when I'd forgotten or had been too busy to eat. There was no one in the store but us. That's the kind of thing that happens when your population drops from fifteen thousand in summer to thirty-five hundred the rest of the year.

"LT," she said, her head cocked to the side. "You better not be here to tell me you're canceling."

"Of course not," I said. Two years earlier, I'd gotten tied up in a case and forgotten a mutual engagement. That led to us yelling at each other across a friend's lawn, which became the night we called it quits. I couldn't even blame that fiasco on being preoccupied with police business, though it was part of it. I was not going to let this investigation get in the way tonight. "I just stopped by to talk to Wink."

"Well, I'm leaving early today, as you can see. I've got something I need to do. If you're looking for lunch, Wink will take care of you."

"Official business," I said.

"If you say so." Doubt appeared on her face as she slipped into her green barn jacket. With her hair in a ponytail, she looked like she did back in high school. "I'll see you tonight then."

"I'll be there," I said, not wanting to sound overly excited. We'd fallen in with each other so easily a few years ago that it seemed crazy we'd never been together. We'd managed this despite both being stung by divorce. While being wary of marriage and not getting any younger, we decided to have a child together—which depending on how things played forward we would co-parent either together or apart. However, our biology wouldn't cooperate. With that weighing on us, things got heavier than we could handle. Maybe I hadn't tried hard enough to make it work. The words we'd shouted across the dandelions that night had only been a symptom.

"You can stop grinning," she said. "It's only dinner."

"I like good food," I said. "What can I say?"

"Sure," she said without much enthusiasm. "Wink's in the back. He should be right out. I'll see you later."

"That you will."

"Don't get ahead of yourself," she said, giving me a little wave as she went out the door. She knew me well. Maybe this was only going to be a check-in. Or maybe she needed a favor. Her ex-husband had been abusive and was as trustworthy as a coyote. If he was bothering her, I'd put an end to it, and she knew that. All she had to do was ask. It wouldn't require dinner. So, I lived with my minuscule hope.

As the door shut behind her, Wink came out of the stockroom. He moved slowly, a big man in denim overalls with a red thermal sweatshirt underneath.

He held up his hands. "I didn't do it." He laughed.

"You've heard about Adam Springbrook?"

"What about him?" His hands came down. Apparently, he had not.

"I found him yesterday. On the Lost Woods property. Shot. Dead."

Wink stopped. A large hand went to his face, his thumb and forefinger wrapping around his chin.

"You don't say."

"It's the truth."

"You're not here for a sandwich, then."

"I've been told that everyone loves him, that he was going to make all of you business owners rich. Is that true?"

"Some would have you believe it," Wink said. After going behind his register station and bringing out the stool that he perched on back there, he walked over and grabbed a couple Cokes from the cooler. He had something to say. He sat down, opened them, and handed me one. He took a long drink out of his.

"Shit," he said, shaking his head.

"You weren't a believer?"

"You know where the road of good intention leads," he said.

"Is there a reason someone would want to fast-track him?"

"You're asking me?"

"Not much happens in Laurel that you don't hear about."

"I do remember when this town was nice and quiet—before you became chief."

"Just my luck. Unless you're saying this is a result of that."

"I ain't. But Adam Springbrook, he was mighty popular with a lot of folks. Those new Chamber types couldn't get enough of him."

"You weren't one of them."

He shook his head. "I'll admit he is bringing more people to town, or at least people with more money. Last year was my best ever, sales-wise."

"Is that true for everyone?"

"Can't say. Some people can run a business. Some can't. But it seems to me that the person most benefiting is—or was—Adam Springbrook. The rest of us are just the feeders nibbling off the shark's pillaging."

"You know anyone who had a problem with him?"

"I couldn't say if it was enough to shoot him, but I know he pissed off a good amount of people."

"How'd he manage that?"

"It ain't a short list. You might want to take a seat and get out your notebook."

I went over to the lunch counter and grabbed one of the tall chairs. I set it down across from Wink. I took a sip of my drink, pulled out a pen, and flipped to a fresh page.

"Let me have it," I said.

"Now, Adam, he had big eyes around here for this town. He was going to do this, and he was going to do that. He did good with that first restaurant, which I wouldn't let my dog eat at even if I could afford those prices, frozen fish and all. He bought the two inns, and did good with those, then bought two more restaurants this fall. He must have a lot of cabbage behind him."

"Those haven't opened yet."

"Nope, but they would have next spring. And he was trying to get more. All of them. I bet you can't find a single owner that he ain't talked to about selling to him."

"That upset people?"

"It ain't so much the 'what' as it was the 'how.' He had a very peculiar way of speaking. More proper than needed. Like on one of those shows on public television. You talked to him, right?"

I nodded.

"Even if he wasn't trying, he kind of made people feel small. It came across that we was running these places just to get them ready for him to take over and make some real money—which we obviously weren't capable of bringing in. He wasn't exactly what they call a people person, and we can be an ornery, prideful lot around here."

"He tried to buy this store?"

"Course."

"What did you tell him?"

"There ain't enough tequila in Mexico for me to take what he was offering. But even if he did put a bundle on the table, what the hell would I do with myself if I didn't have the store?"

"He lowballed you?" I asked.

"He's a bottom-feeder, alright."

"Some people sold."

"He might have made legitimate offers to places that he really wanted. That land for his big project, he may have even paid market. But some offers he made, I know were insulting, just trying to get people to bite."

"I get it." I'd seen the map and its coded circles.

"You might ask around. I did hear that Karen and Rita at Allie's almost clipped him with a frying pan and told him to get the hell out, but that ain't no secret. Rita's told that story all over town. Before you get too excited, that was back in summer. On the other hand, I heard Houston from the Clam Shed is very happy sitting on his ass down in Florida. But if someone's not feeling cheated, it ain't the real estate business."

"Great. Anything else I should know?"

"There's a bunch not too happy about that big project chewing up some woods in town. Lots of deer came out of that parcel."

"I've heard that. Any enough to shoot him?"

"Doubt it," Wink said, shrugging. "It ain't like the town's turning into a parking lot."

"You hear anything else?"

"He was a bachelor, you know."

"So am I. What does that mean?"

"He may get around a little more than you do."

"Everyone does."

"Some married lips might have been kissing more than his ass."

"Who would that be?"

"It ain't right for me to say, not even to you, shit like that. Because I only heard rumors. I don't have firsthand knowledge."

Wink was a proverbial immovable object. It wouldn't be worth pushing him when it wouldn't be too hard to ferret out that information elsewhere. I walked over and dropped my bottle in the bin by the counter.

"You aren't going to be late for dinner tonight, are you?" he said, glancing at his watch.

"I'm not planning on it," I said.

"You could have been a lot smarter when you had your chance. Missing

68

with a girl like Suzy. My son made the same mistake when he moved away after college. Neither of you seems to have a brain in your head when it comes to that. Deke's been divorced twice out there in California, and I still don't have any grandkids. There aren't many better than Suzy on the whole planet, I'd say."

"Don't rub it in."

"Just telling it like it is," he said, laughing.

A thought hit me that made my stomach lurch. "Not Suzanne and Springbrook?"

"She's a lot smarter than that." Wink shook his head. The look with his lips pressed together and his eyes coming up hadn't changed since Deke and I had run around together as teenagers, getting caught doing our share of stupid things. "And don't get your hopes up."

"Do you know something that I don't?"

"Plenty. But that's why you're here, ain't it?"

I thanked him and left. It was lunchtime, I hadn't eaten, and restaurant owners had been added to my list of suspects. I could solve two problems with one stop. George Paquin and Eddie Mancini could wait.

Chapter Twelve

I could never walk into Allie's, even on official business, without an offer to be fed. Karen French and Rita Henderson, the sisters who owned the place, were either the most gracious people in town or believed that I lacked the ability to feed myself. Rita greeted me and seated me at a two-top in the corner of the small dining room. There wasn't anyone in there that I didn't recognize. Half of the ten customers either nodded, waved, or smiled at me. I wondered what kind of reception Adam Springbrook would have received.

Ellie Yarborough took my order, and a few minutes later, Rita was bringing me a massive club sandwich on oversized Vienna bread with a mountain of house-made chips. This was why I rarely ate here. It torpedoed my attempts to stay in shape. By the time I'd finished, the place had cleared. I asked Rita if she could grab Karen and join me for a minute. Puzzled expression on her face, she adjusted the black hair bunched on her head in something resembling a squirrel's nest and headed off to the kitchen. They came out whispering to each other. Karen sat across from me, and Rita pulled a chair from the neighboring table. Karen smiled, her blue eyes poking out from under the bill of the Sox cap that covered her short blond hair. The sisters looked nothing alike.

"Yes, Karen threatened Adam Springbrook with a cast-iron frying pan," Rita said, shaking her head.

Word had traveled fast if they were up on things before Wink. I guessed that was a result of the breakfast crowd they served daily. The broadcast must have started from the Reef House in one direction and Adam's

70

corporate office in the other.

"I'm not here because of that," I said. "I'm here because someone shot him."

"Who told you about our little joke, anyway?" Rita said, looking at Karen like she wanted to growl.

"Front page of the Portland Press Herald," I said. "Not too long ago."

"You can't think it was one of us," Karen said. The sisters gazed at each other, shaking their heads.

"Of course not. You two are a couple of teddy bears. Unless, of course, someone gets on the wrong side of you. What did Adam do to get chased out?"

"He wanted to talk about us selling the place to him," Rita said.

"In the middle of the breakfast rush." Karen rolled her eyes. "On a Saturday. In July."

"I told him that we weren't interested," Rita said.

"And?" I asked.

"He followed her into the kitchen," Karen said.

"That's when you threatened him?"

"At least it was a clean pan," Karen said. "Not even a drop of bacon fat to soil his nice silk shirt. I told him to get the fuck out of my kitchen. He ignored me. The pan encouraged him."

"He seemed to be under the impression that he was doing us a favor," Rita said, "coming here to lowball us. Of course, the formal shitty offer came a few weeks later, at night while we were closed. So, he did have the ability to learn."

"You turned down that offer?" I recalled the red circle around Allie's on Springbrook's map.

"Yes," Rita said. "After we stopped laughing."

"You two have alibis for the last few days?"

Raised eyebrows of the fifty-year-olds greeted me in stereo.

"We've been right here," Karen said. "Hundreds of witnesses."

"At night?"

"You know what time we get here in the morning. We're not doing anything at night. You can check with our husbands about that."

"Were others as bothered as you by Adam?"

"Look," Karen said. "Some have been happy to sell. While I'm sure others didn't have a cast-iron pan handy."

"To clarify," Rita said. "Adam was not out there making people offers they couldn't refuse."

"He was a bit off, that one," Karen said, shrugging. "It wasn't anything malicious, and believe me, we don't know anyone who would have wanted to kill him. But for someone who was frequently trying to get people to do things that he wanted, he could have been way more smooth."

Rita nodded. "He didn't quite understand his place in certain settings. I don't know if I would call him presumptuous or ignorant. The rest of us, having grown up here, have a certain way with each other that respects a distance being maintained without having to think about it. Look at Greg Dehner, who built the brew pub across the river. He's only been here two years, but everyone likes him. If he sees you, he doesn't march over and find an excuse to tell you about his newest plan or what you should do with your place, and how great it would be if it was updated or, even better, completely renovated. Preferably by him."

"That was part of his sales pitch?" I asked, fearing that my suspect list was going to keep expanding.

"No," Rita said. "It was just the way he talked. He must not have realized how insulting he was."

"Or he didn't care," Karen said.

Rita nodded. "Whatever it was, it didn't make him a bad person, but it did make him a major pain in the ass."

I was getting that.

Chapter Thirteen

"This about Adam Springbrook?" Eddie Mancini said when he opened his front door and found me standing there.

"Did you have breakfast at Allie's today?" I asked.

"I did." If nothing else, this confirmed where information was traveling.

"I don't have a problem with that, but you're right. I am here about Adam."

"Let's go to the office over the garage." He must have felt the eye his wife was giving him over his shoulder.

"Well," he said, settling his bulk into the leather chair behind his desk. A fourteen-point buck was mounted on the wall opposite him. Windows looked out into the woods behind the garage. He had more papers stacked on top of his two filing cabinets than he could possibly fit in them. "What do you want to know?"

"When's the last time that you saw Springbrook?"

"We had dinner Monday night, after work."

"But you hadn't been at Lost Woods."

"No," he said. "Not for a week or so."

"You've still got the heavy equipment there. What's going on?"

"There's a couple of reasons. My crew's up north hunting. Bow season."

"And?"

He shifted in his chair, then looked out the window and back at me.

"Waiting on a check," he said.

"You haven't been paid?"

"That's why I let the boys go. We don't work for free."

"How much does he owe you?"

"Three grand. We get some up front, then more as we keep going and reach certain benchmarks."

"That was enough to stop the work?"

"That's a good chunk of change, at least to me. Probably to you, too. The thing with Adam is he pays, but he's a pain in the ass about it. You have to chase him and work him the same way he works you."

"You expected to get the money?"

"I did. But it's hardball."

"Why put up with that?" The other question was how hard the game needed to be played, and did it involve a shotgun.

"Because the money's good. There's a lot of work there."

"Your dinner was business related?" I didn't know many folks who liked hanging out with people who owed them money.

"It was. I'd told him we were pulling the plug until a check came in. I don't think he believed me until he saw the equipment just sitting there. I finally got a call from him asking what the problem was. I explained it. He told me the money was coming. I said okay, but we weren't coming back until we got a check. A few days later, he asked me to have dinner with him. He didn't know I'd already told the boys that they could go bow hunting. He wanted to sweet-talk me, so he brought me to the Reef. He promised that he'd have a check for me on Friday if we got back at it."

"You didn't believe him?"

"You never knew with him. But I didn't say pay me or I'll shoot you. That's what I heard, that he was shot. That true?"

"We're waiting on the crime lab results." If one person heard something, especially this time of year when things weren't likely to get lost in a horde of summer people, it wasn't long before everyone knew, or worse, thought they knew.

He nodded. I waited.

"Adam told me that he would've had a check that night, but he wasn't sure where his accountant had put the checkbook. Now, that was bullshit."

"Had you done work for him before?"

"Sure, I did the new foundation for the Captain Fairweather. The old one was on stilts and stones, for chrissakes."

"You like working for him?"

He shrugged.

"He's pretty particular. He lets you know what he wants and then expects it'll get done that way. But if you do your job right, the way he wants it, he's easy enough. I got no problem with that. It's better than working for someone who doesn't know what they want or changes their mind halfway through. Then they usually want you to do extra and get mad when you actually charge them for it. Springbrook always knew what he wanted and was clear about telling you. Of course, he was tight paying, and getting paid is the point of doing the work."

"Was that a problem with the Fairweather?"

He nodded approvingly, like I'd known something that he figured I hadn't.

"It took some ingenuity on my part, but I got paid."

"What do you mean?" I asked, waiting for a gun to show up in the story while hoping one didn't.

"Mind you, this is after a couple months of calling him and asking for a check. On a Friday morning, first thing, I had a few dump trucks go by and deposit full loads of dirt on the Fairweather's driveway. No one was getting in unless they wanted to drive across the lawn, which I knew he wouldn't allow because he'd just had the grounds landscaped, too. Then I went about my day. I got a call within an hour, and by lunch, I had a check in hand. Only then did I show up with a front-end loader and bring the trucks back. We came to an understanding. Or so I thought, until Lost Woods. That's why I let my guys go hunting. You have to maneuver him. But there's so much work. It isn't easy to pass on it. If you do, some other sucker will take it. It's just tough to know that you've got to work the job and then again just as hard to get your money. You'd think the guy was broke the way he hated to give it up. One of those suits he wore probably cost more than everything in my whole closet."

"What about now that he's not here?" I said. No one had been able to tell me what would happen. I wanted to see if Mancini had perspective that I lacked.

"He's got everything under that new company, right? I'm hoping it gets run like a real business instead of Scrooge McDuck holding onto his money as long as possible to get another ten bucks in interest out of the bank. Someone's got to be liable. I better get paid for what I've done, and I hope it keeps going. He didn't do anything that didn't make money, so I don't know why someone wouldn't want to cash in on his plans. Hopefully, someone who knows their shit and isn't cheap. If I have to wait a bit for them to figure it out, okay. I got other work."

"You seem pretty calm about this." He was one person who didn't have a reason to want Springbrook dead.

"What I've learned," Mancini said, "is that when there's money to be made, these things have a way of working themselves out."

"Do you know anyone less understanding than yourself?"

"I'm guessing there are people out there who don't like getting jerked around for their money, only they're intimidated by him because one, he's got a lot of it, and two, with all his dealings, he represents a ton of potential business. I know for a fact that he still owes Charlie Sarofian for the work he did on the Fairweather right after I finished the foundation. Charlie's got to be some patient. I don't know anyone who actually got stiffed, but I have a few brothers out there who waited a damn sight longer to get paid than they should have. Springbrook seemed to come up with checks right when you were reaching the end of your rope. I don't think he realized or cared that we mere mortals need to pay bills on time."

"Did you know about the bones on the site?"

"The deer? I never laid eyes on them, but my guys saw them. No big deal. From a long time ago."

"You didn't think to report it?"

"Animal bones?" he said, his voice going up as if this were the craziest thing he'd ever heard. Or at least crazier than someone shooting Adam Springbrook.

"Monday night," I said. "What time did you leave the Reef House?"

"We met early at six, so I was probably out of there around seven-thirty. Home before eight, for sure."

"Can I confirm that with Katrina?"

"Of course you can. You know she's home."

"Did you and Adam leave at the same time?"

"No. He was talking with Louie Williams when I took off. I don't know when he left."

I let him know that the worksite was a crime scene and to stay out until I okayed getting back in. He was fine with that, though he hoped it wouldn't be too long before someone would be able to tell him if the project was continuing.

Chapter Fourteen

I returned to the station and found Pettibone waiting for me, leaning on the counter and talking to Estelle. When we got to my office, he looked ready to spit.

"Before we get started," he said, "did you hear about that Fish and Game Club up in Fort Kent that went berserk?"

"Sure. Hard to miss." Despite the legal firearm season not yet being open, three members had staged a gunfight over a deer they each claimed to have brought down. One had died in the hospital, another was in critical condition, and the third was only wounded. Lucky guy.

"I'm getting sent there to sort it out."

"Who's taking our case then?"

"That would be me, too."

"Is this Wisterman trying to fuck with me for the Grimes case?" I hadn't been on good terms with Pettibone's supervisor for a few years now. But when he stayed out of the way, it wasn't exactly a loss. His detective was a good investigator, however.

"I don't know that he'd do that." Pettibone shrugged his wide shoulders. "I think they just need help up there more than you need it down here. Technically, I'll still be working this."

"I'd rather have no one than Wisterman."

"I'm not camping there, believe me. I'll keep in touch. If you get things underway, I'll be back in a day or two. You know the lab guys, and they don't like Wisterman, either, so you have that in common. I have that report." He took a manila folder out of his briefcase and put it on my desk. He gave me the story as I looked through it.

As Bannon had clued me, Springbrook had been shot with a sixteen-gauge deer slug. They were able to estimate the time of death to be between eleven and midnight on Monday. There were over twenty unique footprints in the dirt of the worksite. A few in the center of the site matched the soles of Adam's loafers, but none were found near his body. The only blood they'd found had been directly under where he'd lain, and there wasn't much of it. That likely meant that he'd been carried and placed there. The other onsite footprints appeared to be work boots with similar soles and kids' sneakers. I assumed that Mikey and his gang of bike jumpers weren't the culprits, so we could rule those out for being of value. I asked if they'd gotten fingerprints from Springbrook's car.

They'd found two pair, Pettibone told me, one of which was Adam's. They didn't have a match for the other. I explained that they could have been Talia's.

Pettibone sat back and asked what I'd learned. I told him that I'd found that Adam was a bit of an ass and tight with the piles of money he seemed to have, but neither to the extent that someone would have wanted to shoot him. And that I could be wrong about that.

"It's going to be legwork," Pettibone said, "checking alibis, and following every lead until something pops up."

I nodded. The detective did love to state the obvious.

"You think your officers will be of much help?"

"They'll be fine," I said, hoping.

"How many people in town own shotguns?" he asked. "You starting there?"

"Let's say I don't think there are too many households that don't have them."

He sighed. "At least sixteen gauge isn't as common as twelve or twenty."

"A real break," I said. Sooner or later, he'd come out with something worthwhile. Often, you had to wade through the basics to get to the jewel he'd offer.

"I wish I was here to help," Pettibone said.

"Sounds like you got your hands full in the north country," I said.

"I don't know what they were thinking, as if there isn't a deer behind every tree up there, not to mention the moose."

Chapter Fifteen

Before I could make up my mind whether to go to George Paquin's or the hardware store, Sally Cooper came into the station. She carried a shopping bag full of folders. This case was supplying its share of paperwork if nothing else.

"Mr. Fitzgerald asked me to drop these off for you," she said. "There are financials for the Lost Woods project and for the Springbrook Coastal Group. He wanted me to remind you of your promise to keep them confidential."

I thanked her, then asked if anyone chasing Adam for money seemed to be upset about it.

"I don't think there was anyone that I'd term *chasing* him." She emphasized the word to let me know it disgusted her.

"You must be talking to different people than I've been. He wasn't quick to pay, from what I understand."

"Oh," she said. "That's not true. Some people think they're going to get a check in their hand five minutes after they give us an invoice. The world doesn't work that way. Half the time the bill comes in on a piece of notebook paper that looks like it was scribbled by a five-year-old."

"None of his vendors or workmen were upset with him?"

"Not that I know of. I don't know everything about the investors or the financing, other than what the bank needs and when they expect it. Maybe you can find something in those files that isn't apparent to me, who works with them every day. But if you do, I'll be shocked."

"Where is this attitude coming from, Mrs. Cooper? You sound like you'd rather have me not looking into who killed your boss." I had no problem tweaking anyone with an attitude.

She took a sharp breath and let it out through her nose.

"I don't appreciate the implication that we, including myself, were doing anything wrong, and that led to what happened."

"Who is implying that?"

"Well," she said, lowering her voice, "you are."

"All I'm doing is asking questions."

"I think you enjoy it," she said, standing straight as if working on her posture. "Pressing us like this."

I tried to count. I didn't make it.

"Would you like to come to Portland with me and take a good look at Mr. Springbrook's guts, which were spilling out of his body where someone put a shotgun slug in them at close range, and then see what questions you might have and consider how you might ask them?"

"It's horrid that you would speak to someone this way," she said.

"Consider it your tax dollars at work," I said.

"For your information," she said. "I am not a resident of this town. Thank goodness."

She harrumphed and left.

I opened the first folder, which read Lost Woods #1 on its tab. There was a stack of invoices, one of which was from Mancini for the amount of three thousand dollars. This matched what he'd told me earlier. Springbrook hadn't authorized anything other than cutting trees and clearing land. The additional folders held about a hundred more documents from the Reef House, the inns, and Dante's and the Clam Shed, which had yet to open. There were bills for everything from seafood to electrical work to insurance. Other folders held statements for what looked like commercial accounts at different banks. My checkbook hadn't been balanced in two years. It would take days to get through everything piled on my desk, and I wasn't sure I'd know what I was looking at anyway. I wouldn't have called it fortunate, but I did have other avenues waiting to be pursued. I left the financials where they lay.

Chapter Sixteen

My first stop was the hardware store. Laurel Village Hardware was commonly referred to as Tiffany's, a result of comparing its prices for paintbrushes, screws, and hand tools to New York City jewelry. At least Neal Murdoch knew what he was talking about if you needed help picking out a hose clamp, L-bracket, or lock washer. And if you only needed a quart of touch-up paint, no one wanted to make the drive to Zayre's in Milltowne for something they could get in five minutes. While Neal didn't carry everything, he did stock ammunition. It could be a shortcut to learning who in Laurel had a sixteen-gauge shotgun. As the store was one of the few businesses not circled on Springbrook's map and the afternoon newspapers hadn't come out yet, Neal might remain objective in answering questions.

Murdoch was stationed at the register. My eyes went to the glass ammo case locked behind him on the counter.

"Who buys sixteen-gauge deer slugs around here?" I asked after saying hello.

"I can't tell you," Neal said.

"It says that you're the helpful hardware store on your sign, Neal. Could you try proving it?"

"The thing is, LT, I haven't sold that ammo in years. Not too many folks using sixteens these days. The last box I had, I bought when Nixon was president."

"You're kidding me," I said. It was never easy.

"No joke," he said.

"Do you remember who used to buy sixteen gauge?"

"I couldn't tell you what I had for dinner last night."

I had no reason to doubt him. He was in his seventies. Details hadn't been released, so it wasn't like he was protecting anyone. We were a tight-knit community, but Neal didn't have a dog in this fight.

"No one's even asked for it in years," he said. "They probably just drive up to Milltowne. Even there, a box might last a lifetime."

I sighed. The odds of some kid at a department store remembering who was purchasing what shells would be astronomical. People wondered why my patience always ran short. I thanked Neal and left. At least George Paquin should be home by now.

Chapter Seventeen

I thought Mikey Paquin was going to keel over when he opened the door and saw me standing there. Words did not escape his open mouth.

"I need to talk to your father, please," I said. "Not about yesterday, so don't worry."

He nodded and ran off.

George Paquin came to the door, shaking his head. His hair and mustache were tinged with gray. He invited me in.

"What can we do for you, Chief? Mikey told me about your little accident. He said he ran into you on his brother's bike."

"That's kind of correct, but not why I'm here. I have a few questions about something else."

He shrugged. "Sure, let's go into the kitchen."

He and I sat down at the table. He gave me a glass of ice and a can of Coke and got one for himself.

"Have you had any dealings with Adam Springbrook?" I asked.

"Katie just called and told me that he died," he said, his smile disappearing. The skin around his eyes tightened. "Awful. He was still a young man."

"How did Katie hear?"

"She works the desk over at the Captain Fairweather. I thought you might have known that. She practically runs the place. One of the bosses from the new corporate headquarters told her. They're all in a state of shock. My kids, Alfred and Lucy, worked for him at the Reef House this summer, too. Crazy."

"How about you, personally? Did you see him much?"

"Nope. I'm still fishing, going out every chance I get."

"Are the kids home?" I said, hoping for a chance to start crossing names off my list.

"They're not. Lucy's up in Orono and Alfred's down at UNH."

"How does Katie like working at the inn?"

"She doesn't complain. We need it, with two kids in school."

"Lucy and Alfred, they liked it at the Reef House?"

"They stayed all summer. Mr. Williams, the manager, he was good to them. They're hard workers, though, I can tell you that."

"What about Springbrook?" I asked.

"What about him?"

"I heard you had reason to be, let's say, upset, with him."

He looked over at the sink and clenched his jaw. "I'm not as impressed with him as a lot of people are, to be honest."

"Why is that?"

"He wasn't my kind of guy. I guess he wasn't actually in the Reef too much, which might be a good thing. Williams runs a tight ship, and Springbrook pocketed the money; that's the way I see it. But the kids do well there. As a busboy, Alfred's making fifty bucks some nights. Lucy, she's a waitress and never comes home with less than a C-note, sometimes a lot more. You know how many hours I had to work at their age to make that kind of dough?"

"I hear you," I said. It still sounded like good money to me. "So, what was the problem? I'd appreciate it if you gave it to me straight."

"Why are you asking?"

"Did Katie tell you how he died?"

"She didn't. I don't know if she knows."

"He was shot. We found him at the Lost Woods site."

His mouth opened, and his head came forward as if I'd just punched him in the gut.

"You don't think we had anything to do with it, do you?" he asked.

"What was between you and him?" I said. "I know something's there."

He took a deep breath.

"Springbrook," he said. "I don't know where he got off acting like he did.

If he were at that restaurant more, I might've made the kids quit, no matter how much they were bringing in."

"Why is that?"

"I don't think it's right for him, or any guy his age, to be making a play for the kids who work for him, plain and simple."

"He made a pass at Lucy?" I asked.

"He did. She got her mother's looks. That girl gets a lot of attention, mainly from boys her own age. But she also got her mother's brains. She knew how to handle him. That wasn't it, though."

"What was?" I said.

"The thing is, he showed the same interest in Alfred." Paquin rolled his head on his neck as he tried to diffuse the tension that had tightened his face. "I don't think he cares who or what he goes after, as long as they're young and have a pulse. As lovely a woman as Katie is, she hasn't mentioned him trying anything with her. Maybe she was too old for the bastard."

Or maybe she didn't want her husband getting pushed over the edge. I sat back and massaged my forehead with my fingers. George cracked an ice cube with his teeth.

"To be honest, I didn't hear about any of this until weeks after it happened. It came out at a family dinner at this very table. The kids were laughing like hyenas, telling us the story. They didn't get mad until I told them I was going down to the Reef House to straighten Springbrook out. They might not have been mad at him, but they blew a gasket at me."

"What did you do?"

"Nothing. It's probably lucky I never ran into him around town, because I wouldn't have been able to not say something. If I'd had a few and he showed up at the Dockside, I might have tossed him in the goddamn river. That was months ago. I get Lucy. She's a looker. But Alfred, too? I know times are changing, and if Adam wants to swing from both sides of the plate, that's his business. That they were so much younger than him is what burns me. It's just not right. I would've felt compelled to point that out to him. Lucky for me, I have kids who can handle their business, even Mikey, as you know."

"Nothing came of it?"

He drank his soda. "Look, Chief. I'm nearly sixty. Thirty years ago, I might've tracked him down and throttled him. But I'm not the hothead I once was. I was told to stay out of it, and I did. Katie wasn't even sure that the kids were reading it right, and Adam loved her because of how well she was doing at the Fairweather. If he'd gone so far as putting his hands on one of them, that would have been a different story. I might've knocked his teeth out."

"Okay," I said, nodding.

"How did my name come up in this?"

"A murder investigation kicks over a lot of rocks."

"Shit." George flattened his mustache with his fingers. "My kids can't be the only ones he did this to. I wouldn't call myself exactly open-minded, but there are a few people around who would be less amused than I was. Maybe he tried something with the wrong person."

"Do you have any idea who that might be?"

"No, sir."

"Do you still hunt?"

"Haven't in years. Lucy is one of those animal rights people. You can tell her how many deer will starve in the winter, but she won't believe it. If I was silly enough to bring one home and she heard about it, the roof would come off. You can maybe see why I didn't need to get up in this Springbrook business." He swirled the diluted Coke left in the bottom of his glass.

"Where were you on Monday night?"

"At the VFW, watching football. Saw the whole game, got in late, even though it wasn't much of a contest."

"What time did you get back here?"

"Just after midnight. Christ, it's five minutes away." He took a breath and thought for a second. "When did Springbrook get shot?"

"Looks like a little before that."

"I suppose you want to check my guns."

"While I'm here," I said.

"No problem," he said. "Come on."

We went into the den. There were two shotguns and two deer rifles. True to what he'd told me, they hadn't been fired in what looked like a long time. Neither was a sixteen, and dust covered them like a coating of gray snow.

I got numbers at college for Lucy and Alfred and went back to the station to call them. The George Paquin they described the night they'd told him about Adam was not quite as thoughtful and understanding as the one he'd portrayed. But by the time they'd reached dessert, he'd calmed down to the point where he wasn't doing more than sighing and shaking his head. When I asked them who else Springbrook might have made advances on that summer, they both related that the list of those he hadn't would be much shorter. I was guessing he didn't have much of a governor on his actions. That meant my suspect list would continue to grow. As George had pointed out, not everyone in this town was as forward-thinking and considerate as himself.

Chapter Eighteen

I looked up at the clock after hanging up with Lucy Paquin and nearly screamed. More questionable driving commenced, speed being the issue as I raced home to ditch my uniform and get to the Sea Squall to meet Suzanne. I arrived two minutes early and sat at the bar. My Budweiser was a lone soldier. The couples beside me were drinking red wine out of balloon glasses. I would have liked to relax and narrow down the possible reasons why she wanted to talk to me. But my mind went to Adam Springbrook and the miles I'd put on the Bronco trying to determine who he'd insulted or angered enough to shoot him. The list grew every time I talked to someone.

Thankfully, Suzanne came in before I got locked in on suspects. Jess Consentino, the owner, seated us. My issues seemed small compared to hers. She and her husband Frank had run this restaurant together for twenty years, taking a chance on buying it in their early thirties, a few years younger than Suzanne and I were now. But Jess lost him this past summer. A persistent stomachache that he soldiered through when the snow was melting in March turned out to be a nasty form of cancer, and he was gone by Independence Day. Jess had carried on without him. I couldn't imagine that she didn't think of Frank every time she stepped into the place.

"It's so sad," Suzanne said, as soon as Jess had handed us menus and returned to the host stand. She didn't need to explain.

As close as we'd been, I don't know that Suzanne and I could have ever been Frank and Jessica. They'd never seemed out of step, having met their first day of college and not parting until his death. Suzanne and I had started off as friends in elementary school. She'd been my best friend's girlfriend through high school, and we only found each other five years ago as divorced single adults in this same small town. Though we weren't ready to get married, we did try to have a child. When that didn't take, there wasn't enough to keep us going. I was beginning to understand that I might be a lifelong bachelor. My own marriage had lasted nine months. That fate didn't seem so horrible when I looked across the room and could feel what Jess had lost.

"Thanks for coming," Suzanne said. "And changing out of your uniform."

"I'm sure you have enough to reprimand me for other than my dress," I said, smiling. It had been a last-second decision, and I was grateful I'd gone out of my way to do it.

We ordered cocktails and then sat staring at each other. Minutes seemed to pass. It could have been seconds. We hadn't been together like this in some time. When we'd started dating, our feet would be brushing against each other under the table, with smiles breaking out over it. Now, when our eyes met, they bounced as if the same poles of charged magnets. While we used to take our time and savor the moments, we ordered meals as soon as the waitress returned. Appetizers didn't make the cut. We chit-chatted about Springbrook, which confirmed that she wasn't a fan. She was also surprised that I hadn't used it as an excuse to cancel dinner, knowing "how you can be with work."

I didn't respond to that. Maybe I'd learned from past mistakes.

"I'm sure you're wondering why I asked you here," she said, without the hint of a smile.

"I hope everything's okay." I shifted uncomfortably in my seat.

"It is. Though I have a feeling that you may not think so."

"Okay," I said. This was not to be a romantic let's-get-back-together overture. I tried not to show that realization on my face.

"I have some news."

"Nothing bad, I hope." My mind was trying to process what this could be and coming up blank.

She took a deep breath.

"Not at all, I'm pregnant."

She held the smallest of grins. I coughed as if I'd just taken a shot of cheap whisky. I drank half a glass of water. I didn't have to do the math to know that I wasn't the father.

"You're speechless," she said.

I nodded.

"I'm going to ask you to stay that way when I tell you the rest."

I started worrying. When we were together, had she somehow captured my sperm without my noticing and frozen it? Was that even possible? I was off the rails at an unparalleled level.

"I'm getting back together with Derek. He's the father."

"Derek Anderson? That Derek?" Of course, it was him. There were no others in Laurel. Regardless, I didn't want to believe it. When they were married, he'd abused her. He'd broken her arm, and she'd told me—a friend— that she'd been in an accident because she knew what I'd have done to him. Derek's moral compass pointed in whatever direction the wind blew. I'd kept him out of jail once as an unspoken favor to her when she and I were dating, and he'd gotten mixed up in a gambling ring.

"He's changed," she said.

Only the waitress setting plates in front of us kept me from asking her if she was out of her fucking mind.

"He's an idiot and a loser," I said, after picking up and dropping my fork. She shook her head and frowned.

"I knew you'd say that. You don't want to believe this, but he's been working on himself. He's gone to counseling and AA. He asked me to go to therapy with him, and I did. He's a different person."

I'd just lost my appetite, and there was a beautiful piece of swordfish in front of me.

"Are you crazy?" I said, having counted to ten in my head, and rephrased that response as best I could. It didn't come out as calmly as I had hoped. The folks two tables away glanced over at us.

"Let me ask you this," she said. "When was the last time you saw Derek at the Port Tavern? Or the Rusty Bullet?"

"Someone just told me that he was at the VFW Monday night."

"You're tracking where he goes?"

"Of course not."

"Then why were you asking about him?"

"I wasn't. It came out in an investigation."

"I know he was there. He went to watch the football game with his friends. It doesn't mean that he was drinking."

"You believe that?"

"I do." Her face reddened. She stared across the table, waiting for me to challenge her.

I hadn't seen Derek myself in a long while, and I was okay with that. When I did come across him, he usually couldn't stop running his mouth. Initially, it had been about me and Suzanne being together, and then it became how she'd smartened up and sent me packing. It didn't bother me much, because I'd known he was out of her picture. The one time he threw a sucker punch at me, I whacked him with a beer pitcher—and enjoyed it.

"He hasn't had a drink in fourteen months," she said.

"According to him?" I started to sweat.

"I know he hasn't. And I know that you won't believe me. He acknowledged his mistakes, serious ones, and he's taken responsibility for them. We're all getting older, and the clock is ticking. None of us want to look back and see what could have been. He knew he needed to work on himself, and he has."

"You, Suzy, are a good person. He is not."

"He may never run for selectman or be a big shot around here, but you know what, neither will I. He almost fell off a roof last year. It made him think and question who he was. That's when this started. He had an epiphany."

"You want a child so bad that you'd go back to a man who broke your arm? That's some kind of risk. Have you thought about the kid?"

She shook her head, her eyes moist.

"That's the worst thing you could've said. I think you know that."

"He sent you to the emergency room. He put you in a cast. I can't sit here and ignore it."

"You can and you will." Her arm came up, and her hand flicked back and forth between us. "We aren't together. I am an adult. I know what I'm doing, and you don't know how hard Derek's worked to become a better man. It's rekindled something between us. A true love for each other."

"You've got to be kidding me." I slumped in my seat.

"It's different than what we had. Thinking back, I don't know that we were ever in love."

She looked at me with watery eyes, waiting for me to confirm or deny. I wasn't sure that I knew myself. We'd wanted a child together. But that was as far as we were ready to go. Maybe she was right about that, at least.

"I wanted you to hear it from me," she said, "because I know if you caught it from someone else, you'd fly off the handle."

"Does it look like I'm freaking out?" I said, sitting up and trying hard to look calmer than I was.

"Your face is flushed, your back is as straight as a ruler again, and the veins on your neck are standing out."

These seemed like normal reactions to me.

"I'm going to ask a favor of you now," she said, puckering.

I was pretty sure I heard myself grunt.

"I'd like you to stay away from Derek. Your first instinct will be to track him down and threaten him with something like, 'If you ever lay a hand on her, I'll break your face.' You need to let us live our lives."

I took a breath. Then another one. I finished my water and waited. She'd described exactly what I would have done.

"I will," I said, "if you promise to tell me when he goes back to being who he is and hurts you."

It was her turn to drop her jaw. "I've lost my appetite." She pushed back her chair, stood up, sighed loud enough to be heard in West Laurel, crossed the dining room, and walked out the door.

I looked around, wondering if I had just imagined this. I couldn't understand how she had thought it would go differently. The other fifteen people in the restaurant dropped their eyes to their tables. The show was over.

"Is your dinner okay?" The waitress had approached from the other side of the room. Neither of us had touched our plates.

"I couldn't tell you," I said. I asked her to box everything and bring me the bill at the bar. I walked over with my beer and ordered a shot of Jack Daniels to go with it. I didn't feel the first one go down, so I ordered a second.

"How's it going, LT?" Jess Consentino was beside me with a hand on my shoulder.

"Great," I said. I had a dead body and an ex-girlfriend who was getting back with an abusive partner. Unless a meteor was about to hit the restaurant, things could only get better.

She smiled and asked if she could join me. I nodded. She sat down and the bartender brought her a glass of chardonnay.

"It's not often that people sit down at a table to order takeout," she said, smiling.

"Yeah, I like to do things my own way. Haven't you heard?"

"I've just never seen it before."

"You're one of the lucky ones." I really didn't want to talk about me. "How's business?"

"Good for the off-season."

I wanted to ask how hard it was for her to carry on without Frank, and if she had gotten used to it. I'd been living alone for years, give or take a few, and was accustomed to it. But that didn't prevent me from recognizing the emptiness that Jess must have been experiencing. While we were friendly, we were not on a please-explain-your-life level. There was always work.

"Did you ever do business with Adam Springbrook?" I asked.

"He came in now and then," she said. "Why?"

"He was found dead yesterday, at the Lost Woods project site."

Her breath seemed to get caught in her throat, and she reached out and touched my arm. She swallowed, then took a sip of her wine. She almost spilled her glass when she set it down, its base hitting the bar top at an angle.

"My God," she said, barely able to get the words out. "What happened?"

"He'd been shot."

"Who would want to do that?"

"That's the question," I said.

She motioned to the bartender to give us a couple more drinks.

"Wow," she said. "Here? In this town? There's got to be a mistake."

"Unfortunately, that's not the case."

She grabbed a napkin and patted her eyes. Her hand was shaking.

"I heard he was out to buy every restaurant in town," I said. "Did he ever make you an offer?"

"Are you kidding?" she said, with a sour smile. "Frank would have thrown him out."

I couldn't remember what color circles surrounded the Sea Squall on Springbrook's map.

"He did steal Maureen DiGiovanni from me to go bartend at the Reef House," she said. "He knew she had a following and offered her something ridiculous that I couldn't match. Not to make light of it, but that might make her more likely to shoot him. I can't imagine he was easy to work for, with how particular he is."

She took another drink.

"I'm sorry," she said, placing her hand on my arm. "I shouldn't have said that. He was really going for it with that Lost Woods deal. I know how difficult it can be when you put everything you have into something. And then have it taken away."

"Is it hard to keep on by yourself?" I wanted to slap myself on the forehead. I'd just gone where I wanted to stay away from. Again. "I'm sorry. I don't know where that came from."

"Come on, LT, we've known you for years. I saw what happened over there with Suzy. I know where it came from. You can ask. It doesn't bother me."

"Still," I said.

"We invested our whole lives here. Frank would die if I ever sold it—if he wasn't dead already." She chuckled. "I've got a whole bunch of employees who've been with us for ten, twenty years. They depend on me. What else can I do?"

"I get it."

"It is tough some days, really hard, because there's an emptiness in me that I don't think is coming back. But I like being here. It gives my life foundation, so to speak, like your job must for you."

I took a sip of beer. She was right. But my position wasn't something I'd built, more like what I did to be me.

"Your evening did not go the way you planned," she said.

"No, it didn't," I said.

Jess's brown eyes studied me under black bangs. She was one of the other people in town who ran for exercise. But while I struggled through my runs as if they were something to be survived, she seemed to float along at a clip that I hadn't approached since my high school wrestling days. She'd be out there all the time, even in the middle of winter when I'd be pinned to the couch putting on pounds that it would take me all spring to work off. I realized that I'd be doing some running myself to get over this Derek-Suzanne thing. Stress relief couldn't always come from a bottle.

"At least you didn't end up with a drink in your face," she said, patting my shoulder. "I've seen that happen."

"Not exactly a win," I said.

"Was she your soulmate?" Jess asked, a concerned look crossing her face.

"I couldn't say that she was."

"It might seem awful now," she said, "but in that case, you'll get over it."

Roger Kensington, with a six-two frame and mailbox-sized head, lumbered out of the kitchen and over to the end of the bar. His checkered pants were spotless, but his chef whites were streaked with red, brown, and green. He was one of those long-time employees that Jess had mentioned. We'd graduated high school together, though he'd started a few years before me. People called him Blockhead Roger until my friend Deke Winkedakis, the only other kid in school Roger's size, told everyone to stop or they'd be answering to him. Roger was what was then called slow, but not in a debilitating way. It just took him a while to understand things. He'd started here back then as a dishwasher, and Frank Consentino had brought him along step by step, until now he was a damn good cook. The kid who struggled with simple math as if it were trigonometry had no problems when ratios came in recipe form. He'd been able to step into the top spot when Frank got sick. As far as I knew, the restaurant hadn't slipped. He poured himself a Coke from the soda gun, scowling as he searched the bar until he spotted Jess. Then he found me next to her and fumbled his plastic tumbler. When it hit the floor, the clattering filled the dining room.

"Oh, it's you, LT," he said, as he bent down to scoop it up and started mopping things with a bar rag.

The bartender told him not to worry about it, that she'd take care of it, probably just to get him out of her way. Instead, he wiped his hands on the bottom of his jacket and wandered down to where Jess and I were sitting.

"How're you doing?" he asked me.

"Good. How about you?"

"It could be busier." He shrugged. "I heard Suzy dropped the Derek bomb on you."

"Did it already make the six o'clock news?" I said, trying not to show my irritation.

"No, Annie, the waitress, told me. But I knew it was coming." He nodded.

"You did?" I was afraid to ask how. It was easy to picture Derek bragging about it at the Rusty Bullet or the Tavern, though according to Suzanne, he no longer visited those establishments.

"Yeah, Derek told me."

"Where are you talking to him?" I could already feel the tension run through my shoulders.

"We've been hunting partridge together, out in Brookeville. I got a pointer puppy."

"He must have a good nose," I said.

"It's a girl," he said, nodding from twelve to six. "And she does."

Everyone knew your business here, whether you liked it or not, regardless of season. That's why I tried to lie low, even in summer, when there were people whom I wouldn't see every day of my life. Another reason I might remain a bachelor, as if my inability to get out of my own way wasn't enough.

"Jess won't let me put it on the menu, though, the partridge," he said. He closed his mouth and filled his cheeks with air.

"You know there are health regulations, Roger," she said.

"Those guys never come in here," he said after exhaling.

Jess scowled at him.

"You're probably right," he said. "I better get back to work." He nodded goodbye and returned through the swinging doors.

"Oh brother," Jess said, shaking her head. "Roger thinks he's my protector now that Frank's gone. He's the kid brother that Frank never had if he wanted a gentle giant for a sibling. He's handled the cooking well enough, but he thinks it's his job to watch out for me, too. Annie must have told him that I was having drinks with a gentleman. Naturally, he had to make sure nothing funny was going on. I believe that Frank was my one—you know what I mean—and I'm not looking for anyone else, and who knows if I ever will, but God help the man with Roger if I do meet someone someday. He hates to even squish a fly, but if I were to bring a date in here, they might have to call the National Guard to keep Roger down."

"Well, he seems to think you're safe with me."

"If I weren't, then this town would have a real problem."

That was a fact. I left with two untouched dinners under my arm.

Chapter Nineteen

With Pettibone up north, my officers and I had an eight a.m. meeting to discuss progress with the case. Gwyneth reported that Talia had spent Monday night with her friend, and the gallery owner had even shown her a credit card receipt for dinner at Fore Street. Ted still hadn't managed to find anyone who'd heard a shot in the area surrounding Lost Woods. I told them what I'd learned, that several people had reason to be upset with Springbrook, though it was questionable that their grievances were enough for someone to pick up a shotgun. I asked Gwyneth to hit the VFW and check out who was there on Monday night and find out when they'd left. I knew that she'd head there straight off and warned her that no one would be there until later that afternoon. Ted looked like he was dragging from his stakeout. I sent him home for a few more hours of sleep. The possibility existed that what came next would require him to be sharp and awake.

As soon as they left, a call came in from Fitzgerald. Adam Springbrook had renewed his will after the divorce but had not changed it. He'd left everything to Talia. She'd been made aware of the situation but had not given Fitzgerald any indication that she'd known this had remained Adam's wish. Nor did she know what her plans were. She'd remain a person of interest: Her presence was too much of a coincidence to be overlooked.

I faced the stack of manila folders on my desk. There was no telling how many additional suspects would emerge from that pile, should I somehow be able to decipher them. Of course, whoever killed Adam may have had nothing to do with his investments or business interests. His apparently overactive libido might be more relevant. That was an area that I was confident my department could investigate on our own. The financials were another story.

I picked up the phone and called the one commercial real estate developer I knew who might be willing to help. She was well acquainted with large sums of money and the town. Her family owned the finest private home in Laurel. I was only on hold for two and a half minutes before she picked up the line at her Boston office.

"Is this a social call, LT?" Abby Grimes asked, laying on an exaggeratedly hopeful tone.

"You know me," I said. "All business." She'd suggested that our relationship progress beyond its original professional nature. I'd resisted. One, she was ten years younger than me, and, two, the official business that had brought us together involved her family.

"Have you heard about Adam Springbrook?"

"What has Laurel's pretty boy, big-fish-in-a-small-pond, done now? Is he trying to buy your department or something?"

"Actually, he got himself shot. Dead."

"Jesus," she said.

"Are you familiar with his Lost Woods project?"

"I've read the prospectus for investors. Quite ambitious."

"But you passed on investing," I said.

"Yes, I did. You've already learned that. I'm impressed."

"I can read a list of investors. But I do need a favor."

"I live to serve," she said, laughing.

"I have a two-foot-high stack of folders here, financial documents related to that project and his other businesses. I don't understand them. The body was found on the project site, so I'm thinking there may be a connection. I need someone to translate the P&Ls and statements and invoices for me, to see if there's anyone or anything in there that might provide a motive for someone to kill him."

"How exciting," she said. "Are you going to deputize me and everything?" She was practically snorting as she teased me.

"No, but I will buy you dinner."

"Wow. How could a woman resist such an offer?" she said. "You'll see me in a matter of hours, if that's okay."

"Thank you," I said.

"You sound legitimately grateful."

"Because I am."

"It's unfortunate that we only see each other when something horrible happens."

"Well, what can you do?" I said.

"Do you want me to make reservations somewhere?"

"It's October. We won't need them." Her family owned a sprawling New Englander on a spit of land reaching out into the Atlantic, complete with a separate garage, boathouse, Mako fishing boat, and Hinckley sailboat. Despite that, I don't think that Abby had spent three hours of her life here after Labor Day. "Also, do you know Talia Springbrook, his ex-wife?"

"We've met."

"Well, she's here. Showed up two days before he died."

"You haven't arrested her yet?"

"No. Don't jump ahead. You and Adam, friends or business acquaintances?"

"I'm hoping you're jealous," she said. "It kills me that you keep thinking I'm some naive young thing. Springbrook makes my old friend Ranford look like Gandhi."

"What does Gandhi have to do with this?"

"Exactly," she said. "I'll see you later."

I hoped to be less confused after she dug into the documents.

In the meantime, I outlined my possible suspects, noting the various circumstances and potential motivations that qualified them. I worked through lunch and waited for something to jump out that would separate one from the group. While that didn't happen, the news about Springbrook's will did nudge Talia Springbrook to the top of the list.

Chapter Twenty

"I was expecting you, Chief," Talia Springbrook said, opening the door to her former husband's home. I followed her into the house. She went straight to the kitchen. "I take it you're here because you've heard about the will."

"Yes." I nodded.

"You're assuming that I somehow managed to shoot Adam so I could inherit his vast empire? Or are you thinking it was in a fit of jealousy over another woman, even though we were no longer married?"

"Actually, I just have a few questions."

"Wine?" she asked, picking up her glass from the table. She had her own set of folders spread across it. I assumed they were the originals of the copies piled on my desk. "I know it's early, but this is all rather much."

"No, thank you."

She led us into the TV-less living room. She sat on the couch and straightened the fabric of her black slacks as she waited for me to get settled into a chair across the coffee table.

"Do you mind if I smoke?" she asked.

"It's your place," I said.

"I guess you're right about that," she said. She took a cigarette from a slim silver case and lit it with a matching Zippo. I hadn't noticed anything in the ashtrays on my last trip. This could have been stress smoking.

"I wasn't truthful with you the other day," she said.

"Regarding?" My getting lied to was an occupational hazard.

"Just so you know, Adam dying, well, it's not the best thing that ever happened to me."

"I imagine it's not easy to deal with. On any level."

"While I'm sure there are some who would dance a jig at hearing their former husband has died, and others who would buy the shooter a drink, that's not me."

I hadn't received so much as a Christmas card since my ex left years ago. Not that I wouldn't have flung it straight into the wood stove if I had.

"But," I said, "you are inheriting control of this new business group, right?"

She chuckled.

"How well did you know Adam?" she asked, snubbing out the cigarette that was only half-smoked.

"We were acquainted, I would say. We never had any relations in an official capacity, other than his charitable contributions to sponsor town events. It's not like we were ever called to his places to break up fights or deal with a customer not being able to pay their tab."

She nodded.

"As a businessman, he had his pluses and minuses. He had vision. He had ideas. And once he came up with something, he could sell the devil out of it and get it built. I'll give him all of that. But managing them once they were up and running, that was not his strong suit. The thing I'm getting at is that he's left me a whole lot to piece together. I don't know whether I'm sitting on an organization that will have me printing money or a house of cards ready to tumble. This house is neat as a pin. Everything else he touched is somewhat of a mess. I could be filthy rich or flat broke. As of yet, I don't know. That's what I'm trying to figure out." She nodded to the kitchen.

"Couldn't Fitzgerald and Cooper tell you that?"

"You would think so. But I suspect they might be the highest-paid 'yes men' in the state. They couldn't wait to drop the Springbrook Coastal Group in my lap, as you can see. I haven't even had time to make funeral arrangements."

"How bad off can the company be? His restaurant was packed all summer. The inns never have a vacancy. And he charges an arm and a leg at all of them."

Talia sighed. She tapped the cigarette case on the arm of the couch.

"That's true. But there's something that concerns me. Money's coming in. But there's money going out, too. I'm hoping to find the incoming stream flowing like the Mississippi, with its outgoing counterpart being a dried-up creek. Regardless, I haven't put a down payment on a villa in Capri today."

"Maybe I don't have much of a grasp on business. Why would he keep buying things if he wasn't making money?"

She tilted her head and grinned.

"Maybe you don't. Can I share something with you?"

"Please do," I said.

"Adam didn't call me here just to talk about design."

I waited.

"He wanted more money for Lost Woods. Or, as he put it, he wanted me to become a more substantial investor."

"But construction hasn't even started."

"I'm aware." She snapped open the silver case and pulled out another cigarette, then she hesitated and put it down. "The thing is, Adam never saw the downside. To him, it was only what could be. While trying to get Lost Woods underway, he went out and purchased those other two restaurants and a marina. He was trying to do a lot in a little time. Patience was not in his vocabulary. It will take a while to determine what I've got here. I promise, Chief, to let you know as soon as I figure it out."

This did not make sense to me. He wasn't buying these places on good looks and a white-toothed smile. But it seemed that Talia was in the same place that I was, trying to determine what those stacks of paper meant. I needed to know if there was anything in there to suggest someone would want to put a deer slug in his stomach. At least I'd have Abby to translate.

"Was the investment request why you were upset at dinner on Sunday?"

"You heard about that?" She frowned.

I nodded.

"I was disappointed. Finance isn't my field. Most likely, he was just experiencing a hiccup in cash flow. It wouldn't have been the first time he got ahead of himself. The thing is, if this new company he conjured up goes down, I'll be the one blamed for it."

"You didn't know that on Sunday night," I said.

"No. I was heartbroken because he found himself in that position again. I'd bailed him out before on certain things. I'd hoped he'd learned from those occasions. But the man was allergic to changing his habits. He couldn't help himself from being himself. All ahead full, all the time. Occasionally, he'd get caught short, but he'd always find a way out when things got tight."

"Who else would know about this?" I asked. "And who would have a problem with it?"

"The last people who would know were his investors. He kept the behind-the-scenes under wraps, and as the Springbrook Coastal Group is a privately held company, he could share things in ways that wouldn't bring shade to its activities. And, more than anything, Adam was good at projecting success. If he had gone flat broke, and I'm not saying that he was—because he wasn't—no one would ever have known, not even me. People he owed money to may have looked at him like his pockets were stuffed with thousand-dollar bills and wondered why none of them were being sent their way. I don't know who or how much he owed, but it's easy to see why they could have been upset. Because if they weren't getting paid, it looked like Adam was being a prick, because everything indicated he was swimming in it. If I figure anything out as I dig through this, I'll let you know."

I had yet to come across an aspect of his life that didn't seem to operate on recklessness. But if what she'd told me was true, it certainly undercut one of her motives for shooting him: He'd left her what looked to be, in technical terms, something of a clusterfuck.

"Did Adam own a gun?" I asked.

A gust of air left her mouth.

"Are you joking? Certainly not."

"How about you?"

"Now, I know you're kidding. We are not those people."

Yet, a gun managed to find its way to Adam.

"Do you have any idea why you remained in his will, even after you were divorced?"

"Adam has no other living relatives. Or even people he was close to. I believe it's that simple. His parents are gone. He lost his brother to a skiing accident in Europe a few years ago. He's friendly with a lot of people, but not close to anyone. We knew each other on a deep level and remained friends. Are you married, Chief?"

"I was, briefly."

"Still on good terms?"

"No."

"Well, maybe you're having a hard time understanding our relationship, then."

"Can I ask the reason that you split with Adam?"

"Is this still business, or are you being unprofessionally curious?"

"I've heard things that could have landed him in trouble for other reasons. It would help to know if those avenues are worth pursuing."

She took a deep breath, stood, and walked to the picture window. She paused and looked outside, then turned to me.

"What have you heard, Chief? What are you referring to?"

"He seemed to be interested in both men and women, and he didn't seem to hesitate to take a swing if he saw something he liked, regardless of anything."

"Yes, the sports metaphor. You're lucky that I'm a baseball fan, though I despise those dreadful Red Sox. I believe what you're asking is if Adam was polyamorous or bisexual, those are the terms you managed to skirt, and the answer would be yes. Whether that had anything to do with our marriage ending is none of your fucking business."

"No," I said, "it isn't. I apologize if that's why you thought I was asking. I was attempting to verify information that has been given to me."

"I realize that being from this town, you may not be aware of such things, but they exist all over the planet."

"We're not quite as backward as you think. We have a significant number of people with various sexual orientations here in the summer, and no one has a problem with it. What can be trouble is an employer showing romantic interest in the younger people who work for him, regardless of sex."

She nodded and sighed.

"Adam was the same no matter what he was doing. Business, dating, love, whatever. He only saw good outcomes. If he wanted something, he went for it. And he usually got it. While he could be forward, he would never use his position to force anyone into anything."

"Is there a chance he may have faced some backlash from this...uh... enthusiasm?" I had substituted for the word "bullshit" in hopes of getting an answer.

"He did have a man threatening to punch him because he'd made a pass at both of his kids, one of each, to be fair."

"George Paquin?" Another in the line of those stopping short of telling the truth.

"Adam didn't tell me his name. That was this summer. But nothing came of it, to my understanding."

"You don't seem surprised."

"That's who Adam was. As I said, he would never impose himself, but he didn't see the harm in asking. I think that hot tub out back saw its share of chlorine." She raised her eyebrows and shook her head.

"I'm surprised that he doesn't have a Nobel Prize up on the mantel," I said, nodding to the fireplace.

"You sound bitter." She sat back down on the couch and smoothed over her pants. "Is this personal for you? Why?"

"People do things, and others are left to deal with the fallout. Sometimes that bothers me, yes."

"That covers both of us in this case, Chief. Me, because he was once my husband. You, because it's your job. But Adam was the one who was brutally shot. We're still here, at least. Can we be done? I'm getting a migraine, and those books in the kitchen are waiting for me."

"Can you let me know how that goes?"

"Absolutely," she said. "You'll be the first call when I complete my review, like it was my job."

"We take all the help we can get here in Laurel."

"From what I've seen so far, you can use it."

"Thanks for your cooperation," I said, standing and trying to smile away my aggravation. "I appreciate it."

"I'm sure you do," she said, raising her arm to direct me to the door. "By the way, did you check my alibi for Monday night?"

"That's been taken care of by one of my officers. Your story was confirmed."

"Wonderful. If nothing else, that should free up time for you to find out who actually killed Adam."

"I do have a question, however. You and Adam had a visitor prior to Monday. A woman. Who was that?"

She blinked. Repeatedly.

"How do you know this?" she asked.

"Just doing my job, which might not be as rare an occurrence as you think." I wasn't about to tell her that I'd entered the house and saw the wine glasses in the sink. Her believing that we knew what was going on in town or that Adam's few off-season neighbors were likely to cooperate was going to play in our favor.

"I have no idea," she said. "You know it's possible that Adam could have guests on his own, without my presence or knowledge. That shouldn't be hard to understand."

"True," I said. "You don't plan on leaving the area, do you?"

"Really? Have we become East Germany? Do I not have freedom of movement?"

"I'm not saying that you can't go anywhere. I'm asking as a courtesy in case we have news, or I have another question."

She smiled and shook her head.

"Is written permission required to go to Connecticut to get some clothes sometime next week? I was not prepared for an extended stay. Should I get a lawyer to file something, or can the Reichstag just stamp my papers?"

"If you could just let me know when you're leaving, that would be great."

"I think you will hear from my lawyer. I've been very cooperative. Yet, you're treating me as if I'm a suspect."

"That's your right, and I'm sorry, it wasn't my intention."

"But that's what you've been doing."

I shrugged. I apologized once. That was enough.

If not for Adam's ability to impetuously insert himself into so many others' lives, Talia would have been one of the most obvious suspects I'd ever come across. The math was just too easy: She showed up, and two days later, he was dead. Her alibi, however, got her crossed off what remained a rather long list.

Chapter Twenty-One

I made a detour on the way back to the station. The night I'd informed Maureen DiGiovanni about Adam Springbrook, she'd said that Adam hadn't been an issue at the Reef House. That might have not been the most accurate statement. Everywhere else he stepped, he seemed to be waist-deep in shit. It was worth a follow-up because nothing I'd heard provided the answers we needed. Usually, progress meant narrowing down the number of suspects, and I'd been able to eliminate only one. The tightness in my shoulders was beginning to inch its way up my neck.

"Hey, Mary," I said, once again ignoring that her name was Maureen. When you had a moniker like Mary Queen of Shots, it stuck.

"LT, I don't think you've ever been here." She lived by herself in a pleasant Cape in West Laurel. I'd found her raking leaves.

"I have a few more questions about Adam," I said. "And I need the truth this time."

"What do you mean by that?" she said, leaning the rake against the house.

"I'm not sure you thought things through when I talked to you at the Reef. What you told me just doesn't make sense in light of what I've been hearing."

She went over to her front steps and sat down.

"I don't think I said anything that wasn't true, LT," she said, zipping up her hooded sweatshirt. Before I could get a question out, she'd pulled it back down a few inches. She was not comfortable.

"The other day, you mentioned that Adam was rarely around and was an occasional presence. In the time that he did spend there, did he have problems with any of the employees?"

111

She pushed her bangs to one side and adjusted the bandana struggling to hold them in place.

"Honestly, he never bothered us much. Or if he did, he'd have Louie do it. You could see if he glanced in your direction and then called Louie over, and Louie pulled you aside, it probably came from Adam because you'd done something that the boss didn't like. It was usually something like a shirt being wrinkled or there being a water spot on a wine glass. Louie was on top of things, so Adam didn't have much to say."

"Did that happen often?"

"Hardly ever. As long as things looked right, he was fine. You know when you walk into a bar, as a bartender, you can tell how long it's going to take to get a drink and where the bathrooms are, and which customers have been there the longest. It's like radar. Adam owned restaurants but didn't have that skill. If we were going up in flames, he wouldn't notice. However, if his cosmo was more red than pink, that would be the kind of thing he'd pick up on. But then he'd just tell Louie. Frankly, I don't believe Louie passed half the shit he heard onto us."

"Did Adam ever hit on you?"

"That's a bold question, but no."

"I heard he had interest in some of the younger staff."

"Was that first question some kind of compliment then?" she said, smiling. "You're talking about Lucy and Alfred Paquin. That family gene pool is deep when it comes to looks. If I didn't know better, I'd take a run at Alfred myself, twenty years younger or not. Unfortunately, maturity saves me from those embarrassing moments, no doubt at the expense of some good times."

"Lucy and Alfred didn't have a problem working there after that?"

"It's good to be young. They were in hysterics over it. It was the funniest thing to them that an old bastard—what was Adam, my age, like forty—would be after either of them. They used to kid each other about who he wanted more. Adam has a hot tub over at his place. He did a lot of fishing with that thing."

"Fishing is not the same as catching. Did you get the hot tub offer?"

"No," she shook her head. "I can't even say that I was too old because there's a few around town, age-appropriate for him, that landed in there from what I heard. But I never saw anyone get upset about being asked. It could come off as seeming innocent unless you knew better."

"George Paquin ever drink at your bar?"

She frowned and looked down at her rake.

"No, but I can guess why you're back asking questions. I saw him sitting in his truck in the parking lot one night. He took off after a few minutes."

"He wasn't waiting to pick up one of the kids?"

"No, they were long gone."

"I don't know why he'd think that Adam would be there that late. He rarely was. I never heard that anything came of it, and I hear quite a bit."

"Anything that will help me with this?"

"Adam owned the place, but he might as well have lived in Malibu for his level of involvement in the restaurant and the shenanigans that went on there. They were no different than what goes on in any other restaurant in town. You know the dumb shit that we all do, none of which usually results in an owner getting shot."

"Are you sorry you left the Squall?"

"I love Jess, and even Roger has his qualities, and I felt so bad about Frank. But what Adam offered to pay me, combined with what we charge at the Reef, I'm rolling in it, LT. I can put up with a little fussiness for that."

"Adam ever have a problem with any customers?"

"No," she said, shaking her head. "He wasn't in there often or long enough to get mixed up in that. He'd just drop by, have a few sips of his drink, never a whole one, and take off. It was a show, for the most part. Thankfully, he was better behaved at his own places than at some other spots in town. I heard Karen chased him out with a frying pan, and I don't think he was Jess's favorite customer."

"Do you know why?"

"Well, he poached me, which isn't the greatest from her standpoint. But more likely, he probably told her about the hot tub and offered to put some Mr. Bubble in it for her. That'd be my guess."

I thanked her and left. How someone like Adam projected such success and togetherness when his life was so all over the place was beyond me. It certainly wasn't making my job any easier. I'd heard plenty so far, none of it seemingly enough for someone to reach for a shotgun. I'd circled back to thinking the answer might be in the financials sitting on my desk.

Chapter Twenty-Two

Not far from Mary's, on the town line with Brookeville, Charlie Sarofian was working his latest job. He was another person I'd yet to cross off my extensive list. As I drove the back roads, the temperature dropped, inching us toward winter. I put the heat on in the Bronco. I couldn't go half a mile without having a reason to stop and question someone. I sighed, unsure which of those facts triggered it.

If what I'd heard was true, Sarofian had reason to be placed near the top of the Springbrook grievance list. He'd done a lot of work for him and had yet to be paid in full. But the only times I'd ever come across Charlie were when I stopped by his worksites to talk to Derek Anderson, who constantly skirted trouble. Today, they were building a garage. Sarofian was running a saw in the driveway when I approached him. Derek and another crew member were putting up plywood in what appeared to be a second-floor in-law apartment.

Sarofian stopped when he saw me and shut down the whirring blade. That caught Derek's attention. He looked and dropped his half of a four-by-eight panel. He pointed at me, then started down the ladder.

"Can I talk to you for a minute, Charlie?" I said, ignoring Anderson's approach.

"Sure, Chief."

"Oh no you don't," Derek said, shouting as he charged over.

Charlie shook his head as Derek scurried toward us.

"I told you," Derek said. "I told you he'd be here to hassle me."

"Derek," Charlie said, scowling, "go back to work. Your name hasn't come up."

"Yet," I said, smiling. "I would like to ask you a few questions after I've talked to your boss, if you don't mind."

"Bullshit." He stomped his foot on the driveway. "I know why you're here. You don't think anyone can't see through this?"

"Do you mind if I talk to him first, Charlie?" I said. "So we can put him behind us."

"Go right ahead." He turned on the saw and went back to work. I noticed some grays around his temples. If they didn't stem from having to manage Derek, I would have been shocked.

I walked Derek to the end of the driveway.

"I knew it," he said, jabbing his index finger within six inches of my face. "I told Suzy you'd be up my ass. And goddamn if I'm not right."

"You can get that finger out of my face, Derek," I said. "Before I break it."

His eyes went up as he calculated the odds of me doing that. His hand came down.

"You think you're better than me," he said. "How's that working out for you, LT?"

I sighed. This wasn't the first time I'd have rather dropped him than talked. The restraint required by this job was trying.

"You were at the VFW on Monday?" I asked.

"Yeah," he said. His head leaned to one side as if to get a better view of from what angle I was coming at him.

"Who else was there?"

"There weren't many of us. Who wants to watch the fucking Bengals? Me, Henry Kittle, Fred Labelle, Blockhead Roger, and Pickey. Maybe a couple other guys."

"Anyone leave early?"

"I did. The game sucked. I don't know about anyone else."

"You've been hunting with Roger, I hear."

"That's right. He's got himself a new dog. Damn good one. We been bagging more than our share of partridge."

"Anyone have anything to say about Adam Springbrook that night?"

"He didn't come up," Derek said. "Why are you asking?"

"He was shot Monday night."

"I know that," he said. His hands went to his waist, outraged. "You can't think it's one of us. I guarantee that dandy's never set foot in the VFW."

"Did I say it was one of you?" I wasn't going to explain that very few bar disagreements result in homicides. And in this case, there were plenty of alternate motivations running around town.

"Why else would you be asking?"

"What're you using for a shotgun?"

"I got my old pump Mossberg."

"Gauge?"

"Twelve."

"You know anyone using a sixteen?"

"Most everyone I know uses a twelve. Roger couldn't hit nothing with anything smaller. You could stick me out there with a four-ten and I'd still knock them down."

"I'm sure," I said. There wasn't much Derek couldn't do if you asked him.

"You know that guy Springbrook was a real asshole. Charlie had to bug the shit out of him to get our money."

Giving Derek some rope and letting him hang himself was a good way to get information.

"I wouldn't blame them one bit if Charlie or George took the prick out," he said, nodding.

"I know he owed you guys money. What's up with George?" Maybe I was the only one in town who didn't know that Springbrook was a bisexual Hugh Hefner.

"That bastard was hitting on both of his kids, the boy and the girl. I don't know who'd put up with that kind of shit. I get it for the girl; she's hot. But the boy, too? That ain't right."

"Do you know anyone who'd do something about it?"

"That'd be up to George, but he ain't like that," Derek said. "They can't be the only kids around here that weasel went after, though."

It was rare for him and me to agree on anything. I started to say something, but hesitated. Then I couldn't help myself.

"Were you drinking on Monday?"

"You think I was so fucked up I don't know who I was watching the game with?"

"No. Suzanne told me that you'd quit."

"That ain't your concern, is it?" He shifted his head back, out of punching range.

That was when I normally would have threatened him. But he was right. And I'd promised I wouldn't. I wasn't sure what approach I should take. I'd broken his nose once, and it hadn't changed him.

"If that woman shows up anywhere with so much as a scratch on her little finger," I said, "I'm going to hold you responsible. Know that." I battled to say it in a non-threatening way. But after the words left my mouth, I knew I'd failed.

"That's a low blow. I ain't that person anymore."

"Let's hope not." He tried to match my stare. Then he nodded and went back to work.

I talked to Charlie Sarofian for fifteen minutes. He did have to chase Springbrook for money. He was still owed five out of twenty thousand for the work he'd done renovating the Captain Fairweather. Payments had come in dribs and drabs. He hadn't thought to go over there and nail the doors shut like Mancini. He told me that he'd called the office every day, and then got Springbrook's home number and called there every night. That's when the money started coming. He was at least getting paid, if not at a rate he was happy with. His concern was that the money would now stop with Adam out of the picture. I didn't know what to tell him.

He mentioned that he hadn't been asked about doing any work at Lost Woods. While he guessed they weren't that far along in the planning, he said that he'd take roofing jobs before he worked for Adam again. I didn't bother asking him if he had a shotgun. I assumed that he did, and if he'd used it on Springbrook, that wouldn't have been something that he'd have been willing to share.

Chapter Twenty-Three

My desk was covered. The financials from the Springbrook Group spread from edge to edge. In their center was a standard legal pad. It contained my list of suspects and bullet points of their potential motives. I was staring at them, knowing I'd be adding names and killing more trees once those business documents had been translated. I could have been in a trance when Estelle buzzed and put a call through from Gwyneth. She was at the VFW and told me that I might want to get down there because she'd come across something important. I hung up, but before I could grab my keys from the pegboard, Marv Fitzgerald walked in with his arms full of manila folders.

"There's more?" I said. *Moby Dick* probably held fewer pages than I'd accumulated. "How?"

"Believe me, this is nothing out of the ordinary. As I said at our offices, if there are things that could lead you to Adam's killer, we will provide anything you deem necessary."

That wasn't exactly what they'd said then, though reminding him of that wasn't going to help.

"These are the latest profit and loss statements from the Reef House, the Captain Fairweather, and the Seagrass Inn," Fitzgerald said. "I've also included the purchase and sale documents from Dante's, the Clam Shed, and Babe's Marina. They should match up with the information provided earlier. I would again ask that you keep these confidential. I would not want this information to get out to the general public, nor should you have reason to release such data."

"I'm just trying to find out who shot Adam, Mr. Fitzgerald. I'm not looking to get into discussions of economics, real estate, or the price of oysters with anyone."

"Good to know," he said, adjusting his wire-rim glasses. He took a breath, not picking up on my desire to leave. Maybe he thought I stood in front of my desk to receive all visitors. "Have you talked to Talia Springbrook regarding the will?"

"Yes," I said, thinking I might as well see what he thought while I had him here. "Can I ask what her specific reaction was when you shared the details with her?"

"She seemed to be okay. I wouldn't say that she was excited, overwhelmed, or surprised. Appeared to take it as the course of business. She did tear up at times, I should note."

"Do you know her plans?" There was always a chance that what she'd told me was not the truth. That had been proven again and again.

"I don't. I'm sure that you realize it's a lot to process, not just the death of a former spouse, but to inherit a burgeoning hospitality enterprise. It's one thing to consult or invest, and another to be sitting at the top. I made myself available to her, of course."

"Thank you for letting me know, and for the information," I said. Not all of his colleagues, officers of the court in name, at least, had been so forthcoming in the past.

He left, but I didn't bother looking through the new documents. Until Abby got here to tell me what they contained, examining them would be a waste of time. And I had Gwyneth waiting for me at the VFW. I wondered how many of the workmen who frequented that place Springbrook owed money because I'd have bet my house that they all owned shotguns.

Chapter Twenty-Four

I'd made it nearly halfway across the lobby when Abby Grimes strolled into the station. Few people entered smiling. She was an exception. Estelle grinned. As an old friend of my mother's, she'd been hoping that I'd settle down with someone, and prospects were dwindling. Of course, with Abby younger than myself and our relationship stemming from a case that ripped apart her family, I couldn't help but question the wisdom in letting things advance beyond the casual flirting that Abby relentlessly pitched at me.

"I'm here and at your service," she said.

"Thank God," I said. Gwyneth and the VFW could spare two more minutes. I did an about-face and brought her into my office.

"I need a translator," I said, showing her the papers and stacks of folders carpeting my desk. I went around and pulled a chair from in front, placing it next to mine. But not too close.

"Wow," she said. "The inner sanctum, like being in the Bat Cave."

"I know you're a drinker, but this early in the day?"

"Shut up," she said. "What exactly do you need from me?"

"Those," I said, "are the financials from Lost Woods and the Springbrook Coastal Group. To me, they might as well be written in Latin. I need you to look them over, confidentially, I might add, and tell me whose money is screwed up or missing or in jeopardy enough to have wanted to shoot Springbrook over it."

"That leaves me with several questions," she said. "The first being, am I supposed to ignore what I see here, for the purposes of real life?"

That was an interesting place for her to start. Her business was commercial real estate. But in Boston. I shouldn't have been surprised that she'd look for an angle.

"That would depend on what you mean by that. I can't have what's in here getting out to a newspaper or around town. I'm guessing that you might know some of the investors. I promised Fitzgerald, Springbrook's lawyer and the guy you may have just passed in the parking lot, that this information would remain within the department. I realize that you can't very well forget something that you've learned from doing this. But you can't tell anyone what you've seen. It could compromise the investigation or feed information to a guilty party. We don't know yet who's responsible."

"This is a real thing," she said. "I get it."

"Thank you."

"So, if I can't leverage this top-secret, proprietary information, what's in this for me?" She smiled widely.

"My eternal gratitude? The satisfaction of helping get a killer off the streets?"

"That's not enough." She pushed the folders into the center of the desk.

It was hard to ignore how her smile triggered one of my own.

"I'm afraid to hear your demands," I said.

"I didn't think that you were afraid of anything. But let's start with dinner tonight. I'm staying at the Compound, but I don't think your friend Mr. Trout will have the kitchen stocked this time of year. I called him and told him I was coming, so at least the place will be habitable."

"Have you been here in the fall?"

"Please," she said, shaking her head. "It's sleepy enough in the summer. Now it's practically deserted. How do you stand it?"

"Some call it peace and quiet," I said. "Usually, there aren't entrepreneurs getting shot."

"Times are changing," she said, picking up a folder. "Is there a decent restaurant open? You know I'm not fond of the Tavern or Allies, and the Dockside is closed for the season."

"There's the Sea Squall," I said. They were going to get pretty tired of me over there. I wasn't sure the Reef was open, which was the only other place she may have been interested in.

"That will do." She opened one of the folders and glanced at the stack of papers. "Do I have to do this here? Can I bring these to the Compound?"

"My office isn't nice enough?"

"I don't want you looking over my shoulder expecting me to come up with something brilliant."

"Have at it. I was on my way out when you came in."

"You trust me, then. To leave the premises with them. That's important in a relationship."

"I wouldn't have called you if I didn't. But don't get carried away."

"Jesus, you are an open book." She shook her head and moved the chestnut hair that was creeping over the side of her face.

"I think the term you're avoiding, one favored by the horde of federal authorities that were here a few years ago, is rube."

"Well, I wouldn't go quite that far. It didn't turn out so great for them, did it?"

"Not for any of us."

"Remind me of why I came?"

"Because, at heart, you're a good person, though you make quite an effort to avoid admitting it."

"Maybe I just like you," she said, standing.

"I don't think that's it," I said, gathering the folders and putting them into a box for her. While I had no background or training in psychology, I couldn't help but think her interest in me stemmed from some sort of hero complex, if there was such a thing. I was just a guy who tried to do his job, but somehow in her eyes, I was more than that. I imagined that she'd come to see it my way eventually. In the meantime, I wasn't inclined to venture out onto that ice just to see if it would crack. "But I will carry these out for you as a small token of my appreciation."

"How gallant," she said, snickering.

"Let's meet at the Sea Squall at seven," I said. "That should give us plenty of time to get some things done."

"A little early for dinner, isn't it?"

"In October, in Laurel, that might as well be midnight."

"You know what Eric Clapton says," she said, following me through the lobby. "That's when it all hangs down."

"I was just hoping for some swordfish."

"Aim higher, Chief Nichols. Aim higher."

Chapter Twenty-Five

J ack Shelton was behind the wood-paneled counter that served as the VFW's bar. Gwyneth stood across from him, arms folded across her chest. An American flag covered the wall to their right. Rows of alternating round and rectangular tables filled the rest of the place, each spotted with gold glass ashtrays. Jack ran the bar in his retirement. He was wiping the bar top with Murphy's Oil Soap. I guess that's what made it one step up from the Rusty Bullet, which seemed to operate on the belief that long-seated grime only added to its character. He nodded at me and put down his rag.

He came around and sat on a bar stool. The color television mounted on the wall was sharp and clear. Jack walked over and turned it off.

"Would you like a soda, LT? I've offered your officer one, but she won't bite. I've been telling her that I'm quite harmless."

Gwyneth rolled her eyes at me.

"Go ahead," she said, "tell the Chief what you told me."

"Yes, ma'am," he said and winked at her. I don't think he realized that was a dangerous game.

"Officer Robinson was asking about who was in here Monday night. It was the usual crew: Henry Kittle, Fred Labelle, Blockhead Roger, Derek Anderson, and Ed Pickey. We were watching the game."

"But not George Paquin?" Gwyneth said.

"No," Jack said. "He left way before kickoff. Right after the news was over." That was something.

"Anyone stay for the whole game?" It would be nice to be able to cross someone off the suspect list before we started after Paquin to see what his real story was.

"Are you kidding? Bengals and the Chargers. It was lousy. Roger got a call just before halftime. Jess was looking for him. Something was up at the restaurant. He went right out the door. But no one made it to the second half kickoff."

That made them all unaccounted for at the time of death.

"Adam Springbrook's name come up that night?"

"No, sir. But I don't think any of them have been working for him."

"Everyone drinking?"

"They don't come for the decor, Chief."

"Derek Anderson, too?"

He raised his eyebrows. Of course, there were probably fewer people in town who knew that Springbrook had been shot than that Derek was back with Suzanne and she'd dropped the bomb on me at the Sea Squall.

"It isn't good business to talk about my customers."

"I've been told he quit."

"Oh, LT," Jack said, waving me off. "Beer ain't drinking. Used to be he never had a High Life without a Seagram's Seven to keep it company. Haven't seen that in a long time, to his credit."

"Yeah," I said. I didn't like hearing it, but there wasn't much I could do. Promises.

I already had George Paquin on my follow-up list after hearing that Mary had found him lurking late at night in the Reef House's parking lot. Maybe Paquin hadn't been as understanding as he'd claimed. But he'd have to have been very upset and extremely patient to wait this long to do something about it.

"Let's take a ride," I said to Gwyneth in the parking lot. "I know where we can find George."

126

Chapter Twenty-Six

I t was a little early for me to be visiting the Rusty Bullet, but this wasn't a pleasure trip. Like most of those who worked on the pier, George was known to have a pop before heading home, especially on a Friday. If we were able to find him there, I wouldn't have to horrify his son by appearing again at his door.

Gwyneth and I practically filled the place by ourselves. That's what happens when a bar is smaller than a double-wide. Paquin sat with Jim Wilton on the last of the eight stools. Duke, the bartender, did a double-take when he saw me. I couldn't remember ever visiting in uniform.

I said hello to Paquin and Wilton. Their eyes narrowed over their noses, wondering if they had mistakenly parked near the pier's one fire hydrant.

"George, can we talk outside, please?" I said.

He sighed and nodded. "What'd you do now?" Wilton said.

"Shut up," Paquin said. Wilton laughed.

We went down the three steps and stood off to the side next to our cruiser. He looked everywhere around the pier except at us.

"George," I said. "You told me that you were at the VFW on Monday night. We checked. You had one drink and left before the game started. Where were you?"

His hands alternated tapping their corresponding thighs. I half-expected him to take off running.

"I'd rather not say," he said.

"Were you with Adam Springbrook?"

"No. I didn't have anything to do with that. Christ."

"Then where were you?" Gwyneth said, eyes trained on him. "Not telling us isn't an option. This is a homicide investigation."

I was surprised—and glad—to see her jump in.

"I was somewhere else." Now he was studying his shoes.

"Where would that be?" I asked.

"Do I have to say in front of the girl?" he said, nodding at Gwyneth.

"That's Officer Robinson," I said. "She's a real live policewoman. So cut the shit."

"It's kind of a delicate situation," he said quietly.

"You might have a different opinion," I said, "if you'd seen the condition that Springbrook was left in."

He took a deep breath. "Is this confidential?"

"Just answer the question, sir," Gwyneth said.

His face reddened, like he wanted to tell her to lay off, but thought better of it. A wise decision.

"It's my understanding," I said, "that you weren't as easy-going about Springbrook and your kids as you claimed. You were also seen this summer lurking in the Reef House parking lot. Your kids had both left for the night, so you can file that excuse."

"What liar told you that?" he said, jamming his hands in his pockets.

"Do you think you might cooperate better if we went down to the station?"

"Come on," he said. "You don't have to get all bent out of shape."

"Last chance. Where were you?"

"Fuck," he said. "Rick Powell's place."

"He can verify that?" His eyes met mine for a fraction of a second, then shot off.

"Not exactly." He sighed and looked past us to the harbor.

I opened the back door to the cruiser. "Get in," I said.

"Daisy could tell you."

"Not Rick?" I asked.

"Come on, man," he said, looking down. "Are you going to make me spell it out?"

Powell was the first mate on a trawler out of Portland. They left for days, even weeks, at a time. I was beginning to see why Paquin hadn't wanted this spilling out.

"I'm guessing that you weren't visiting to take out the screens for winter. How long were you there?"

"Until midnight, or so." Paquin's wife had probably gotten the same story that we did.

"When you left, where did you go?"

"Straight home. Honest." To him, this was the worst kind of alibi.

A knowing look came over Gwyneth's face. She'd put it together.

"We'll need to check that out," I said to Gwyneth.

"You can't," he said, his voice cracking. "Rick's back."

It took effort not to laugh.

"I'll send Officer Robinson. I'm sure she'll be discreet."

"I hope so. I haven't done anything wrong."

"I don't know if Rick would agree with that," I said, "not that it's any of our business."

"You provided false information to an investigation," Gwyneth said. "Do you realize that?"

"That can't be illegal," he said. "Everyone lies to the cops."

"Maybe you better get right to the bottom of it, Officer Robinson. If Rick Powell happens to hear your line of questioning, that's just the way it is. We can't have people thinking it's okay to jerk us around, and it isn't our job to cover for an asshole who doesn't respect the fact that we're trying to determine who killed one of his neighbors."

"Got it, Chief," she said.

"Come on, LT," George said. He kicked the toe of one work boot into the heel of the other. "That's not what I meant."

"Well?" I said, waiting for an explanation.

"What Daisy and I were doing has got nothing to do with damn Adam Springbrook. If you're so hot and bothered about this thing, go talk to Earl Goodwin. His wife was fucking Springbrook half the summer, and I know he wasn't happy when he found out. Almost everyone who worked at the Reef House knew about it. My boy Alfred's friends with his son Jimmy. It was all he could do to keep him from letting on. Earl's the one you should be harassing, not me. I didn't do more than yell at him that one time."

"You told me you didn't do anything," I said. I folded my arms across my chest to keep my hands from turning into fists. It was hard not to take all this lying personally. It was widespread and unending. And, of course, it was coming from people who claimed to have nothing to do with Springbrook's death. I didn't understand it.

"I dropped off some shrimp for Louie Williams, as a favor, once. For him, not the restaurant. I ran into Springbrook in the parking lot. I was just off the boat. Had a few in me. I told him that he better think twice if he wanted to keep harassing the kids who worked for him, that he might get a boot up his ass. I don't think he even knew who I was. He just kind of nodded and slipped through the kitchen door."

If I hadn't already checked his guns, I would have made a trip to the house. His relationship with the truth didn't appear to be a close one.

"Address, please, of Daisy and Rick Powell?" Gwyneth asked, taking out her notebook. I could have told her that, too, but let her do her job.

"Sixty-seven Fernwood Drive," he said.

"You're not going to bring this up in front of Rick, are you?" he asked, looking from Gwyneth to me.

"We can't predict how these things will go," Gwyneth said, no sympathy evident on her face.

"That's all I need," George said.

"What time did you leave the Powell house?"

"Right after the game. We did have it on."

"Did you go by Providence Hill?"

"Yeah, it's on the way."

"Did you see anything there?"

"No. I was pretty tired. Long day."

"I can imagine," I said. "Get out of here."

"Can I go in and finish my beer?" he asked.

"There's no law against it," I said. We watched him scoot back into the bar.

"It's like a bad episode of Dynasty," Gwyneth said. "Only without the money and glamour. What the hell is going on in this town?"

"I wish I could tell you," I said, shaking my head. She didn't even know these people. I did, and it made it that much worse. I wanted to tell her it hadn't always been like this. But, standing there in a dive bar parking lot, I wasn't sure about that.

Chapter Twenty-Seven

I was lucky to catch Earl Goodwin's office open this late on a Friday in the off-season. His new secretary showed me right in. It must have been the uniform. Earl sold the vast majority of houses in town, but I couldn't recall him being involved in any of Springbrook's dealings. That may have been the least of his issues with Adam. Earl asked me to sit down. We chatted about how his boys were doing, his son Jimmy playing quarterback at Bates. The secretary brought me a coffee. When stories of his offspring's athletic exploits came to an end, I started working.

"I hear you have an ax to grind with Adam Springbrook," I said, sipping something of much higher quality than we had at the station.

Earl shifted his bottom in his chair. A navy blazer hung off the back of it. The pictures of the coast and sailboats framed on the walls were summer-drenched shots of sunshine and blue skies. Outside the window, everything was brown and gray.

"What are you talking about?" he said. His hands moved from the desktop to his lap to the arms of his chair.

"You tell me, Earl," I said.

"I have no idea what you're trying to get at," he said, tightening the knot of his red tie.

"Let's start with that he doesn't use you for his acquisitions," I said.

"That's his choice. He has his own team and lawyer, Marvin Fitzgerald. He doesn't need me. Probably saves him a whole half of a point."

"Have you discussed this with him?"

"I'm one person in town who never sucked up to him."

"Is that because of Cindy?" I said. This was not a comfortable subject to broach. "I've heard that they had some sort of relationship."

"That's nobody's business," he said. He ran a hand through his brown hair. "Including yours."

"This is a murder investigation. I go where it takes me."

"Of course," he said, settling his hands flat on his desk. "I wasn't happy to hear that he got shot. But I wasn't crying into my beer. I'm sure you can figure out why. I assume he overplayed his hand with someone less reasonable than myself."

"Think back. You weren't upset when you found out what was going on?"

"You can't be serious," he said, his face reddening, "that you'd think I'd have shot the man over that."

"Some people do tend to take that sort of thing seriously, as you just noted."

"I am not one of them. Though I shouldn't say that, to be honest. As you have your ear to what passes for pavement in this town, you know that Cindy and I have had our share of challenges. We've been getting help, however. We're past all that and doing better." That might explain the new receptionist. The previous one and Earl had a relationship that extended beyond typing and getting coffee. On a previous case, I'd held that over him to get information. With my own relationship track record, I was not one to make judgments. However, I had yet to meet the person who was more innocent than they claimed to be.

"Where were you on Monday night?"

"At home. With Cindy. Who was also home. She didn't do it, either, if that's where you were going next."

"I wasn't." But it would have been wrong to eliminate a suspect based on gender. Quite a few women in town accompanied their husbands into the woods during deer season. It's just that good-looking businessmen weren't usually the game.

"Can anyone verify that you were together?"

"Nick was home, too. We were looking over college catalogs. He's not going to follow his brother to Bates. Too small for him."

"Nobody outside the family?"

"It must be horrible to think so poorly of people you know that you feel the need to ask these questions. We could never do something like that. How do you live with yourself?"

"I don't have much of a choice," I said. "No one wants to live with me." I took a breath. "Though I've never fucked around on anyone who has."

His cheeks puckered as he considered a response.

"Did you confront Springbrook when you found out about him and Cindy?"

"I caught word of it around Labor Day. Cindy didn't deny it when I told her what I'd heard. It wasn't even like that. I asked her about it, and she told me it was already over. Of course, I've seen him around since then. We run in some of the same circles. I might have been having a cocktail at the Sea Squall when he happened to be there. We crossed paths as I was coming out of the bathroom."

"What happened?"

"I told him that he better do his best to stay out of my way."

"What did he say to that?"

"He brought out that phony smile and said, 'Noted.' That was it." Goodwin shook his head. "I would have liked to have been at the Squall the night that Jess Consentino slapped him, right in the bar. That flustered him for once, I heard. He ran right out the door. There's no telling what he said to her to elicit that response. I would have paid to see it, however. He's not the nicest person on the planet, though he worked hard to give the opposite impression."

I had to concentrate to not grind my teeth. Earl was just short of gloating that the man had been shot while he had nothing to do with it, and Jess had failed to relate that she'd slapped Adam in the middle of her restaurant when I'd asked her about him.

"As for where I was Monday, you can talk to Cindy. You can talk to Nick. There's no Goodwin conspiracy going on. Cindy was quite shaken when she heard. But I'm also sure Cindy wasn't the only woman in town that he's taken advantage of. He was a sleazeball of the highest order."

"I will be following up with her. And Nick. Just so you know." That didn't mean he'd been wrong in his assessment of Springbrook.

"Can you do me a favor, at least?" he said, straightening up. "The boy isn't aware of his mother's activities. Neither is Jimmy, for that matter. Is there a reason things can't stay that way?"

"I'm not in this to hurt people," I said.

We shook hands over the desk.

"You know," he said. I stopped and turned. "He did owe a lot of people money."

"Anyone in particular?" I said.

"If you did work for him, you had to chase him for your check," Earl said. "He should have been a fucking juggler because that was what he was good at. Money, people, you name it. It's one thing for some of these bigger outfits to not get paid. But the small guys, shit. Springbrook wasn't so popular at the Tavern or the Bullet as he was at the Sea Squall or the Reef House. The investors got a little better treatment than the workingmen, at least as far as the money went. But you'd never know it with the way he carried on. I'm glad that I wasn't mixed up in any of his deals. People still talk to me when I run into them on the street."

I left his office feeling worse about my chances of narrowing down a suspect. The question may have been: Who didn't want to shoot Adam Springbrook?

Chapter Twenty-Eight

I drove back across town, not feeling great about having to insert myself in the middle of what should have been private family business. I wasn't sure what anarchy meant in theory, but it seemed like it was what was going on in Laurel. Everyone I'd come into contact with these last few days had their lives disrupted in some way by one man: Adam Springbrook. Day-to-day living was not supposed to be this hard on people. I rolled to a stop in the Goodwins' driveway and banged the steering wheel as if it were the one responsible.

Cindy Goodwin offered me coffee, tea, water, and beer, all of which I turned down. We sat across from each other at the kitchen island. She didn't seem surprised to see me. The outgoing tide drained from the river behind us.

"Earl told you I was coming to ask about Adam Springbrook?"

She nodded.

"Let's start with where you were Monday night, please."

"We were home, the three of us. We were going over college catalogs with Nick."

They'd had time to get this story straight, if I wanted to think like a cynic.

"You understand why I'm here, right?" I said.

Cindy nodded. She was not smiling, nor was she frowning. "I suppose everyone in town knows about us by now."

"I couldn't say. I just heard myself."

"From who?"

"That's not important."

136

"Maybe not to you." She shrugged. Cindy had a pleasant face, with smooth skin and strawberry blond hair that fell feathered about her shoulders. She was probably in her mid-forties and thick in her body. As pretty as she was, she didn't seem the type that Springbrook would have been interested in, considering his pursuit of Lucy and Alfred Paquin, twenty-five years younger, and the fashionable look of his ex-wife, Talia.

"I don't need to get into all the details, but can you tell me how you and Springbrook, uh, got together?"

"We met around town. You know how the summer circuit works. He can be quite charming. I fell for it." She got up and poured herself a cup of coffee. "It was a mistake. I did it for stupid reasons."

"Would you like to share those?"

"Not particularly. I wasn't too happy with Earl, or feeling good about myself. I was an easy target for a handsome man. I should have known better."

I nodded.

"This past summer? That's when we're talking about?"

"We started up around the Fourth, and it was over by August. Your basic summer fling, as if I was a dumb college girl."

"It ended because?"

"I stopped calling him. He stopped calling me."

"It was mutual, you would say?"

"That's right. I began to see what a fool I'd been, and I got the impression that for Adam, there was always another bus coming around the corner."

"No hard feelings?"

"I don't know about that, but really, it just ran its course. I was relieved, to be honest. That's not my life, that kind of thing."

"And when Earl found out?"

She smiled. "He handled it as well as one could hope. He wasn't happy, of course, and it got a little chilly in here. If the kids weren't home, maybe the fur would have been flying. But their presence kept us grounded and made us realize what was important. If something good could come from something bad, I guess that would be it. Earl had reason to be understanding.

We went to marriage counseling. Things are better now. Except, of course, for Adam."

"Earl and Adam didn't have any problems afterward?"

"We never talked about it. Let sleeping dogs lie, as they say."

I left the house believing that neither Earl nor Cindy were the ones who killed Springbrook and left him in the woods. I guessed that half the town had they the chance, would have swerved through a puddle if they'd seen Adam standing on the sidewalk. But that was a long way from blasting him point-blank with a shotgun.

Chapter Twenty-Nine

My next stop was the Sea Squall. While I had a hard time picturing Jess Consentino wielding anything more lethal than a corkscrew, I couldn't let her slapping Adam in public go without a follow-up. I'd learned not to make assumptions. And I knew better than to do my questioning when I came in later for dinner, seeing as it was the only place that Abby would likely find acceptable.

They were just getting open at five, so I went in through the kitchen. Roger was chopping lettuce with a chef's knife. Another cook was pouring oil into a fryer. Hood fans were purring over an enormous stock pot. Roger kept chopping but looked up when the door closed behind me.

"Shit," he yelled. He'd clipped the edge of his finger.

"You okay?" I asked, looking over.

"Yeah, nothing serious," he said, examining the cut. He grabbed a kitchen towel and wrapped it. It didn't turn red, so I assumed he was right about it being nothing major.

"What are you doing here?" he asked.

"I'm looking for Jess."

"Why?" he asked.

"It's my business to ask the questions. You better focus on your chopping before you lose your trigger finger and can't hit any more partridge."

"Okay," he said. "She's in the office, I think." He looked down, then up at me, then down again.

The office was under the stairs that went up to the loft. The door was open, so I waited on the threshold and knocked on the frame. Jess had her hair in a bun, and she wore oversized glasses more suitable for a librarian than a restauranteur. She put down the *Wine Spectator* she was reading and asked me to come in.

"What can I do for you, LT?" she asked.

"Adam Springbrook," I said. "I'm hearing that you hit him. You failed to mention that the other day."

"Oh, that," she said, shrugging. "Honestly, it was no big deal. I don't see where slapping him after he insulted me months ago has any relevance to what happened this week."

"Why don't you leave it to me to judge its importance? I'm not saying that you shot him. I'm just wondering why you didn't tell me it happened."

"He made a comment that I didn't like. I wasn't about to stand for it. It was while Frank was in the hospital. I may have overreacted. It was a stressful time. I probably shouldn't have been working, but this is our only source of income. I had little choice."

"What exactly did he say?"

"I'd rather not repeat it." Her eyes went over my shoulder, then focused back on me.

"That bad?"

"Worse."

"Business or personal?"

"Business, which is personal for us."

"Okay," I said, determined to wait her out.

"He intimated that with Frank soon to be gone—something I wasn't ready to accept—I would need a new partner—Adam, of course—or want to sell to him directly. Can you imagine someone saying those things at a time like that?"

"I can't," I said. The more I learned, the less sympathy I had for the man.

"Do you blame me?" she asked.

"I'm not exactly known for my patience and understanding," I said.

"You're not going to drag me downtown and put me under the lights?"

"I don't think so," I said, smiling.

Jess was just one more person with reason to dislike Springbrook. Motive was never going to be a problem with this investigation. Maybe it was time to shift focus to means and opportunity.

The soda gun went off behind me. Roger was getting another Coke. He drank more soda than anyone I knew. That's where Jess's eyes had been going. He must have been standing there the whole time. I let my gaze rest on him. Most people caught like that would have retreated to the kitchen. I don't think Roger knew better.

"He's worried about everything without Frank around," Jess said. "He probably wants to make sure that I'm not in any kind of trouble. Maybe it's even worse, and he thinks you're here to ask me out on a date."

"I don't believe in torture," I said.

Jess laughed.

"I'm sorry I didn't bring it up before," she said, scrunching up her face and shaking her head. "It's a little embarrassing. I should have shown more restraint."

"And, of course, where were you on Monday night?"

"I was here. We had a pipe come loose in the kitchen, had a bit of a flood at the dish machine after closing. I was dealing with that."

"That's why you called Roger, to come help?"

Her head jerked an inch to the left.

"Exactly," she said. "I can run a mop okay, but a wrench, not so much."

I nodded.

"If you want to know the truth, Adam wasn't my favorite person. I could give you a list as long as my arm of those who would cosign on that, too. But that doesn't mean I was happy to hear what happened. I wouldn't want that for anyone, just to be clear."

"You're a real humanitarian, Jess," I said.

"I try, LT," she said. "I try."

"I have one more question," I said, "and you might not mind this one quite as much. Can I get a table in an hour or so?"

That brought a look of relief to her face, her jaw relaxing. At least doing my job had not gotten me blacklisted. Abby would be happy. I thanked her and went out through the kitchen. Roger was standing by the back door, drinking his Coke.

"Roger, can I ask you a question?"

"Sure, LT."

"Why are you always watching me when I'm here?"

"I'm not."

"You seem pretty thirsty whenever I'm around. I assume you spend most of your time cooking, otherwise, don't you?"

"I sure do."

"Good man," I said.

Chapter Thirty

I found myself at Wink's just before closing. I had time before meeting Abby for seven. I came in, said hello, and walked around the aisles as if I were looking for something, waiting for Suzanne to leave. We hadn't spoken, and I didn't care. Derek had probably already told her that I'd threatened him. That was too bad. I would have done it for any woman in town, and just because she'd had the misfortune of dating me didn't mean that I'd do less to protect her, whether she requested it or not. She left, saying goodbye to Wink but ignoring me.

"You're a smooth one, aren't you?" Wink said as the door closed behind her.

"It's a curse," I said.

"What brings you in, LT? I'm guessing it's no accident, no matter how long you were going to wander around pretending to look for something."

"You should have my job."

"Don't want it," he said.

"I need some help understanding what's going on."

"With Suzy?" He looked at me like I couldn't be that stupid.

"Jesus, Wink, you must think I'm a real dumbass."

He shrugged and lit up a Marlboro.

"It's everyone else."

"What do you mean?" he asked and nodded to the stools at the lunch counter. He went to grab a couple beers out of the cooler.

"I know you didn't think much of Springbrook, and probably for good reason. I'm finding that he had a real toxic effect on this town. I don't just mean with the restaurants and inns and the commerce. I mean with the people. It's like I don't know anyone who I've been talking to."

"You haven't been smoking any confiscated materials, have you? You know everyone around here."

"It's that I can't get a handle on what I've been hearing. I talk to one person about a reason they might have been upset with Adam, and, of course, they deny it. Then the next words out of their mouth are telling me why one of their friends had even more reason to hate the guy. They're turning on each other. I've never seen it before."

"Excuse me, Chief, isn't that what you want when you're running an investigation? Isn't it worse when people won't tell you anything?"

"It's given me an unbelievably long list of suspects. Everyone's happy to share whatever rumor they heard about this neighbor or that one. Some of which have to be true, and others I know can't be. With what that guy did to get people to behave like this, maybe we're better off without him. Though I won't be pinning a medal on whoever killed him. Laurel doesn't seem like the town I grew up in."

"What you got here," he said, "is people acting like people."

"Like bad people. And Springbrook was the one with all the money."

"It doesn't matter how much or what someone has, LT. They always want more. Whether it's Randolph Grimes or Boomer Woodman, or Suzy and Derek, they want more: more money, more love, a bigger house, a better car, more lobster in their traps, more fried clams going out, a better boyfriend, a prettier girl, whatever. People want. The problem lies in what some will do to get it, which you're familiar with in your line of work. It's what gives you job security."

"I get that. But people used to act a certain way, look out for each other. When Deke put that dent in your Lincoln, hitting a boulder at a keg party in the woods, I would've never given him up for anything."

"You were kids, and all you wanted was not to be in trouble. You had nothing to lose. To some joker, if it's one of his friends who killed Springbrook, and they didn't care for Adam themselves, it could make them seem like part of it. The real people who come out ahead are the ones who don't want anything."

"Everyone wants something. You just said it."

"See," Wink said. "There's your problem. You're surprised by that."

"There's plenty of people who didn't like the man. It comes down to him always acting in what he thought was his own best interest, regardless of anyone else. But I don't know that makes him evil. You, or Rita and Karen, or Jess Consentino, could tell the man no, and nothing would come of it."

"That's some logic," Wink said, nodding. "What do you make of it?"

"He must have done something to one of these people that put them in a position where they couldn't say no, that went beyond what he did to everyone else."

"There you go," Wink said.

"That still leaves me with a town full of people turning on each other."

"You're confusing the hell out of me, Tim. Doesn't that help you figure this out?"

"I guess it does." I had to unearth the one person he'd pushed too far. That much was clear. "But the thing is, for weeks I had a bad feeling anytime I drove past that Lost Woods cut on Providence Hill, and it started long before anything happened to Springbrook. Now I get the same vibrations just driving through town. I've never felt things like this before. Something's not right here."

"We do have a killer among us. Maybe you *should* feel that."

"This is a different bad. I can't put my finger on it. I understand the logic behind what I have to do. What I don't get is picking up on it without having to think. My shoulders and neck are as stiff as boards."

Wink sighed and nodded his head.

"Maybe everyone feels it," he said, "and that's what you're seeing."

"Do you believe that?" I asked.

"Of course not," he said, laughing. "But they might. I ain't no mystic but, you know, people can be funny. Strange things happen. For a million reasons. Don't take it personally."

It was my turn to shrug.

"Could be," he said, "you realize that one of those people giving up their neighbor is lying. You just haven't figured out who it is yet."

"Yeah, that's crossed my mind."

"Good thing you're a wily veteran of police work."

"It's supposed to be peace and quiet this time of year," I said. "I'm already sick of it."

"That don't make you a bad person," Wink said. "Plenty of other things will qualify you for that.

Chapter Thirty-One

"You ain't going to do this, are you?" Nate Trout said. I'd been changing for dinner when he called. All that entailed was ditching my uniform for fresh jeans and a dress shirt.

"What do you mean?" I said, having an idea, but willing to let him work for it.

"You and Abby?"

"She's doing me a favor. I need help with the financials from Springbrook's company, and as you know, I don't have EF Hutton in my Rolodex. It's not like a date or anything."

"Does she know that? For some reason I can't understand, since you clocked the old man, she's got a crush on you. She's come downstairs in three different outfits and asked my damn opinion."

"I've tried to make it clear that she and I wouldn't be a good idea."

"You could be doing a better job communicating that." He chuckled. "Speaking of doing your job, you uncovered who killed that asshole yet?"

"Working on it," I said. "You have a lead for me?"

"Could be anyone. He pissed off a lot of people around here."

"I'm finding that out."

"Just use your head with the girl. She's got you nailed as some combination of John Wayne and Lee Majors. She's well into her twenties, but right now she's reminding me of my daughter at prom time."

"I know you're bullshitting me. Isn't it that you're worried I'll piss her off and she'll get back at me by firing you, and then you'd have to go out and get a real job instead of that setup you have babysitting a house?"

"If I was, I'd be right to do so."
I couldn't argue with my best friend on that one.

Chapter Thirty-Two

J ess Consentino put on a pleasant face as she led us to a booth in the back of her restaurant. The time that Trout had said Abby spent getting ready had paid off because I couldn't stop grinning. Her blue eyes were luminous, her hair was shining, and she appeared to have achieved this level of grace with ease. A long winter lay ahead, and my chances of coming across a woman this fetching during that ice age were small, to say the least. Anyone sitting across from her would have had a tough time resisting. Yet, I was determined.

We ordered drinks, and she brought out a notebook from her oversized leather bag.

"Let's get right to business," she said. "Even in the minimal time I've had to look things over, it appears that you don't have any shortage of suspects. All that land he purchased for Lost Woods, he made it appear that he was paying above market, but he wasn't. He'd provided the sellers with specs and comps for properties from interior locations, and, as we know, Laurel is on the coast. That makes a difference. But as none of them had their own agents, they bought it. The prices were still probably more than they'd thought their land was worth, and presumably, Adam didn't hold a gun to them to sell. If the property owners were mad enough to shoot him over that, I couldn't say."

I explained how people were happy until the term "million-dollar project" appeared in newspaper coverage.

Her eyes rolled.

"The workmen," she said, "are another story. Adam owed a lot of people."

She then listed off a string of names that I was familiar with: Mancini, Sarofian, and others.

"What I don't understand," I said, "is why he would ever be short of money. He just started clearing the land at Lost Woods. His restaurant is always packed, and there's never a weekend vacancy at his inns. He had plenty of investors. Did he just like to not pay people? Didn't he care?"

"Are you familiar with the float?" she said.

"As in the opposite of the Australian crawl, an inflatable water toy, the toilet part, or a wooden structure supported by flotation devices that you find on a lake?"

"None of the above," she said. "It's a component of business strategy. There are two kinds of entrepreneurs. One is conservative and spends money as it comes in or has expenditures budgeted on a schedule. The other is the kind that Adam was. They get sufficient backing and jump in, knowing or hoping that they'll have cash flow to direct as needed. This, you might understand, is like flying by the seat of your pants. The money generated by the inns and the Reef House isn't only paying their bills, it's also getting funneled into the construction of Lost Woods and work being done to upgrade the new restaurants. I think that's one of the reasons he started his corporate group, so he could move money around more easily. It's a slippery slope, and things can go haywire if you get caught short. For example, he learned that the pilings of the Clam Shed needed to be redone, which I don't think he was expecting, though he should have realized it. So, some of the funds targeted for the Lost Woods startup went there. Another unexpected problem was having to get additional permitting from the state EPA, and what that entailed due to a change in ownership. It wasn't cheap, and that's not even considering what Fitzgerald cost him. If you're playing the float, situations like that can be fatal. Adam weathered it, but that means Lost Woods gets held up, and he's probably got the people working there waiting on checks. He shuffles things around to keep everyone just happy enough to keep everything moving forward. Construction goes in fits and starts depending on cash flow and him sending money where it's most needed. The other problem is that, coming into winter, the earnings from the existing businesses slow down to a crawl, compared to the avalanche of summer. Dante's and the Clam Shed, being seasonal, are not going to produce income for another six months. That was a risk on his part, of course, buying these places right after the season. He knew that he'd be sitting on them but was willing to do it. What he probably didn't estimate correctly is how much money he'd have to sink into them to get them the way he wants."

"I thought those places were gold mines. What was wrong with leaving them like they were?"

"Nothing, for most people. But Adam had these great expectations. He wanted a sophisticated brand aesthetic for his Coastal Group, whether he was serving fried clams in those little boxes at the Shed or Alaskan salmon on white tablecloths at Dante's."

"Springbrookville," I said.

"What's that?" she said, her eyes focusing on me.

"He had this vision of turning Laurel into some sort of jet-set resort town. By himself. That's why he was buying everything that he could get his hands on. He had it mapped out in his office. I saw it. He was the dog who had to piss on every tree. Someone should have told him that you can't have everything."

"It's a little late for that," she said.

"Maybe somebody did tell him," I said, "with a bullet."

"Damn," Abby said.

That person was still out there, too.

"I'm glad I don't have to clean up this mess," Abby said, putting her notes back in her bag.

"Is this whole thing a house of cards?" I asked. Talia may have had reason to be worried.

"I wouldn't go quite that far. It seems like he was very adept at managing the chaos. I imagine that he pushed a lot of people to their limits in the process, however."

"And maybe one over."

"Was it the best way to do things?" she said, shaking her head. "I guess not. It's not how I run my business. As you would enjoy pointing out, I'm much too young for crow's feet, and operating like that would bring them like rain in spring. Apparently, he could deal with it."

"Are you happy that you didn't invest in Lost Woods?"

"Of course. I'm also glad that I wasn't one of those poor stiffs doing work for him."

I sighed, still not having reached the point where my list of potential suspects would thin—or stop growing.

"Would investors be aware of this?"

"They probably had no way of knowing. They're not seeing what I'm wading through for you. They got projections, and based on how busy his properties are, they probably looked good. Adam never gave the impression that he was doing anything other than cashing checks. If you saw him, everything was as it should be and tracking beautifully. Behind the scenes, of course, it was messy as hell. But unless the curtain comes up, no one sees it."

"How could he be out of money if all he'd done was start clearing the land?" My head hurt trying to think this through. "It sounds like a pyramid scheme."

"It's just business. It's not always as neat and tidy as it appears. Adam was a very charismatic man. He exuded success. It doesn't matter who you are and what you have; people attach themselves to that, and if they can make money at the same time, even better. People see without really seeing, if you know what I mean. I'm sure he had no trouble getting investors, and if he did need to raise more money, I bet that wouldn't be an issue."

"Does that make you smarter than everyone then, by not getting involved?" I asked, smiling.

"I wasn't going to wait around for the return. I was fairly sure it would eventually pay, but Springbrook Coastal Group was not going to be in the black anytime soon, even if things went as planned."

"It doesn't seem like the right way to operate," I said.

"No guts, no glory," she said, smiling. "If you look at what he paid for these places and that land, then what he sunk into them to upscale them, that's a lot in the expense column. And outside of ten weeks a year, cash flow is limited, though I assume his marketing would address the development of off-season business. His timing could have been better, too. But if these properties were up and running by next summer, he might have been fine. Or more than fine. I don't know quite yet. I've still got paper to push."

"Now I get why those old-school businessmen had three-martini lunches." She nodded. I was getting an education.

"So," I said, "I can eliminate investors from the suspect list? Even if someone found out about this shady accounting, it wouldn't be something that they'd shoot him over, would it?"

"Killing him certainly wouldn't help them get their money back. Of course, they'd have every right to be upset if their investment in Lost Woods got filtered to Dante's. But putting a bullet into Adam wouldn't fix that. And to clarify, I haven't seen any correspondence from an investor questioning anything he was doing or asking for a return of funds. It's not unheard of, but no one doing this kind of investing would expect such a request to be fulfilled."

I relaxed and took a sip of beer. Finally, I could cross off a series of names from my list of suspects. That I hadn't yet had the chance to look into them nearly struck me as funny.

"Now," Abby said, "these vendors who are getting jerked around, that's another story."

"Meaning?" I asked, wondering if it was worse than I'd been told.

"People had to rattle a lot of cages before they got money. Who is that guy that you talked to, Mancini? He's owed. Some contractor hasn't gotten fully paid yet for the work he did on the Captain Fairweather two years ago. Springbrook let out a little line at a time. No one wants to spend money on lawyers, so Adam kept them on the hook by giving them what he could get away with. Then they hear about something like Lost Woods and see more business for themselves and hope that Springbrook will have his shit together by then, because they see more work coming their way, somehow forgetting what it took to get paid the last time they signed on with him. Or they're sure it will be different this time around. Because that's how people are."

"But it won't be," I said.

"Of course not," she said, raising her glass.

"Christ, you're making my job sound good." I looked up at her, and she was grinning. "You know, you just used a fishing reference. You're finally speaking in a language that I can understand. I usually have to visit the town library to figure out what you meant."

"You asked me to help. I'm trying."

She reached across the table and patted my hand. Her touch was warm.

"You're blushing," she said, smiling wickedly. "What Adam was doing is called speculation. He never thought he would fail, because he never had. It's not like how you, and I don't presume to know how you live, would look at your salary and figure out how much of a new car you can afford, factoring in your existing mortgage payment."

"I drive an eight-year-old Bronco."

"Of course, but you don't imagine that your salary is going to go up by fifty percent next year because you're going to take over policing Wellport and another seventy-five percent the year after that because then you're going to get Milltowne, too. It seems that the way Adam thought, there was only one direction that things were going to go: Up."

I let out a deep breath. She was right. I couldn't envision dealing with that constant level of risk in business, never mind life in general.

"The more he put into it," she said, "the more he expected he'd get out of it."

"Does that actually happen?"

"There are a lot of millionaires out there who would tell you it does."

"What do you think?"

"I'm a little more analytical, as well as a bit more risk-averse."

This took us through cocktails and an appetizer of oysters and shrimp. Abby did make reference to the shellfish being legendary for putting lead in one's pencil. I tried to ignore it.

"Do you remember," I said, "once telling me that you didn't do civil servants?"

"Is that why you think I'm here?" she asked.

"Jesus, Abby. Why is it that you have the impression that I'm never aware of what's going on?"

"Whatever are you talking about?" she said, laughing.

"Your body language," I said, glancing at her hand, still on mine, "low-cut sweater, eye make-up, and smile are sending a very clear message."

"Okay, detective. You got me." Her grin vanished. "It's not polite to call someone out like that."

"I'm supposed to just go along?"

"Would that be so terrible?"

"Don't you see the psychology that's at work here?" I said. "I feel like I'm some sort of hero figure to you because of what happened with your father."

"You can entertain whatever fantasy you like," she said. "That doesn't make it true."

Of course, I'd gone too far. Another habit I feared I'd never shake.

"I will admit," I said, "that if I'd run across you in some bar in Boston and we hadn't previously met, I probably would've made a fool of myself trying to impress you."

"You in Boston," she said. "That's funny."

"I've been to several of your old boyfriend's clubs."

"Sure you have."

"And some dive between the Sub Woofer and Kenmore Square. It made the Rusty Bullet look like the Ritz-Carlton."

"The Rusty Bullet might be the only place in town that I've never been to. My brother would have died before going there—which he, sadly, in fact, did. I wasn't about to go on my own."

"Lots of local color."

"You'll have to take me sometime."

"I'd be delighted."

We talked for another half hour over dinner. Somehow, she got me to tell her about my failed marriage, a story she hadn't heard. She was aware that I'd had a girlfriend a few years ago. I didn't tell her that two days earlier, I'd thought there might have been renewed interest. I was suffering enough embarrassment from those already familiar with the story.

Abby insisted on having drinks at the bar afterward, Gran Marnier. The sickly sweet orange liqueur was not my favorite. I introduced Abby to Jess, who she'd been acquainted with from summer visits. That this was the second time this week that I'd been in with a woman, thankfully, didn't come up in conversation. Nor did my visit earlier that day. Jess usually saw me once a year when I took the department out for an end-of-summer splurge.

"Making progress on the Springbrook case?" Jess asked as if I hadn't talked to her a few hours earlier.

"I'm getting there. Shouldn't be long." It wasn't the truth, but it was the best way to stop more questions.

"Wow, you're on the ball, aren't you?" she said, nodding.

"What are you talking about, LT?" Roger said. I'd had my back to the service end of the bar and had a hard time taking my eyes off of Abby, so hadn't noticed him come out. He had another tumbler of Coke in his hand.

"I was just introducing my date to Jess. Is that okay with you?" In his eyes, everyone was a suspect when it came to his boss. I knew he was well-meaning, but my patience had worn out with his impression of a watchdog.

"Sure," he said, smiling. "Good for you." He nodded and beamed at Abby, now positive that I didn't have an interest in Jess.

"I'm Abby," she said, giving Roger one of her best smiles.

"Roger," he said. "I went to school with LT. From way back."

"What was he like then?" she asked, having already picked up that Roger wasn't the swiftest boat on the river.

"Nice. State champion, too."

"Impressive," she said, glancing at me. "I'm trying to get him to take me to the Rusty Bullet tonight. Don't you think he should?"

"If he won't, I will," Roger said, grinning.

"I couldn't do that to Roger," I said. "So please, allow me. We'll ignore that I've been running around all day."

"That place will cost you," Jess said. "But these drinks are on me. Good to see you again, LT." She walked around the end of the bar, put her arm around Roger's shoulder, and led him back into the kitchen.

At least Duke would have something to get that Gran Marnier taste out of my mouth.

Chapter Thirty-Three

It took two Jim Beams and a Budweiser to vanquish the orange syrup coating my tongue. Abby, drinking beer with me, enjoyed the Rusty Bullet. The few lobstermen there barely bothered to glance our way. She told me about the condo conversions that she was doing around Boston. When she asked if I was buying her breakfast, I told her that I'd be glad to. I wasn't expecting her to follow with the "Should I nudge you when I get hungry?" line. I informed her that she'd have to call, as I would not be accompanying her to the Compound. My real mistake was anticipating that she'd go home after I sidestepped her request.

She hadn't even tried to kiss me when we parted at the pier. But there were her headlights in my rearview mirror, two car lengths behind me, not taking the left that would have taken her home to River Road. She followed me through Cape Laurel and onto Route Nine to the backside of Gray Gull Beach. Her beams tracked the Bronco right into the driveway, where she parked behind me.

She was smiling when she stepped out of her Mercedes. The air was crisp and clean, a hallmark of fall. I was frozen next to the driver's side door of the Bronco, asking myself what was the harm. A beautiful woman stood before me in the moonlight, her dark eyes sparkling, her coat open. She might as well have been Halley's comet. I wasn't going to be able to hold out. I wondered why I was even trying.

"I think you may be lost," I said, shaking my head.

"I must have gotten confused," she said.

"I doubt that very much."

"Well?" she said. "Aren't you going to invite me in?"

"Sure," I said, with a groan. We were both adults, and her family's case was two years in the rearview. If I wanted to be honest, Abby wanting this to happen had probably made it inevitable.

"Look," I said, walking to her, readying myself to give one last speech about how things could get complicated between us. It would be some bullshit, for sure, and she wouldn't listen. But I felt obligated to do it. Then I thought of my father telling me that you usually regret the things that you don't do, rather than the things you've done. My hands went to her waist, and I pulled her to me.

That's when the shot rang out, peppering the garage door behind us.

I closed around Abby and threw her to the lawn. As I dove to cover her, another blast echoed. My left calf seized as I landed on top of her. Of course, my thirty-eight was in the Bronco's glove compartment. I blanketed Abby and raised my head to scan the woods across the street where I thought the shots had come from. Limbs snapped as something crashed through the brush, getting away. It wasn't Bambi. I waited, taking no chances with Abby until all I could hear was our own heavy breathing. You'd think a police officer would be safe in his front yard, date or no date.

"If you wanted to get over on me like this," Abby said, "you should have just asked."

"I wish you'd made that more clear. I guess following me home wasn't indication enough." I rolled to the side. "I think we're safe now."

I tried to stand up and fell right back down, landing beside her.

"Is someone still out there?" she asked, pressing into me.

"No, I pulled my calf diving on you. That's what happens when you date an old person. Don't move."

This time I got on all fours and eased my way up. I put my hand out to keep her on the ground until I was sure. Then I reached down to help her up. My calf was locked. It wasn't the first time I'd had a cramp like this. I'd spent many years wrestling and working out to the point of exhaustion. Now I couldn't even fall correctly. Pathetic.

I limped to the Bronco to jump on the radio. The forest across from my house was enclosed by roads on all four sides. Unfortunately, they were miles long. We needed to set up a perimeter as soon as possible. Even with half the trees naked of leaves, the woods were thick. I requested Gwyneth, Ted, and the state police to my house immediately. The good news was that when I'd told Jess that I'd been making progress, I hadn't been wrong. Someone was worried enough to shoot at me. If I only knew which of the many suspects I'd questioned was sufficiently spooked to pull something like this, I'd have Adam Springbrook's killer. Unfortunately, I had no idea who I'd rattled.

I told Abby to go into the house. She wouldn't. We waited, leaning against the Bronco. If my calf wasn't throbbing, I would have considered grabbing a flashlight and heading into the woods after the shooter. Realistically, that may have only resulted in me getting lost. I wasn't much of a tracker.

"I thought it was boring up here," Abby said, brushing grass and leaves off her shirt and brown leather jacket. "I've spent the last ten years in Boston and New York and never heard a gunshot."

"Good way to sober up, at least," I said.

"You don't think there's still someone out there, do you?" she asked, looking at the pistol in my hand.

"We better go inside," I said, not wanting to take the chance of someone coming back with Abby out in the open. I put my arm around her, and we started over. I was limping, and naturally, having strained it, my calf was killing me. Sirens wailed in the distance. I opened the door.

Her eyes glistened in the moonlight as she studied me. I forced mine back across the street where the shots must have come from.

"I don't think you pulled a muscle," she said.

"I'm hobbling like I'm eighty years old."

She made a face and pointed at my calf. I looked down.

"As an athlete, myself," she said, "I don't recall ever bleeding from a pull. I'm not a doctor, but I'd say you got shot."

There were a series of spots dotting my jeans over the meat of my left calf. They were the black of the dried blood that covered Adam Springbrook's chest.

CHAPTER THIRTY-THREE

"I don't suppose you have a jealous boyfriend out there, do you?"

"It's not that," Abby said. "I figured getting someone to shoot you was the easiest way to get your pants off. You better add an ambulance to your list of calls."

"I've been shot," I said, confirming something that I wouldn't have believed possible, not in Laurel, Maine, in the off-season, in my driveway. Somehow, I felt cheated.

Chapter Thirty-Four

I t wasn't long before my house was a circus. Ted and Gwyneth had come and left. They were driving concentric circles around Oak Ridge Road, Route Nine, Old Gull Road, and the Milltowne Road, which surrounded the woods across the street from my house in various extended and looping configurations. Then they were to check a list of houses incorporating the suspects I'd questioned these last two days to see if anyone wasn't home and to check car hoods for warmth, clueing us that they'd recently been driven. My faculties seemed to be unaffected, as the list had come right off the top of my head: Bill Tatum, George Paquin, Charlie Sarofian, Ed Marinella, and Earl Goodwin.

Randy Kingston, an EMT from the fire department, had my leg up on the kitchen table. Dr. Martin was on his way. Pettibone was driving down from the Arctic Circle, but his investigative team had already flooded my front yard and the woods across the street with klieg lights. One tech marked space on the opposite road shoulder, determining where the would-be assassin had hidden. Another was pulling birdshot from my garage door. Randy, laughing, told me that Martin was going to do the same thing to the meat of my calf, but given his age, certainly with less precision.

"You aren't going to be running much in the next few weeks, LT," he said. "It will hurt just to walk."

"Great." I'd sent Abby upstairs to get a pair of my Nike shorts so I wouldn't have the whole town in here gawking at my plaid boxers. She'd returned with them and stood looking over Kingston's shoulder. She was making a variety of faces, none of which seemed to indicate that I was seriously

162

wounded. Kingston held up my pants. Dried blood covered them like black polka dots.

"If they were using buckshot," Kingston said, "you'd be a lot worse off."

"So you've got that going for you," Abby said. "Which is nice."

"*Caddyshack*? Now you're spoiling me." Usually, she was spouting a quote from some left-handed poet of the eighteenth century, someone, of course, that I'd never heard of. This probably wasn't a good direction for her.

"You're lucky that you didn't get hit," I said.

"No," she said. "You're lucky. I would have had to move in and have you nurse me back to health."

"Randy, check her head; she might have a concussion."

"I'm not getting into the middle of this," he said, looking back and forth between us. He was swabbing my leg with alcohol. I was sipping Jack Daniels with ice. My leg hurt. If Abby hadn't been there, I would have probably been whining about it.

Dr. Martin arrived with his black bag. Like every person who'd protested when I told them they should go to the hospital, I did the same. He shook his head and looked out at me from behind his black-framed glasses.

"I don't have much in the way to numb things, LT. That's one reason to go to Southern Maine Med. The other, of course, is that a sterile atmosphere will protect you from infection. From the looks of things, I wouldn't be surprised if some actual germs were lurking close by."

"My germs are very clean," I said. I hadn't known that Abby would be crossing my threshold, or there wouldn't have been a stack of dishes littering the sink.

"You can gut it out, or we can move it to the hospital," the doctor said.

"I can take it."

"Famous last words," he said, making eyes at Abby.

"At least you won't need stitches. And Miss Grimes will not have to venture into the woods to get you a stick to bite down on while I pull out the little itty, bitty BBs."

"Now you're making fun of me."

"They barely got through your jeans. Of course, it wouldn't hurt to come in for an X-ray tomorrow to make sure that we got them all."

"I think I'll manage."

"That was less of an offer and more of a prescription, just to be clear."

Out came the stainless-steel tweezers. When I was a kid, I hated getting shots. This didn't look to be any more enjoyable. I motioned for Abby and held up my empty glass. I took comfort in seeing that Dr. Martin's hand was steady as the forceps approached my leg. I braced myself and shifted my eyes to the clock over the sink. The little black lead planets came out one by one. My head was underwater by the time he was done, but I hadn't whimpered. That would have been embarrassing.

Dr. Martin agreed with Kingston's assessment that buckshot would have been worse, an opinion that I didn't think required a medical degree. He also said that we were lucky that whoever shot at us had lousy aim, as the garage door and driveway had absorbed more pellets than I had.

"Birdshot, it looks like," he said. "You only got hit with ten of them. Miss Grimes, I don't know where you were in relation to him, but if they only missed him by that much, you're lucky that you didn't catch any."

"I told her that following me home wasn't a good idea. Some people you can't tell anything."

"If you're going to keep drinking, I'm not giving you any painkillers," Martin said.

"Fine by me."

"Aspirin, it is, then. Just so you know, your brain will do strange things when your body is faced with trauma like this. You may not be quite as sharp as usual with the stress."

I let out a long, slow exhale as he finished coating the calf with antiseptic and started bandaging. Fred Green, the state police lab tech, came in as Dr. Martin was telling me to stay off my feet. I didn't bother replying that wasn't an option, as not only did someone kill Springbrook, but the same person had shot at me and Abby. The bleeding may have stopped, but the investigation was about to get ratcheted up in a major way.

Green looked down at the pellets that Martin had deposited in one of my soup bowls. He pulled out a Baggie that held more of the same.

"These are sixes or sevens," Fred said. "Quail load, which everyone uses for the birds we got here because it won't obliterate them. Or your leg, for that matter. You've got a much more robust grouping on your garage door. That must have been the first shot. The second, which clipped you, also nailed the siding between the edge of the garage and the house, behind your walkway."

"Can you tell what gauge the shotgun was?"

"Not from the shot, so much, but from the grouping. If the shooter was in the woods across the street, he must have had a gun with full choke, because the spread doesn't widen out too far, and the distance is thirty-five yards. Based on the amount of pellets in your garage door, I'm guessing it was a sixteen, but I haven't counted the individual pieces. We will do that. It does look to be less than a twelve. Springbrook was hit with a sixteen-gauge slug, so that wouldn't surprise me."

"It's the same gun, you think?"

"We won't be able to tell from the pellets. But it makes sense if we confirm gauge from the spread."

As I sat there with my leg still on the table, it occurred to me that any of my suspects could have had a sixteen and stashed it, knowing I'd be looking for one. I'd been taking people at their word and not expecting them to be unusually devious. That seemed to have been a mistake. If they shot Springbrook, they may not have left the shotgun sitting in a rack as if nothing happened—whether they expected me to show up at their house or not. It seemed that I might have to get some search warrants and make a few repeat visits. At least I knew that the gun wasn't sitting on the bottom of the Atlantic.

Shortly after Dr. Martin left, Gwyneth and Ted arrived. They came through the door and marched into the kitchen. Gwyneth started to say something, then stopped. She looked at Abby. We were both drinking Jack Daniels now. The confused looks on their faces revealed that this may have been the first time they considered that I had a life outside of the police force. I told them that she'd been shot at too, so could hear whatever it was they'd found out. I tried to keep my personal and professional lives separate,

165

but I'd never been shot before.

"Well?" I said. Ted glanced at Gwyneth.

"Sorry, Chief," Gwyneth said. "We didn't find anything. No cars leaving the area, no signs of anyone on the list being out."

"Not even one warm car hood," Ted said. "It is Friday. You'd think someone would be up to something."

"It's October," I said.

"I went real slow searching, too," Ted said. "I had the spot trained on the woods, looking to see if there was a sign that someone had trampled their way out. Nothing."

"Maybe the staties will find something across the street," Gwyneth said. "They've got it lit up like Fenway Park."

"What else do you want us to do?" Ted asked.

"Take a ride through town. Even though it's a Friday, this time of year, no one should be up. Maybe you'll see something, maybe you won't. If you see a light on, call me on the radio. I don't want you approaching anyone on your own."

"You're supposed to stay off your feet," Abby said.

"You can give me a piggyback," I said.

"Gladly," she said.

"Is that alcohol, Chief?" Gwyneth asked, always with regulations in mind. This was not a bad thing, I reminded myself.

"Medicinal purposes, Officer Robinson," I said.

"Hey, Chief," Green said, coming back into the room. "I looked all over across the street. I found one of these. It's a sixteen." He held up a plastic purple cartridge in a clear evidence bag. He'd been right about that. Then he proceeded to tell me that he'd found an area on the roadside where it dropped off into a stream and that he'd found the withered tall grass on the side of the road pressed down. Unfortunately, they'd left nothing but the one shell. He'd seen a path through the brush that had gone straight back into the woods and ran onto one of the deer and dirt bike trails that cut through there. He'd be back in the morning to see if there was something he could follow. Daylight would help.

It was nearly four o'clock by the time everyone left. My calf was throbbing. Abby and I sat across the kitchen table, my leg propped on a chair but now resting on a decorative pillow from the couch. I couldn't believe that I owned a decorative pillow. I wondered where I'd gotten it, then recalled that Suzanne had bought me a set while we'd been dating. My mind was fading, as predicted.

"What happens now?" Abby asked. Our glasses were empty. As tired and beat as she looked, I could only imagine the specter that I presented.

"You're going home. I'm going to bed."

"What if something happens?"

"You mean besides getting shot?"

"You could start bleeding or go into shock."

"I've suffered worse from a bee sting."

"Don't be an ass, LT. It doesn't suit you."

More than a few folks in town would have disagreed with her, at least this week.

"Do you have a problem with people trying to help you?" she asked, letting out a sigh.

"Following me home almost got you killed," I said. "I think you'd be safer at the Compound."

"That big house is scary enough without a gunman on the loose. I don't want to be alone."

"I'm the one who put you in danger."

"Maybe they were after me. Did you ever consider that? How many people know that I'm looking over those books?"

"No one."

She made a pouty face. I couldn't tell if she was serious.

"Unless you want to count Nate Trout," I said. "And he'd never let anything happen to you, now that you've given him that caretaking job. I can't imagine anyone would want to take a shot at you, besides myself for following me home."

"That sick sense of humor of yours is very endearing," she said. "I know that you're just trying to piss me off. It's a defense mechanism, and I'm immune to it, which you should realize any second now."

The concern on her face was genuine.

"Okay, I'll set up the couch."

"No. I'm staying with you."

"As you wish," I said. Why let random pieces of birdshot get in the way of whatever this was going to be?

* * *

I had no experience with psychedelics, and it could have been that my brain was indeed continuing to scramble as Dr. Martin had warned, but from the first kiss, until we fell asleep in each other's arms an hour later, it was, to sound like a hippie, what I could only call cosmic. Otherworldly. Maybe it was the combination of trauma, aspirin, alcohol, and exhaustion, or it could be that the chemistry between us made it so. The proximity to the possibility of death hours earlier could have made being alive and together that much more vibrant, as well. But whatever factors were at play, Abby and I together were a slow-burning inferno that flashed into an out-of-body experience of heat and desire. As we drifted off afterward, I could feel myself floating.

This was not how my mind worked. Nor was it how I could have described previous sexual experiences, a great number of them being meaningful and fantastic and far from what I would have called lacking. Since I'd picked up those vibrations from the cut on Providence Hill days earlier, my conception of reality had warped. It appeared there was little I could do about it now, other than to go with the flow, as someone more enlightened might say.

I awoke that morning with Abby wrapped around me. I didn't want to move. But there were things to be done. I slipped out from under her. She didn't wake up. As tired as if I hadn't slept, I limped to the bathroom, then downstairs to the Mr. Coffee. I was pouring the water when the pounding on the door started.

Chapter Thirty-Five

I wasn't ready for this. I hopped to the hall and grabbed my thirty-eight from the drawer. Then I dragged myself to the side door that went into the garage. The calf could have been worse. I took it as a win that it only felt like it was getting stabbed with a dull fork rather than being filleted with a knife. I wondered how long I could hold out before I went for that X-ray as an excuse to get something stronger than aspirin. Who and whatever was waiting for me out front wouldn't give it a rest, and I worried that the pounding would wake Abby, and she'd come down and answer it. As best I could on a leg and a half, which is not to say silently, I slipped outside through the garage, gun pointed at the door, only to find State Police Detective Rick Pettibone standing there.

"You can stop now before you split the thing in two," I said.

He saw the gun and raised his eyebrows. "Good morning to you, too."

"This used to be a town where a guy didn't get shot in his front yard."

"I'm sorry I left you alone on this," Pettibone said. "Never should have happened."

"Maybe someone shoots you on your lawn instead. You're a bigger target than I am. They may have hit you somewhere that counted."

"Well, I'm here now. Drove all night. Let's find this fucker. It's tied to the Springbrook case?"

"Has to be," I said.

"Someone doesn't like where you've been poking around."

"That was my conclusion."

"Do you have a list of suspects?"

"Sure do. But I've seen fewer names in a phone book. We know that the shooter used the same gauge shotgun, a sixteen. Only they used a bird load on me and a deer slug on Adam. Lousy shot, too. They must have been a lot closer to Springbrook."

I pointed to the birdshot that was embedded in my clapboards.

"The techs found that the shooter was across the street, prone, reaching up to the side of the road."

Pettibone's head swiveled as he estimated the difficulty, or lack thereof, of the shot. "How do they miss you?"

"They caught me in the leg. The doctor took ten of the little suckers out of my calf."

"You have coffee going?"

"Just put it on."

We were heading in when Gwyneth and Ted showed up, already in uniform. If I had driven by on patrol, with all the cars strewn about, I would have assumed there was a party going on.

I poured coffee for everyone, and we sat around the table. My officers reported on what they'd found last night after I'd sent them on their way. Which was nothing. All the houses on their list had been dark. Car hoods had been cool.

"But when I was driving through town," Gwyneth said, "I did notice one thing that seemed odd."

Abby appeared at the entrance of the kitchen. With all the chatter, I hadn't heard her coming down the stairs. Everyone stopped talking and looked at her. She must have heard us, however, because she'd put on some clothes. She was wearing the jeans she'd had on last night, with one of my flannels over a T-shirt. Her hair was loose and messy.

"This is my friend, Abby Grimes," I said.

"I never got the pleasure, Ms. Grimes," Pettibone said, standing. He'd been aced out of the investigation of her brother's death by his supervisor, who then got replaced by a US Marshal of questionable ethics. Ted and Gwyneth stood, as well, when they saw Pettibone do it.

"We were just discussing the case," I said, hoping she would get the hint and take her coffee into the living room, though I doubted that was something she'd be inclined to do.

"As I was shot at, too, and I'm here as a consultant, I'd like to hear what's going on," she said. "If you don't mind, of course."

I was out of chairs, and she was not to be denied. I stood to give her mine. She shook her head and leaned back, hopping her ass up onto the counter.

"Consultant?" Pettibone asked, directing his baritone at me. A foghorn would have been only slightly more forceful.

"I needed someone to read through the financial documents from Springbrook's business holdings. I couldn't make heads or tails of it, and I didn't want to wait around while I sent them out. There are potential suspects among the investors and vendors. He had some questionable accounting practices, come to find out."

"Not questionable from his viewpoint," Abby said, correcting me. "But if he owed you money and you knew what he was doing, well, that could make someone upset."

"Good to know," Pettibone said. "Where are we on these folks?"

"There's a list. The question is who on it owns a sixteen-gauge shotgun."

"The local hardware store doesn't even sell ammunition for them," Gwyneth said.

"How do you know that?" I asked.

"I checked two days ago."

"Very good, young lady," Pettibone said.

"Chief Nichols had already been there," she said. Then she smiled at him. "And I'm not a young lady. I'm a police officer and would like to be treated as such with the respect that I'm due."

Abby nearly choked on her coffee.

Pettibone nodded and twirled the ends of his handlebar mustache. "I'm sorry, Officer," he said. "Noted."

"Do we have our list of suspects?" Pettibone asked.

"Before we get to that," Ted said. "I did notice something last night when I was driving home."

"Let's hear it," I said, motioning for him to continue.

"There were lights on at the Sea Squall. Usually, they leave one on in the bar window facing the street, so it's not completely dark. But it seemed that there were lights on in the back, too."

"Is that unusual for a restaurant?" Gwyneth said. "On a Friday?"

"I can tell you in July they stay open until one," Abby said. "In October, things may be different. We were some of the last customers yesterday, and we left before ten."

"We'll need to follow up on that," I said.

"When did you drive past?" Pettibone asked.

"It must have been well after midnight," Ted said.

"And Jessica Consentino slapped Springbrook this summer," Gwyneth said.

They'd been reading my case notes, too. I was impressed.

"Why don't you two go by and see what she has to say about it?" Because I couldn't picture Jess wielding a shotgun like The Rifleman didn't mean we were going to ignore something we were looking for.

Gwyneth and Ted took off, leaving the three of us. Pettibone looked from Abby to me with a puzzled expression on his face. With all that had been going on, I hadn't had a moment to consider how we appeared. I didn't know if she and I were smirking at each other or stealing glances like goofballs. But Pettibone picked up on something. He told us that he'd take his coffee outside and then drive me into the office so we could go over what I had.

Abby stayed seated on the counter. I was awkwardly standing next to the kitchen table, unsure if I should take her in my arms and see if the electricity remained. My other choice was to stay where I was and maintain a safe distance. If the clock over the sink hadn't been ticking, the room would have been completely quiet. I don't think I felt any more awkward at my first junior high homecoming dance.

"So, was it as horrible as you thought it was going to be?" she said, as if reading my mind and enjoying a twist of the knife. "I mean us together, not us getting shot."

"Far from the worst thing that happened yesterday," I said.

"First, the Bat Cave, and now you're not even pushing me away. Are the walls coming down?"

"Not entirely. I almost got you killed."

"You can't be responsible for that. But you are responsible for feeding me. You promised breakfast." Now she was smiling slyly.

"That doesn't look like it's going to happen." I nodded outside, where Pettibone was waiting for me.

"Then dinner?"

"Absolutely. You're going to stick around a bit, then?"

The front door slapped open, and footfalls crossed the living room. I assumed that Pettibone had heard something about the case. But it was Nate Trout bursting into the kitchen, breathing like he'd run the five miles here from the Compound.

"What the fuck is going on?" he said. He looked at me, then Abby, then settled on me. "You got shot?"

"In the leg," I said. "As you can see, I'm alive and well."

"And you were there?" he said, turning to his employer. The tufts of white hair that remained over his ears were unkempt and disheveled as if he'd been pulling at them. His face was red.

"Yes, Nate. And I'm perfectly fine. No reason to worry."

"Jesus Christ, is this connected to the Springbrook thing?"

"It's looking like it," I said.

"Abby, I don't think you should be staying here," Trout said.

"I've been telling her that," I said.

"You two worry like old men."

"We are old men," I said.

"Hardly," she said.

"Are you going back to Boston?" Trout asked.

"Certainly not," she said, grinning. "This is where the action is."

"You two are going to give me a heart attack. This is nothing to joke about."

"Can you give us a minute, Nathan?" she said, nodding to the door.

"I'll be right outside," he said.

Abby smiled at me once he left the room.

"He's going to offer his services as a bodyguard," I said.

"I've already got one," she said. "You."

"That doesn't seem to be working."

"I think I can work out a compromise. I'll head to the Compound for the day. You can go find your shooter. Nate will calm down, and there's some work that I can get done there. After all, I just can't sit here waiting for my wounded man to limp back home."

"I'm glad that I know you well enough to cut through the sarcasm," I said.

"I'd say you know me very well now, don't you?"

"I certainly know you better."

"And?"

"I'm looking forward to dinner."

"I told you it wouldn't be so bad."

"Let's just make it through the day without getting shot," I said.

"That seems reasonable," she said. She slid off the counter and came straight for me. She hugged me and rested her head against my shoulder. If Trout and Pettibone hadn't been waiting, we may not have left the house, regardless of the lack of food in the refrigerator.

Chapter Thirty-Six

"Wow," Pettibone said, sliding the financials and my accompanying notes back across the desk. "Who didn't this guy owe money to?"

"Me and you," I said. "That might be it. And I still got shot."

"There's two ways to look at it. If someone killed him, they'd have to know they'd likely be writing off getting their money. Someone would have to be right mad to do that. But if they realized they weren't getting it anyway, then what's stopping them, other than the obvious?"

"From what I've learned, he did pay. But slowly, and he had to be rousted for it. He just kept reinvesting whatever money he had coming in." I sighed. "It would help to know who owns a sixteen-gauge. I've checked several households already. But I didn't toss the places, just noted what was on the various gun racks. I haven't found one yet."

I'd sent Gwyneth to Millville to check with the department store, but of course, they had no idea who bought what shells or if any customers were from Laurel. There was just too much traffic. Another reason to lament people not supporting local businesses—you didn't know who was up to no good.

"Let's look at who thinks they're sitting dead center in your sights."

We were working our way down the list of suspects I'd questioned. The phone kept ringing. Word was out, and people kept calling to see if I was okay. I supposed that was nice. If I had been so inclined, I could have imagined that they thought if someone would shoot me, they wouldn't hesitate to shoot anyone. I was asked if it was safe to leave the house. I wanted to answer that unless they were the police chief, dating the police chief, or planning to build a massive resort, they had nothing to worry about. Instead, I told people everything was fine. Then, correspondingly, my calf would throb. Eventually, a call came through for Pettibone. Two more of the club members in the Fort Kent case had gone after each other with rifles, taking sides in the original dispute. He argued for five minutes, stating that a police officer had been shot here, and that should take priority over a bunch of wackos living out a Hatfield and McCoy fantasy. He hung up the phone, overruled, and let out a torrent of curses that I'd never heard him use. He apologized for that and confessed that he was required to drive back north. He left, and I worked. I sat with my leg up on my desk, sending Gwyneth here and Ted there chasing alibis. A killer was on the loose in our small, formerly friendly town where everyone knew each other, and there were nearly a dozen people who had something of a reason to kill Springbrook, a guy lined up to make everyone a pile of money. The case wasn't without its contradictions and complications.

After two hours of accomplishing nothing on my end, Gwyneth and Ted were able to report that Goodwin had been in Augusta at a dinner at the state house as part of some real estate lobbying concern. Charlie Sarofian had been at the Port Tavern until closing. George Paquin had been home with his wife. Bill Tatum had been with his. Not even the women who were suspects and didn't own shotguns were viable. Jess Consentino had been dealing with a recurring broken pipe in her kitchen. Talia Springbrook had been in Portland. Cindy Goodwin was home with her son. If I didn't go so far as to remove them from the suspect list, I did run a line through their names. My only conclusion was that I was missing something somewhere. That wasn't exactly comforting.

I sat with my leg up on the desk, shuffling through pages and pages of paper, making more notes and outlines that only served to reshuffle ideas and thoughts I'd already had. A day of steadily rising frustration laid out in front of me. I wasn't making progress, nor could I get out and do anything about it.

At noon, Estelle put another call through, letting me know it was my friend, "that cute Miss Grimes."

"LT," Abby said, "you need to come home. Right now."

"What's wrong?" I was instantly on my feet. "I thought you were going to the Compound."

"I was out for a while and came back, and now there are two people here and they're demanding to see you."

"Did you tell them I'm at the station?"

"I did. But they don't want to go there. They said to tell you that it's Suzanne and Derek and that once I did, you'd come here."

"I'm on my way," I said. Because getting shot wasn't painful enough, I had those two camping at my house. Luckily, Ted had left his cruiser when he'd gone off with Gwyneth. It was an automatic. I could make it home on my own. Another victory.

Chapter Thirty-Seven

Suzanne and Derek leaned against his truck in the sun, their jackets unzipped. Suzanne's mouth was closed, and her eyebrows were arched toward her nose. I recognized the look: she was mad. Derek's head was at an angle, looking across my lawn. If she were here to bitch me out for warning him, this would be a quick visit. I wasn't listening.

"We need to talk to you, LT," Suzanne said.

"Are you not familiar with my job?" I said. "Or where the station is? And that I'm in the middle of a murder investigation? And that I got shot last night?"

"Sorry about that, LT," she said. "We heard from Wink. Are you doing okay?"

"Just a flesh wound, as they say."

The grimace on her face indicated she didn't find that funny.

"We saw the Bronco here, and we're not idiots," Suzanne said. "We might have some information, and Derek wasn't comfortable telling you at the station."

Before I could ask why that was, certain that it would spike my blood pressure, Abby came out of the house and joined us. We formed a small circle between the cars.

"I take it you've met," I said.

"She was kind enough to answer the door and call you for us," Derek said, nodding and looking at Suzanne.

Suzanne sighed.

"I heard Adam Springbrook was shot with a sixteen-gauge," she said. "Is that right?"

"Word gets around, and, miraculously, sometimes it's true. That's correct."

"Was it the same gun last night?"

"It could be," I said.

"Go ahead, Derek," Suzanne said.

"You know I been hunting with Blockhead Roger, right?" he said, sighing.

"Yes."

"He uses a pump sixteen."

"What?" I said, unable to stop myself from shouting.

"After we went this morning, he asked me if I'd hold it for him."

"The day after we got shot?" Abby said, her voice rising, too.

"Abby," I said.

"I didn't know what was going on," Derek said. "I ain't a cop. I thought it was just in case we went hunting later, and he was coming from work. He said he didn't want to leave it around the kitchen at the Squall. You know, they got a lot of kids who are busboys and that shit. I assumed he didn't want them fucking with it. So he asked me to hold it. It was Suzy who asked whose gun it was when she saw me bringing it into the house. I wasn't going to leave it out in my truck."

Citizen of the year, I thought.

"Then she asked if it was a sixteen. When I said that it was, we came right over. She knew that's what Springbrook got clipped with. I didn't have no idea. Roger would never shoot anyone, if you ask me. But, Suzy, as you know, she isn't one for taking chances."

"I asked you what he used last week, and you said he had a twelve."

"That's what I thought. I wasn't paying attention, I guess."

"You didn't notice his shells were purple and yours were green?"

"Nope," he said, shaking his head and looking down. "Sorry."

It didn't surprise me.

"Do you have it with you, at least?" I asked.

"It's right here," he said, patting the tailgate. His head jerked nervously to the right as he spoke. "The thing is, he had me hold it earlier this week, too. He was keeping it at the Squall. I'd pick up the dog and meet him at whatever spot we were hunting, because he came straight from work in the afternoon and didn't always have time to drive around. He had me hold it after we went on Tuesday. But he kept it after we hunted on Wednesday. Then he had me take it again after we went this morning, and Suzy saw me with a new gun and asked where I got it. When I told her what was going on, she said we needed to get right over here, in spite of the fact that she's supposed to be at work already."

I nodded. Adam gets shot; Derek gets the gun. Nothing happens, and they go hunting. He takes it back. I get shot, and he returns it to Derek. Not a hard pattern to follow. I didn't think that Roger had a beef with me, though he'd been watching closely anytime I'd been in the Squall. He could have thought I was after Jess. He heard me questioning her, and he'd been there when I said that we were closing in. He may have gone too far in his imagined role of her protector. The question was what would he be protecting Jess from? And where did Adam Springbrook fit in? The slap had been months earlier. There had to be more to it. I may have been on the right trail and not realized it.

"He left at halftime, the night you were watching football at the VFW?"

"He could have," Derek said. "But I left early, too, so couldn't say what he did, really. Now that I ain't touching the stuff and have settled down, I tend to not hang out as much."

This wasn't the time to debate whether beer was considered drinking.

"If you ask me," Derek said, "that probably ain't the gun that you're looking for."

"I didn't hear anyone asking you," Abby said.

I would have said it myself, if I wasn't interested in getting more information out of him. This was the kind of banter that had bartenders groaning when Abby and her brother set up shop in their stations.

"You're in the middle of this, because why?" Suzanne said.

"I was asked," Abby said.

"Roger ain't the smartest guy," Derek said, looking from one woman to the other. "But he wouldn't know Adam Springbrook if he hit him in the face. And why would he shoot you, LT?"

180

"Good question," I said. "Why would he have given you his gun?"

"He didn't say, other than he didn't want to leave it lying around the restaurant," Derek said. "I just guessed he didn't want the kids and the cooks messing with it."

"I know how you don't believe in coincidences," Suzanne said.

'You're right about that," I said. "Let's see it."

"Okay." Derek opened the driver's door and started to reach for it behind the seat. I stopped him and asked Abby to grab a blanket from inside. I didn't want fingerprints getting disturbed. She took off for the house.

"So," Derek said, nodding at me, "G-Two."

Suzanne elbowed him in the ribs. Her scowl deepened and her eyes flicked on Abby as she returned. One of those fork-like pains spread through my calf. It was hard to ignore the timing.

"I know I ain't your favorite person, LT," Derek said, "with me getting Suzy back off of you. But that doesn't mean I want to see you killed. Especially if it's someone else doing it." He laughed. The three of us stared at him.

"That was a joke," he said, dropping his head. "Probably not a good one."

"Thanks, Derek," I said. "I was hoping."

"You don't have to be an ass about it, LT," Suzanne said.

Abby laughed.

"What's so funny, G-Two?" Suzanne said.

Abby looked at me, eyebrows raised. She wasn't aware of her nickname. She and her brother had been named the Gold Dust Twins by Laurel's bartenders and waitresses, who they had regularly terrorized with poor behavior: G-One and G-Two for short. I wasn't about to explain now. Suzanne's eyes returned to me. If she was calling Abby by her nickname, she wasn't happy, or at least less happy than finding out her future second-time-around husband could be an accessory after the fact to a murder.

"I never knew the town was so lively this time of year," Abby said. "People getting shot. Bitter, high school sniping. It's like a black comedy."

"Okay, Abby," I said, cradling the shotgun, wrapped in its blanket. "Anything else you know, Derek? About Roger and what he might be up to?"

"I just hunt with the man. The only thing I'm shooting with him is woodcock and partridge."

I thanked him and Suzanne for coming over. As soon as they left, I got on the radio and tracked down my officers. I asked them to step on it and come get me. I let them know that we'd finally gotten a lead, a shotgun that popped in and out of someone's possession tied to the dates of the shootings, and that we'd be picking up the suspect.

While the shootings had to be somehow connected to Jess Consentino, Roger would have to tell us what set him in motion. I didn't anticipate that being a problem. We knew where to find him. They served lunch at the Squall on weekends in October. We'd be there in fifteen minutes.

When I got off the radio, Abby was grinning at me.

"Let me get this straight," she said. "That's your old girlfriend?"

"Sure is."

"She dumped you for that guy?"

"I wouldn't put it like that."

She smirked. "What does she know that I don't?"

"You don't really expect me to answer that, do you?"

"Oh, I'd like to hear it. Very much."

"Haven't I been trying to warn you off me?"

"I thought you were just playing hard to get."

"No, you didn't."

"We're too far down the road to turn back now," she said.

"We haven't even left the house," I said.

"So, what are we going to do?" she said.

"I'm going to work, and you're going back to Boston."

"If you think that's happening, you really aren't too bright."

"I've heard that before, too," I said.

"I don't plan on moving in, if that's what you're afraid of. When everything's settled here, I'll go back. Gladly."

"You're not safe here with me. The shooter's still out there. It was Derek and Suzanne showing up here this morning. It could have been Roger."

"I wasn't anyone's target. I just happened to be in your vicinity."

"That's my point."

CHAPTER THIRTY-SEVEN

"You're not safe, either, until you track this guy down."

"Which I'll be doing shortly. You've helped all you can. And it's unnerving me to know that you're in danger here."

"You're getting quite dramatic," she said, laughing.

"Not to mention that you're somewhat distracting, outside of everything else."

"I'll take that as a compliment. I never knew there was so much excitement in the offseason."

"There isn't, usually. My ex-wife could tell you that. She couldn't stand it."

Abby stepped closer. She smiled and reached out to run her fingers through my hair.

"That is very distracting, for example," I said.

"It's not horrible, though, is it?"

"I'm not complaining. But I'm responsible for you being here. Naturally, I don't want to see anything happen to you."

"Have you considered," she said, her eyes fluttering, "that these events which have brought us together could be the universe at work?" She wasn't trying to get me going. It was a serious question.

"I try not to contemplate things like that."

"Really?" she said. "What do you think about?"

"How to keep you safe. Who shot Adam Springbrook, likely Roger Kensington, and if so, how can we grab him without getting anyone else hurt? Why everyone in town has these hidden resentments and grudges. People have been acting like everything's fine, but underneath, it's a sea of crazy. Everyone I questioned pointed their finger at someone else in less than a minute. Usually, I can't get people to tell me shit. I've been doing this job awhile. I know there are bad people out there. But I never assumed that *everyone* had that potential, and it would surface here in October when nothing ever happens. Speeding or cheating on your taxes is one thing. Killing is another. There haven't been any tears shed for Springbrook, and considering how he was, maybe that's okay. But someone pulled a trigger on him—and us. I don't know what to make of it, to be honest. I'm not sure it's something I want to dwell on, other than in finding out who did it, because that's my job and what needs to be done. What I'd like to do is watch the World Series and football and go to a high school wrestling match or run on the beach. I don't need to spend hours like some philosopher, trying to judge the soul of man and good and evil and all that. I'm not wired for it."

"How can you not be?" she said, her eyes focusing. "You deal with this all the time, whether it's that backwoods nut or my father or whoever else you come across."

"That's the thing. I deal with it on a practical level. They're exceptions and oddities. But with this, everyone in town is losing it, even if they didn't do business with Springbrook."

"You've got it now," she said. "When you haul this Roger in, it will all be over. Then you can stop worrying about the greater ramifications."

"I hope you're right."

"You shouldn't be too torn up over Adam getting shot. He was no innocent being. It's not like those poor girls a few years ago. Or my brother."

"I'm not explaining it right. It's fucked up, the way this town reacted, with people saying anything to get out from under suspicion, even if they didn't have anything to do with it."

"Maybe they have guilty consciences because they don't care that he got shot. Or would have liked to do it themselves."

"I don't know," I said. "I might be able to relax if I wasn't concerned about a round of buckshot coming through the window tonight when you're sitting next to me."

"You won't have to worry about that once you pick up your man."

"Let's hope not."

"Aren't you glad I stayed?" Her smile was only slight. She wasn't teasing.

"I am. I don't know why I made such an issue out of us getting together. But, as a result, now I feel responsible for you."

"Maybe you should give me a gun."

"That's not happening," I said, chuckling.

"I may not be the marksman my mother is, but I do know how to handle one. I wouldn't have missed us from across the street with a shotgun."

The Grimes, through her mother's family, were related to the Remingtons, the famous gun manufacturer. I'd seen Abby's mother handle a pistol. She was a better shot than I was and likely everyone else in Laurel, too. That didn't mean I was handing her daughter my backup Smith and Wesson.

"Regardless," I said. "I'd feel better if you were in Boston. Where people won't be shooting in your general direction. You can always come back."

She moved closer.

"I don't think you really want me to go," she said.

"You can tell that because I just asked you to? For the fiftieth time? I don't know how many more shootings or heart-to-hearts like this I can handle."

She put her hands on either side of my head and smiled. If I wanted to avoid what was coming, I could have pivoted on my good leg. She planted one on me. A heat wave, like whisky going down, rippled. This was another argument that I was going to lose. I was trying to think about too many things on too deep a level, and I wasn't used to it.

She pulled back, putting a hand on my chest.

"You have a problem with that?" she said. Her blue eyes, dark like the ocean in winter, froze me in place.

By the time Gwyneth and Ted pulled into the driveway, I'd convinced her to go to the Compound for the day, or at least until we found Roger. That probably brought my pulse down all of one full beat per minute.

Chapter Thirty-Eight

Roger would be surrounded by knives, pots, and cast-iron pans, all potential weapons. If somewhat less lethal than the shotgun that we already had in our possession, they were still things to be wary of, especially when going in with rookies. But I didn't want to wait for state police help or have to turn Pettibone around. Even with me on one leg, this should be something we could handle. When we arrived at the restaurant, I had Gwyneth park in the lot behind it. I sent Ted to the front door. Should Roger try to make a run for it, he was fully capable of taking him down.

It being October, there wouldn't be a packed roomful of tourists in the vicinity of our target. I limped over to one of the windows that opened onto their prep station. A cook was spinning lettuce in a top-looking thing at the three-bay sink. I couldn't see Roger. Gwyneth and I went to the door. Every step jabbed my calf. We entered the kitchen, hand on my holster. I didn't think Roger would bolt, especially if I put a smile on my face and asked for Jess. I said hello to the prep cook, who stopped his vegetable shower when he saw us. There was a wall between the prep kitchen and the main line. I put my hand up to keep him from asking questions. It was always better to act like you knew where you were going, and it didn't hurt that I was familiar with the place. I took a deep breath, tried to look relaxed, and peg-legged around the corner to the main line. There were two cooks. One watched burgers and some fish on a grill. The other was flipping broccoli in a sauté pan over a flame. Neither were Roger.

"Roger here?" I asked the one closest to me, his eyes on the halibut.

"Not today."

"Do you know where he is?"

He shrugged.

"How about Jess?" I asked.

"Probably the host stand."

We went through the swinging door to the right and out into the lounge. I half-expected to find Roger at the soda gun pouring himself another Coke. But he wasn't there. That didn't mean there was nothing to see. While one of the Surrelle sisters manned the host desk, Jess stood at the end of the bar in a full-on discussion with Talia Springbrook.

She noticed us making our way over and stopped talking.

"Chief Nichols," Talia Springbrook said, not seeming to notice that her friend had slipped into a mild state of shock.

"Funny to find you here, Ms. Murphy," I said.

"You mean you haven't been tracking my every move, the widow with so much to gain?"

"I have not. But it is somewhat curious that you and I keep crossing paths."

"In a town this size, this time of year, I'd think it would be impossible not to," she said.

She had a point. But I figured if I kept playing dumb, someone would tell me something meaningful sooner or later.

"I wasn't aware that you two knew each other," I said. Jess had a look on her face like she'd massively overbooked the place and had a line out the door. Less than half the tables were occupied. I was tempted to ask Talia if she was here the night that her ex-husband got slapped, but passed. Nor was I about to inquire if they were commiserating over losing husbands. Maybe that's what they had in common.

"Of course, we do," Talia said. "I cannot handle that awful lounge at the Reef House. I come here quite often when I'm in town."

"You're going to continue with the project?" I said.

"That hasn't been decided. I'm sure you realize that these things don't come together overnight."

"He doesn't want to hear about that boring business, Talia," Jess said. She glanced at Gwyneth, waiting patiently behind me. "I'm assuming that you're not on another date, LT. What can I do for you?"

Jess glanced at Talia. Gwyneth watched the kitchen doors. She wasn't taking for granted that, because we hadn't seen Roger, that didn't mean he wasn't here. I asked Jess to step away so that I could talk to her. This was getting more tangled by the minute, and I was allowing myself to get sidetracked. That had to stop.

"Roger isn't in the kitchen," I said. "Would you know where he is?"

"He called out sick."

"You talked to him?"

"I did."

"What did he say?"

"That he had something going on and that he couldn't come in. He sounded dreadful, and he doesn't have that filter. I didn't need the visuals of whatever illness would keep him out. He would never not be here if he could. I have absolute trust in him."

"He's home?"

"I would assume," she said, scanning the restaurant as if she had some task to complete and I was keeping her from it.

"Can I ask you another question?" I said. She nodded, her lips pressed tight together. "Have you seen a gun around the kitchen?"

"A gun?" Her head pulled back, and she started shaking it.

"A shotgun, to be precise. Something that Roger might be hunting with."

"I don't remember seeing anything," she said. She started twirling the bracelet on her left wrist with her right hand. "I mean, he could have put it in a closet in the kitchen with the mops or something. I know he's been coming in before noon to do prep, then going hunting in the afternoon, and coming back to run dinner service. I'm sure I wouldn't have known if one was here. It's not something we'd keep hanging around."

"Okay," I said.

"Is Roger in some sort of trouble?"

"I don't know about that," I said. "But we would like to talk to him. If he does come in, could you please notify the station?"

"He won't come in now after he already called out."

CHAPTER THIRTY-EIGHT

"If he does, though," I said.

"Sure," she said. "I'll let you know."

"One last thing, does he know that you slapped Adam Springbrook?"

"I'm not sure. We never discussed it, me and him. But he may have heard about it. People in this town do enjoy talking about things that aren't their business."

"Has he ever met Adam?"

"I doubt it. They don't exactly move in the same circles."

She was right about that.

"Would Roger know that you and Adam had issues? Is there any reason for him to think he needed to protect you from him?"

"Of course not, because there were no issues. You've grossly mischaracterized our relationship. Adam and I put that one silly incident behind us right after it happened. We were laughing about it the next time we saw each other, in fact."

"When was the last time Adam was here?"

"It must have been a few weeks ago," she said. "He was not a regular customer, but still came in every now and then."

"I do have another question. What happened here Monday night?"

"What do you mean? We had our usual community supper for five-ninety-nine. We do a lot of business at that price, believe it or not. I let Roger leave early because he likes to watch the game, and we don't have a TV."

"Roger was at the VFW, and you called him there?"

"I thought I'd already mentioned that. We had a water pipe under the three-bay come loose. I was closing up with the dishwasher. There's a lot I can do around here, but plumbing's not on the list. I asked him to come back and fix it."

I nodded. "Thank you."

Talia had finished her wine, and when we returned to her, she said goodbye to Jess and told us that she'd be leaving unless we had some legal objection. It was and was not a joke. I told her I'd walk out with her, and had Gwyneth go around and get the car.

Talia and I stopped on the sidewalk.

"You're moving okay for someone who got shot," she said.

"It could have been worse," I said.

"Is who killed Adam the same person that went after you?" she asked.

"Working on it. You could help me with that."

"How so?"

"Who was the third person over at the beach house earlier this week?"

"I told you it was just me and Adam."

"When I was looking for you, the back door was open. I noticed there were three wine glasses in the sink. One of them I assumed was Adam's. The other two had different shades of lipstick. You've been wearing the same color whenever I've seen you, so they both cannot be yours."

"My," she said. "You are an observant one."

"And the answer would be?"

"I don't know. I'm not one for doing dishes when Adam has someone coming in. He must have had a guest while I was in Portland, a woman I'd say, given your keen observations. He was somewhat popular, I hear. Just because there were three glasses doesn't mean that they were all used at the same time. Adam abhorred doing any kind of domestic work. That glass could have been there for days."

"Was it Jessica?"

"I didn't know thirty seconds ago, and I don't know now. But I highly doubt it."

"I'm trying to find out who shot Adam—and me. I'd think you'd have a vested interest in that."

She gave me a smile.

"I'm doing my best to help. I'm sorry if I don't know everything you'd like me to. And I get the feeling that I'm still a suspect, and my motive would be because I wanted to take over a precariously financed and perhaps overzealous resort project. That doesn't make sense to me."

"I didn't say that."

"You don't say much."

"I find it's less trouble that way."

190

Chapter Thirty-Nine

Blockhead Roger lived in West Laurel, fifteen minutes out of town, in a small ranch with a detached garage. Apple Blossom Lane was a pleasant dead-end side street. His back lawn ran up against a state-owned conservation forest. I could feel the sweat rise under my arms and on my neck. Not because we were going after someone who was armed, but because there were two rookies in my care. I presumed that the shotgun we had in our possession wasn't the only one he owned, and if he wasn't afraid of pointing it at me and squeezing the trigger, he wouldn't hesitate to do the same to them. Why he felt compelled to protect Jess Consentino to this extent remained to be seen. But she had to be in the middle of it. Or maybe Roger and Springbrook weren't unacquainted. He'd stolen her best bartender. Perhaps he'd come after her chef with an offer, as well, something that Roger might have seen as a threat rather than an opportunity.

I had Gwyneth and Ted stop their cars at the end of Apple Blossom to block off the street, a row of humble ranch houses. People lived comfortably and quietly here, without the propensity to make a showplace of their homes, something becoming more prevalent along the beaches. I laid out what we were going to do. They both protested when I said that I'd be the one knocking on the door. Gwyneth didn't hesitate to share that the way I was hobbling around, I'd be a sitting duck. When I asked them to relate the experience they had in approaching armed suspects, they looked at each other and sighed.

We approached from the side, cutting over from a neighbor's yard. Roger's Datson pickup wasn't in the driveway, but Gwyneth nodded when she checked the garage. I had Ted go around back, should Roger bolt for the woods. I watched the house for movement. There wasn't any. Gwyneth and I hung close to the garage, eyes glued to the curtains and door. I waved her over behind me. She jogged, and I hopped to the door, lodging the fork firmly in my calf. I was glad I hadn't made time to grab those painkillers. Under these circumstances, one needed a clear head, or at least to not be drifting off in alternating clouds of rage—the bastard had shot me—and distraction—I had Abby waiting for me when this was over.

I went to the concrete front step and pressed myself to the right of the door. Gwyneth flanked it on the left. What I presumed to be his new hunting dog went off like a rocket. It sounded throaty and ferocious. I could already feel its teeth locked on my good calf, the result of which would be complete paralysis. I knocked anyway. Footsteps sounded behind the door.

"Roger, it's Chief Nichols. This is police business. We need you to open up and come out." Gwyneth watched me, hand on her pistol. Her face had gone from smooth to tight. "With your hands up and empty."

"LT, I don't want to. You might shoot me."

"Why would I do that?"

"Because of this monkey business with that Springbrook guy."

"Roger, come on out. Enough people have been shot this week." I hoped he'd listen. Things didn't need to get ugly.

"Leave me alone," he said.

"What happened on Monday night?" I said.

"Nothing."

"We both know that's not true. Come out. I don't want to have to bring in the state police."

"If I come out, what about Princess Leia? I don't want anything to happen to her."

Gwyneth looked at me and shook her head. He'd lost his mind. He must have been in this up to his neck, and it was too much for him. I took a deep breath. Did they have blow-up dolls of Star Wars characters? And how could a grown man become so attached to one? I didn't even want to think about it, though I supposed anything was possible based on what had been going on in Laurel this week.

"Roger, we don't want anything to do with Princess Leia. We only want to talk to you."

"If I come out, you need to promise not to take her to the pound."

Of course, it was the dog.

"We won't shoot your dog, Roger," I said. "We like dogs." Gwyneth nodded in agreement. I wanted things in the simplest terms that he could understand.

"You need to promise you won't send her to the pound in Milltowne. I don't want her caged up. It's not right what they do to them over there."

"I won't send her."

"Promise."

"I promise I won't send your dog to the pound. If you come out now with your hands up."

"Okay, we'll come out then. Don't shoot."

"Make sure your hands are up and nothing's in them."

The door crept open. "Stay," he said.

My hand was on my gun now, too. He came down the two steps and walked past us. I told him to take three more steps and turn around. Roger stopped five yards in front of us. His large mitts were empty and up as if he were signaling a touchdown. Sweat moons spread from under the arms of a red Patriots sweatshirt. He saw our guns out and whimpered.

"Okay, Roger," I said. "This doesn't have to be difficult. I'm going to pat you down. Come over here, put your hands out, and lean against the house."

"I don't have anything, LT."

"I'm going to make sure. Just do it." Gwyneth watched while he came back and pressed himself against the clapboards. I checked him. He wasn't carrying.

"Don't get upset, but I'm going to put the handcuffs on next. I have to do it." I assumed that if he knew what was coming step-by-step, he'd be better able to handle it.

"I know what to do," he said. "*Adam Twelve* used to be my favorite show."

I took one arm at a time and put the handcuffs on him. I called Ted from the back and sent him and Gwyneth to get the cars. We waited, the dog sitting in the doorway where she'd been told to stay.

"I screwed up, LT," Roger said. He shifted his weight from one foot to the other. His eyes were on the ground. "I'm sorry."

"I know, Roger."

The cruisers pulled into the driveway. I told Ted to call for the state police lab techs. They'd go through the house. I led Roger to Ted's cruiser and put him in the back seat. I left the door open.

"What about Princess Leia?" Roger asked.

"Go ahead and call her," I said.

He whistled, and the dog came bounding down the steps. She turned and walked over in front of us. She looked at Roger in the car. He told her to sit. She did.

"Right now," I said. "We have some questions."

"I did it, LT," he said. "I'm the one who shot that guy." He started crying. He tried to wipe his eyes with his shoulder, but couldn't quite reach.

"You're sure about that? That's what you want to tell us?"

"Yes," he said.

"Do you have any other guns in there?" First things first.

"In the hall closet."

"What do we want to do about the dog, Chief?" Ted asked.

Princess Leia, with her brown head and soft orange eyes, was sitting there looking at Roger and probably wondering why he wasn't calling her to come with him. I held out my hand and she sniffed it, watching me warily. She had brown spots the size of plates on each side and scattered flecks running over her body, with another spot on her rump and tail. She was a good-looking pointer. Gwyneth stepped over and patted her head. Her tail wagged just a little. Her eyes were fixed on Roger. She must have picked up on something bad happening.

"Is there a leash for the dog?" I asked.

"Hanging in the kitchen closet. But you won't need it. She'll do what you tell her."

"Just the same, she might get upset when you go off without her."

"Princess Leia isn't like that." He tried wiping his eyes again, but couldn't. A spot was growing like a shadow on his shirt where his tears were falling. He seemed more upset about leaving the dog than his pending legal issues. "Her rug's in front of the fireplace, and her food is in the closet, too. You're going to need all that because you aren't taking her to the pound. Right?"

"I promised I wouldn't, and I won't."

"Okay."

I had Gwyneth shut the car door and then went into the house to secure the remaining firearms. The way things were going, I wasn't sure where they might wind up in the investigation, nor did I want them left out in the wild. The front door opened into his living room. The kitchen was behind it through an open doorway. I found a deer rifle and a twenty-two in the closet, and, more importantly, boxes of sixteen-gauge slugs and number six birdshot. I took a paper shopping bag and put them in it. The most shocking thing was that Roger's neat little place showed none of the lifelong bachelor tendencies that surfaced in mine. No dishes sat in the sink, nor were there stacks of newspapers and magazines scattered about. The plaid curtains on the windows were bunched on the bottom with ribbon. A matching set of flowered porcelain coffee, sugar, and flour jars was neatly arranged on the counter. Paintings of the coast, most from places I recognized from around town, covered the walls. One was of Abby's Compound on its peninsula. If I wasn't taking him away, I might have asked him to come over and decorate.

When I came out, Gwyneth and Ted were standing next to the cruiser, watching the big man. Roger was sniffling but trying not to. I put the rifles and shells in the trunk. Princess Leia started whining.

"Are you okay with dogs?" I asked Gwyneth. "She seems to like you."

"Sure."

I went back in and came out with the food, rug, bowls, and leash. I called Princess Leia over. She came, looking up with expectant eyes. I clipped the leash on her and petted her a bit. Her tail wagged. Then I loaded the fifty-pound bag of food and the rest of her things into Gwyneth's cruiser. I gave her the address to Suzanne's house on Cape Laurel, where Derek was now living. If he hunted with the dog, I was sure that he'd take care of her, and even he couldn't be as bad as the pound. I told her to let them know that Roger had been arrested. Even though Princess Leia was a pup, she was well-trained, and I couldn't imagine that she'd be a problem for them.

Roger started blubbering when Gwyneth and the dog drove off.

Ted read him his rights, and we left for the station.

Chapter Forty

Things didn't get any better for Roger once we locked him up. He didn't want to make a phone call. Not even to Jessica. He only asked what we were doing with his dog. His face clouded when I told him we'd brought her to Derek.

"She don't like him too much," he said. "Unless we're hunting."

"Well, everyone loves Suzanne. She'll probably be the one taking care of her anyway."

"I hope so," he said. That seemed to calm him down.

Surprisingly, the dog had not been foremost in my thoughts.

I left Roger in his cell and went to the office. I called Jess Consentino for him. She wasn't at the restaurant. Nor was she answering at home. I didn't imagine she'd be out running in the middle of a workday and assumed that she'd turn up in one place or another soon enough. Then I called Laurent, the district attorney, at home. I followed that up by contacting Pettibone and letting him know that we had a suspect in custody. From the way Roger had talked at the house, it wouldn't take much to get a statement. That would be something different, even here in Laurel.

Ted and I took Roger into the conference room. I got out the tape recorder and went over his rights with him again. He said he didn't want a lawyer. He just wanted to say what happened, that he'd done everything by himself. This, of course, is what a person would say who wanted to keep someone else—Jess Consentino, in this case—out of it. But Roger wasn't one loaded with guile. It should have been impossible to feel bad for the guy who shot me, but that was the path I was traveling. Whatever he thought he'd been doing

197

to help Jess, he just didn't have the ability to anticipate the consequences.

"Let's start with Monday night. What happened when you left the VFW?"

He heaved a sigh and started to sob. I waited. He wiped his eyes.

"I was watching the game with Derek and the guys and Jessica called me there. She told me that she needed my help and to come down to the Squall right away. So I left."

"Is this because of the broken pipe?"

"What broken pipe?"

"The water pipe on the three-bay sink."

"Oh yeah," he said, his eyes shifting from side to side. "That pipe."

"What happened when you got to the Sea Squall?"

"I—I—came in the kitchen door. That guy, Adam Springbrook, was yelling at Jess. They were in the kitchen. She was crying. I told him to knock it off. I got mad, real quick. He told me to shut up and mind my own business. It was bad, LT, how upset she was."

"What did you do?"

"You know that my folks both died the year after we graduated. If it wasn't for Frank, I don't know what I would have done. He was like my best friend, and, if he wasn't my dad, he was as close as a guy could get. He taught me the kitchen and how to cook. It's about the only thing I can do any good. And then he got sick. It was terrible, LT. One day he was fine, just he had a stomachache, and then three months later, he was gone. But you know Frank. He wasn't worried about what was happening to him. He was worried about Jess and me. He asked us to look out for each other. I promised him I would, just like you promised to look after Princess Leia and not send her to the pound. I couldn't live with myself if I let anything happen to her. Jess, I mean."

"Okay, but what happened that night?"

He stopped and wiped his eyes.

"I couldn't take it, that guy yelling at Jessica. I told her to leave, and I'd take care of things. Once she left, I told him that if he didn't get out and never come back, I was going to pound him. He said that if I laid a hand on him, he'd sue Jess and put me in jail, and he'd own the Sea Squall. I didn't know what to do. Then he said he was going to own it soon enough anyway, and the first thing he was going to do was fire me. My shotgun was in the kitchen closet for hunting, so I grabbed it and told him that I didn't think so. I knew that he was the guy buying every place in town. Mary Queen of Shots works for him now. He stole her from us. But I know she don't like him. He wasn't anything like Frank. I made him get in my truck and brought him out to the woods where his new giant place is supposed to go, that he snookered from Bill Tatum and those guys. I shot him. I shouldn't have done it, LT. I know it. But what he was doing to Jessica wasn't right. And he was going to buy the Sea Squall and fire me. I hear what everyone says. He does whatever he wants. Frank wouldn't have stood for it. He'd have died before he let that happen. Frank said that when he and Jess were ready to retire, they were going to see to it that I could buy the Squall from them. I didn't even care about that. I'm not getting it now anyway. But I couldn't have him treating Jess like that and owning the place, after all we put into it. I couldn't do that to Frank. I'd promised him."

"You didn't think just to scare him, maybe throw him out like a bouncer or something?"

"You know that outside of a kitchen, my brain doesn't work too good. Frank would talk things over with me, so I could see what to do. But Jess always tells me to try to think for myself. I'm just not good at it, and I made a big mistake."

"Frank was a great guy," I said.

"I guess I could have used him that night, but I couldn't let nothing happen to Jessica and the Sea Squall, LT. At least that asshole isn't going to wind up with our restaurant."

"What about Friday night?"

"What about it?"

That answer vanquished much of my sympathy. I put my leg up on the table and showed him the bandaged calf.

"When you shot me and my friend."

"Oh," he said as if remembering something from back when we were kids. "I saw you at the Squall. You said you were going to the Rusty Bullet and that

199

you had almost figured everything out. You said that to Jess at the bar, and I heard it. You barely ever come in, and then you were there a lot. I figured you were close to catching me. I didn't want to get caught. I went to your place and waited for you to get home. It was dumb, LT. I'm really sorry."

"Derek tells me you're knocking partridge and woodcock down like beer cans, yet you missed us by a good bit."

"I guess I really didn't want to hit you, down deep. You always treated me right, even in school. I knew that I'd done something wrong. I'm sorry. I shouldn't have done it."

"Did Jess know what happened?"

"No, sir," he said. He put his cuffed hands on the table and shook his head shoulder to shoulder. "I made her leave as soon as I got there. I told her I would talk to Mr. Springbrook myself."

"What did you tell her when he turned up dead?"

"I told her that I didn't do it. That it must have been someone else."

"She believed that?"

"Sure, she did. She knows me. I've never done anything like this before."

"How did his car get back to his house?"

"I took his keys and drove it there and hid it in the garage."

"How'd you get home?"

"I walked back from Bishop's."

"That's a long way."

"Five miles or so. I've been walking a lot hunting, and you know, Jess runs ten miles some days, so I can hoof a few and it won't hurt me."

I wasn't quite believing all this, that Jess just left them alone and then disregarded it when Springbrook turned up dead. She was too sharp for that. She had to have known.

"Jess didn't mention any of this to me when I questioned her."

"She didn't know. That's why."

"She sure knew she called you at the VFW, and that Springbrook had been at the Squall, which she lied about. And, according to you, you told her that you'd take care of things."

"She knows that there's a million people in town who don't like him. We weren't the only ones. She thought someone else did it." His hands came down from the table to his lap. He looked around the room. There was nothing to see.

"Anything else you want to tell me?"

"Jess didn't have anything to do with it. I didn't tell her a thing. She had enough trouble with Frank dying and trying to run the restaurant. I was just looking out for her the way Frank would have. I know I was wrong. Now I'm going to have to pay. I don't have a problem with that, as long as Princess Leia finds a good home."

"Springbrook got shot with a deer slug. You've been hunting partridge and used birdshot on me. Where did that slug come from?"

"Always keep one in the field jacket, LT. You never know when a big ol' buck is going to cross in front of you. I guess I forgot to put another one in there. I kept the jacket at work, too, with the Remington."

I sighed and nodded.

"And that's the truth?" I said.

"All of it."

I clicked off the recorder.

"You need to get a lawyer," I said. "Or we can get you a public defender."

"Okay," he said.

I turned it back on.

"Did anything else happen at the Squall that Monday night?"

"Nope. I pointed the gun at him and made him get in the truck with me. He was scared, so he did it. Then I let him out in the woods."

"Where'd you shoot him there?"

"In the stomach."

"No, where in the worksite?"

"Out in the back. I didn't think anyone would find him."

"And everything went just as you told me?"

"Honest to God," he said, looking down into his lap.

That, too, remained to be seen.

Chapter Forty-One

I knew Laurent would be happy. We had a confession. Pettibone would be happy. He'd be able to focus on his fish and game club case up north. People in town would be happy, with a killer off the street. Though, admittedly, few had been torn up about Springbrook himself. Yet, I wasn't happy. Jess Consentino needed to be dealt with. Despite what Roger had told me, even if she had left when Roger said, she would have had to have her suspicions. This pact that she and Roger had made to look out for each other was not to be overlooked, with a murder involved. She wasn't Roger. She had to know that if she was covering for him, as he would for her, she'd be implicating herself in a crime. She'd told me she hadn't seen Springbrook in weeks. It would be hard to argue that she wasn't an accessory, before or after the fact. I'd bring her in and let Laurent sort it out. I'd also need to let Talia Springbrook know that we'd made an arrest. But that could wait. I left Ted to watch over Roger and drove back to the restaurant where the trouble had started.

Jess still hadn't returned to the Sea Squall. Quinnie Surrelle, the host attempting to run the place in her absence, looked a bit unkempt going over the seating chart for the evening. Two cooks were doing prep, and two waiters were out back smoking. No one knew where Jess had gone, nor had she left a number where she could be reached. That she couldn't be found was edging me into worst-case-scenario mode. If she was running from this, maybe she had reason to be. She'd made a mistake in hiding what happened. I'd seen it before: Someone makes an incredibly bad decision and the whirlpool it creates sucks everyone down to the bottom, a place they never imagined themselves.

The Consentino house stood halfway between downtown and Bishop's Beach to the south, on Pine Street. Her car wasn't in the driveway or garage. I knocked, not expecting a response and not receiving one. When I returned to the Bronco, I radioed the station and had Ted notify Gwyneth. Jess drove a SAAB 9000, and I wanted her out looking for it. I wanted the state police searching, as well.

I kept on to Bishop's Beach. There are many times when one is surprised on this job. And finding Jess's car in the Springbrook driveway was an all-timer. Maybe it shouldn't have been. It seemed too convenient. I knocked and waited.

Talia opened the door. Her hair was stacked on her head, and she had glasses on.

"Chief Nichols," she said. "What can I do for you?"

"I'd like to talk to you," I said.

"Now might not be the best time."

"Is Jess Consentino here?"

"Yes."

"Well, I'm looking for her, too."

"As I said, not really a convenient moment for us."

I started counting to myself so I didn't come out and tell her that I didn't give a shit.

"This is official business, Ms. Murphy."

"So, we don't have a choice?" Her smile was slight, her eyes glassy. If she had been driving, I'd be questioning her on what she'd had to drink and asking her to walk a straight line.

"Not really."

"Well, come on in then," she said, stepping back and swinging the door open. Jess Consentino was seated on the couch. She had a wine glass in her hand. She looked almost as bad as she had at her husband's funeral. Her eyes were red and her mascara had run. Her hair, neat and confined earlier that day at the Squall, now had several strands that had broken free.

"I'd offer you a glass," Talia said. "But being in uniform and on official

203

business, I'm guessing that's not allowable."

"Well, thank you anyway. I'll have to pass whether that was an offer or not."

Jess wouldn't look at me straight on. Talia picked up her glass on the coffee table and asked, instead, if I'd like to sit down. I declined.

"Actually," I said, "what brings me here concerns both of you." I paused and waited to see where their eyes went. I had no way of knowing what Jess had told her about Roger and what had happened prior to the fatal event on Monday. Jess looked at her glass and took a sip. Talia adjusted the sleeve of her black shirt.

"We have a suspect who has confessed to Adam's killing."

Jess shook her head and looked down. "Roger."

"That's right, Roger Kensington."

Talia looked over at Jess. "That's the employee you were talking about?" Jess nodded.

"I thought you said that he wasn't capable of such a thing." The pitch of her voice rose. "Shooting Adam and dropping him out in those woods. It's horrible."

"I honestly didn't think he was," Jess said, looking from Talia to me. "Of course, I was hoping that he hadn't done it. He's admitted to this?"

"Yes." I leaned back. "You two discussed this possibility?"

"I wouldn't say that," Jess said. "I'd let her know that Adam had stopped by the Squall the other night and that it didn't go well."

"Something that you kept from me," I said. "You told me that you hadn't seen Adam for weeks."

"I didn't want to complicate things for you," she said, her hands shuffling in front of her. "I never believed Roger was capable of something like this. I wouldn't allow myself to think it."

I pressed my lips together and breathed through my nose. This was an attempt to squelch my asking her if she thought I was an idiot.

"This Roger, he shot Adam, for sure?" Talia asked.

"As well as myself."

"Why?" Talia asked. She looked over at Jess, who was shaking her head.

"Adam was having a disagreement with Jess, and Roger had promised Frank he'd look out for her. He'd worked for her and Frank since he was a kid. He was concerned for her, the restaurant, and his job. He told me that Adam had threatened to have him fired, should he be purchasing the property, which I hadn't known was a consideration."

"That was never going to happen," Jess said. "I made that quite clear to them both. Roger must have been confused." She looked to Talia. "He's limited, intellectually."

"What were you discussing with Springbrook Monday night?" I asked.

"He wanted me to partner with him and then open another restaurant at Lost Woods."

"This was also something that you failed to mention at the time."

"I didn't find it relevant. I didn't know it had anything to do with Adam's death."

"Then why did you call Roger?"

"I had a pipe leaking on the three-bay. That Adam showed up was a coincidence and incredibly bad luck for all of us."

"He only told me that you needed help and had asked him to get there as soon as he could. He didn't mention the pipe until I reminded him of it."

"That's Roger. Have you seen a flooded kitchen, LT? I needed him."

"But what he found was you crying and Adam threatening him."

"It was too much to handle for Roger. I can see that now, and I'm sorry I left him there. Between all that was going on, with the water and Adam's offer that I wanted nothing to do with, I was overwhelmed and not thinking straight. I asked him to get Adam to leave, and I ran out of there. I couldn't take it anymore. We've had an incredibly difficult time since Frank died. I didn't know Roger would go that far. But Adam did threaten to take the restaurant and fire him, which anyone could see would never happen. Maybe anyone but Roger."

I turned to Talia.

"Were you aware of these, what should we call them, proposals?"

"Not specifically. But that's who Adam was. If he saw a business opportunity, he didn't sleep on it. He moved when a thought struck him."

"At nine o'clock on a Monday night?"

"Why not? It's business hours for a restaurant. He probably knew that Jess would be there."

"No one thought any of this would be worth relating to me?" I said.

"We're not trying to hide anything," Talia Murphy said. "It seems to me, Chief, that you have one dumb fuck who went over the edge and snapped. I don't know why you're badgering us. And if you're wondering about how quickly things move in business, talk to your girlfriend."

"Excuse me?" I said. I didn't know who she meant. In the few days she'd been here, it was possible that she'd heard about both Suzanne and Abby.

"Convenient that Abby Grimes," Talia said, "a developer, was given immediate access to the financial documents of Springbrook Coastal. She didn't waste any time putting an offer in on the Lost Woods property. She was here this morning."

"She made an offer on the land?" I said, not having to appear like I was surprised.

"Oh," Talia said. "You weren't aware of that?" She finished the wine in her glass, pulled the bottle from the ice bucket on the table, and poured more. "You had her looking over the finances. Of course, I'm sure it was only to tell you if there was anything there to worry about. How were you to know that they had nothing to do with my ex-husband's killing?"

"Regardless," I said, not liking what she was implying. "I'm going to need to talk to you, Jess, on an official basis, about this. That will be done in my office. Right now."

"I've got a restaurant to run and we're shorthanded."

"I just left the Squall. They're managing."

"Do I need a lawyer?" she said, folding her arms across her chest.

"You're not under arrest. I'm trying to find out what happened."

"Didn't Roger tell you exactly that?"

"His statements need to be corroborated. You're welcome to have a lawyer present if you want one. Maybe you could get one for Roger. He wouldn't call one for himself."

"What good will that do if he's already confessed?"

CHAPTER FORTY-ONE

"Your compassion is breathtaking," I said.

"I don't think I like your tone, Chief," she said.

"I don't think I care."

"I hope you can understand, Chief Nichols," Talia said, "why we all might be a little upset."

I raised an eyebrow. "Yes, a man getting killed will do that."

"Jess," Talia said, "I can call Fitzgerald if you want."

"There's no need," she said. "I haven't done anything wrong."

As she'd been drinking, I offered Jess a lift to the station. She declined. She drove there flawlessly, with me right behind her.

Chapter Forty-Two

Jess sat in one of the folding chairs. I'd brought Gwyneth in from patrol and sent Ted home from monitoring Roger to grab some sleep.

"Tell me what happened Monday night," I asked. I nodded to Gwyneth, who held a legal pad and would be taking notes.

Though she had driven like she hadn't had a drop, Jess looked pale. If she hadn't been seated, I would have been on my toes. I thought she might faint.

"Do I need to get a lawyer?" she asked, for the second time.

"You just turned an offer for one down," I said. "You are not under arrest. I'm just asking some questions. But it's up to you."

She took a deep breath.

"I was closing the restaurant when Adam Springbrook came in. That pipe was leaking. My nerves were shot. He'd called earlier to let me know he was coming. When he got there, he looked like he'd been drinking. He told me that he'd decided that we were going to open a restaurant together at Lost Woods."

"What did you say to that?"

"That I wasn't interested."

"What was his response?"

"He wasn't going to take no for an answer. He gave me a number of reasons why he thought it would be a great idea. I told him I'd be passing, nevertheless. He said in that case that he'd run me out of business. With all the places he owned and the pressure he could put on certain vendors, he claimed he could do it."

"Could he?"

"He was confident, but I doubt it."

"What did you say to that?"

"I told him no—again."

"That's when you called Roger?"

"Yes. No. I'd already called him because of the pipe."

"When I talked to him, he didn't say anything about a flood."

"He didn't get far with it that night. I'd somehow managed to shut off the water right before Adam arrived. But Roger came in and found Adam threatening me and the business, and he got flustered. You saw for yourself how he is around me. Adam made the mistake of starting in on him, too. Like I said, I got overwhelmed and ran out the door."

"You left Roger to deal with him?" This didn't make a lot of sense.

"I thought Adam would leave, too, and Roger could fix the pipe. I couldn't have helped him with that, anyway."

"Where did he keep his gun?"

"I didn't know he had one at the Squall."

"How could you not?"

"I was aware that he was going hunting and coming in early for prep so he could do it. But I don't run daily inspections of every corner of his kitchen. I guess I just thought he kept it in his truck. He worked sixty hours a week and never complained. If he wanted to go off and hunt between lunch and dinner service, and it was easier for him to go from there, why would I stop him? He deserved it."

"When Adam turned up dead after you'd left them together, you didn't think anything of it?"

"You know how gentle Roger is. I wasn't aware of when Adam was killed. How was I supposed to know that it was that night?"

I folded my arms in front of me.

"Did you ask Roger about it when you heard Adam had been shot?"

"No."

"I don't believe you."

"You're implying that you think I did something wrong. If you're going to ask me any more questions, I want a lawyer present."

"What could you be guilty of?"

"I'm guilty of nothing. But I don't like where you're going with this."

"Why did you slap Springbrook this summer?"

"That again." She shook her head and took a deep breath. "That was the first time he asked about buying the Sea Squall. I didn't appreciate it, with Frank in the hospital."

"Yet, you're friends with Talia."

"The enemy of my enemy is my friend," she said. "Isn't that how the saying goes? Not that we were enemies with Adam, just in competition." She looked at me hard. "I'm done explaining things to you."

"You had no inkling of Roger's involvement in Adam's death?"

"Of course not."

"Despite what happened in your restaurant?"

"I left before anything happened. It was too much for me. If Adam was visiting the Squall that late, who's to say he didn't have other stops? He knew people all over town for a variety of pursuits, let's say."

"And Roger didn't seem at all weird to you?"

"Roger is Roger. He's been the way he is since forever. You know that as well as anyone."

"You didn't ask him what happened after you left?"

"It's not my job to figure out who did what in this town. It's yours."

"That's a convenient answer."

"I'm serious about that lawyer. Unless you want me to stare at you and not speak, I'd like to leave. I'm glad to make an appointment for tomorrow, which will give me time to get an attorney. Because I'm done. I mean it."

"I have a problem believing things happened the way you and Roger are telling me."

"That's on you. Roger doesn't lie about anything. He doesn't have it in him."

But he would do it to protect her.

"Roger wouldn't have needed a gun to get Adam out of the Squall," I said.

"If that's your determination, you can take it up with him."

"How long have you and Talia known each other?"

210

CHAPTER FORTY-TWO

"Since Adam started coming here."

"I didn't know that."

"Why would you?" Jess said.

"Do you know how to use a gun?"

"What's to it?" she said. "You point and pull the trigger, from what I understand."

"Have you ever done it?"

"For real?"

"Yes."

"Of course not."

I hadn't liked any of her answers, but they couldn't all have been lies. I told her that if she planned on leaving town, she needed to let me know. And that I'd be contacting her in the morning to set up a meeting for tomorrow afternoon, which would give her time to find the lawyer she wanted. She asked to see Roger, and I gave them five minutes together. She could not have been oblivious to what happened and the possibility that Roger had killed Springbrook, even if she had left when she claimed on Monday night.

Chapter Forty-Three

"You're here," I said. Abby was sprawled on my couch with a book, one of my science fiction novels, a remnant of my high school reading habits.

"I'm not going anywhere until you figure out who shot us, and you feed me. I believe you've already taken care of the first requirement today."

"It was Roger, the cook from the Sea Squall. He admitted it."

She swung her legs over and sat up.

"Kind of strange, isn't it?" she said, putting down the book.

"What?" I had my doubts, at least in the precision of his account, and that things had gone down precisely the way he and Jess were claiming. But if Abby was at the point where she was reading my mind, I could have been in more trouble than I thought.

"The guy's a hunter. He can shoot a flying bird, but barely clips us from across the street?"

"People get stressed," I said. "It's not easy to shoot a human."

"Tell that to Adam Springbrook." She stood. "Where are we going for dinner? Your refrigerator is like Death Valley. Nothing lives there. Are we going to have to drive to Portland to find a place open after eight o'clock?"

"I imagine you worked up quite an appetite," I said. I hadn't meant to bring this up first thing, though I did plan on asking her how she could have moved so quickly on that land. As tired as I was, maybe I realized I wasn't going to be awake much longer.

"What are you talking about?"

"You're wheeling and dealing all over town, I heard. You've already made an offer on the Lost Woods property. The case isn't even closed."

"You know what I do for a living, right?" she said. "Isn't that why you asked me here?"

"I had the new landowner and her friend accuse me of being underhanded and out of line for letting my girlfriend look at the finances."

She shook her head.

"You told me not to share the information with anyone, which I did not," she said. "I asked you what I was supposed to do with what I'd seen. You didn't seem to have a problem if I kept it to myself, which I've done."

"It looks like you saw an opportunity and jumped on it, using knowledge that you weren't necessarily supposed to have."

"You provided me with that information. Literally handed it to me."

"I know that, and that you arrived here with no ulterior motives. There's no way you could have known what you'd find."

"Then what's your problem? You think I got carried away and couldn't help myself because I'm a Grimes and a money-hungry bitch?"

"I didn't say that."

"But you're bent out of shape because whoever you were talking to, and I can guess who that is, questioned your precious integrity. You know better, so why do you care?"

"This is a small town, and in my position, I have a certain reputation to uphold."

"That sounds like something my father would have said."

"That's not fair."

"Please. It's business. You weren't the one who made the offer, so Talia Springbrook or Murphy or whatever she's calling herself, can fuck right off. If you must know, she was listening with both ears and practically leaped over the table to kiss me when I told her what I'd give her for that land. That's who you were talking to, right? And maybe her pal Jess Consentino?"

"So, you'd build Lost Woods?"

"Hell, no. I'd put houses up there."

"This is a done deal?"

"Of course not."

"Then why didn't you at least wait until the case was closed?"

"Maybe you should work faster."

"I'm doing the best I can. I've got the shooter in a cell."

"I apologize if my actions, which you earlier did not—and should not—have a problem with, tarnish that halo you think is floating over your head. I can't see it myself, but apparently, you believe other people can."

"You're getting a little carried away."

She took a deep breath.

"You think I took advantage of this situation. You asked me to come here and help, and I did. You were grateful. Now, because I made an offer on a property, which is in no way illegal or immoral, and that, in some way I can't understand, makes you look unethical to a couple of bitter widows who don't care that a man's dead except in how it affects them, you're mad at me? Christ, LT, take a step back and think. You didn't care what my father, as reprehensible as he was, a man who had actually accomplished things, thought of you. But those two make one comment that's completely out of bounds, and you're butt hurt."

"I just asked you about it, that's all," I said.

"Bullshit," she said. "Fucking hick town. I should have told you to find an accountant to do your work—if they even have them up here."

"What are you yelling about?" I said. "I asked about you making an offer on a property. And now you're all pissed off."

"You didn't ask anything. You pretty much implied that I was up to no good and taking advantage of something that you think I shouldn't have. It's not the offer that fries you; it's that some people might think the pure and honest Tim Nichols set up his friend to take advantage of a distraught, confused woman as if she were a drunk teenager at a frat party. You know better. If they hadn't said anything, you would have had no problem. Grow a pair."

"Of course, the possibility that what you did might have jumped the gun on this doesn't enter the conversation."

"We both know that I've done nothing wrong. Someone will buy that land, or someone won't. Unlike certain people in this town, I won't be bullying anybody into it, either. I don't need this shit, LT."

"You think I do?"

Car doors closed outside.

"What now?" she said, looking over my shoulder. "Not these two again."

She sounded even angrier.

I turned to see Derek Anderson's truck. He, Suzanne, and Princess Leia were walking up the driveway. Of course, they would show up in the middle of this. Abby and I hadn't even made it twenty-four hours after reaching a new level in our relationship, if one could call it that, before having a blowout.

I sighed and opened the door. Suzanne took the leash and sent Derek back to the Dodge.

"To what do we owe the pleasure this time?" I said, glancing down at my watch to make a point. "You've brought the whole family."

"LT, we can't take this dog," Suzanne said, leading her right into the house.

She unclipped Princess Leia, who brushed past me and jogged over to Abby. The dog sat at her feet and looked at Suzanne and me.

"Why not?" I said. "Roger made me promise that I wouldn't bring it to the pound in Milltowne. Derek hunts with her. He said the dog is great. And he's Roger's friend. What's the problem?"

Derek laughed as he entered the house. In his arms were the dog's rug, the bag of Burger Bits dog food, and two plastic red bowls.

"That dog hates me," he said.

"Impossible. You hunt with her. She's a pointer."

"Won't listen one bit," he said.

"We've got a kid coming, LT," Suzanne said. "That's enough. Not to mention that I'm allergic, which you could have remembered from when we were kids. We've had her for all of six hours, and I'm stuffed up. Derek's right, too. She's an angel for me, but won't listen to him at all."

"You don't know anyone who wants a good dog?" I said.

"We aren't the ASPCA," Suzanne said. "You sent her to us with your officer. We're telling you that we can't take her. So, here she is."

"It's a stupid animal," Derek said. "It's got one job, and when it ain't doing that, it's useless. She only likes Roger. If that dog knew it was me who was going to shoot one of those birds, she'd let them stay hidden. I just happen to be there."

Princess Leia let out a low growl.

"If I weren't allergic, I might consider it," Suzanne said. "But the dog hates him. Seriously."

"Dogs are known to be good judges of character," Abby said, scratching behind Princess Leia's ears. Derek missed it as he was depositing the dog's worldly possessions in the corner of the room. Suzanne did not. I'd be lucky if they didn't end up throwing punches.

"Didn't you have a dog when you were a kid?" Suzanne asked. "And didn't you teach it all sorts of tricks?"

"Sure, we had a cocker spaniel, Rico. But I don't have the time now. You need to work with a dog to get them good. How am I supposed to do that with my job?"

"A smart guy like you can figure it out," Suzanne said, hands on her hips. "It's not our problem."

"I promised Roger that I wouldn't take her to the pound."

"Also, not our problem."

It was just like Derek to hunt with a dog and still manage to have that dog so dislike him that it wouldn't live with him. Though, I'd rather go to the pound than live with him, too.

"You've got to be kidding me," I said.

"You're the one who made the promise," Suzanne said.

Abby laughed. That did not make me any happier.

"By the looks of things around here," Suzanne said. "You could use some good companionship. Unless, of course, your friend is moving in."

"Oh," Abby said. "We wouldn't do that. We'd live at the Compound. The dog would have a lot of room over there. She'd get a diamond-studded collar and filet mignon for dinner."

Derek stood with his hands tapping his thighs, watching them go back and forth. I looked to him for some help, hoping he had brains enough to tell Suzanne that they'd dropped the dog off and could move along. No such luck, of course. If something was lousy for me, by default, he imagined that it was good for him.

"Well, wherever you two wind up," Suzanne said, bowing and holding out her arms. "I wish you all the happiness."

"What," I said, "was that?"

"I don't think Suzy likes your girlfriend," Derek said. "She usually isn't one for snottiness."

The dog didn't even peep with Abby working her fingers behind its ears.

"I think you better be going," Abby said. "Before I release the hound."

Suzanne shook her head, and they walked out. I didn't know what to think.

"To be honest," Abby said, "I've always wanted to say that."

"Great," I said.

"You know, she's right," Abby said.

"About what?"

"That you could use some companionship. Because I've had just about enough of this place."

She picked up her pocketbook and went out the door, too.

"Abby, come on," I said, following her as far as the front porch. Princess Leia came up next to me, wagging her tail.

Abby stopped. My heart fluttered as she turned.

"And for the record," she said. "If anyone asks, I'm not your fucking girlfriend."

"Rest easy, Abby. That's what I've been telling people."

I watched Abby get in her car and drive off without looking back. The dog trailed me into the house. At least she had food. I picked up one of her dishes and filled it with water. I gave her a piece of American cheese from the refrigerator, which wasn't completely barren. I put the dog's rug in front of the wood stove, and when I told her to lie down, she circled it and did just that. I sat on the couch and waited for Abby to come back, wondering how I'd managed to screw things up so quickly. Abby's overnight bag was still here, so I assumed that she'd return. The dog looked at me. I told her that she hadn't exactly hit the jackpot. While I didn't tell her that I wasn't going to keep her, no matter what both women said, I did let her know that she wasn't going to the pound. I called her over and patted her. We watched some television, waiting. At one in the morning, I broke down and made myself a peanut butter sandwich.

Princess Leia. How many times would I find myself explaining that name before I could find someone to take her, as if telling the Little Tim story over and over wasn't bad enough?

Chapter Forty-Four

I'd fallen asleep on the couch waiting for Abby to return. Princess Leia had slept on her rug a few feet away. I'd woken up at seven o'clock with a stiff neck. I sat up and grabbed the phone.

"No, she didn't spend the night here," Trout said, his voice dripping with sarcasm. "She's supposed to be at your place."

"Well, she didn't come home last night."

"Home?" Trout said. "What? You got a regular love nest going on over there?"

"We kind of had a fight."

"Already?" He cackled. "You're never getting married again. What did that last, three days?"

"I can count."

"Did you try her place in Boston? Or her office? Though she usually won't go in on a Sunday."

"I've called everywhere. She's not answering. At either place."

"Maybe she knows it's your dumbass calling and doesn't want to talk to you."

"How would she know that?"

"Women have a way, I'm telling you. What were you fighting over? I hope it wasn't china patterns for your registry." He laughed.

"She'd been talking to Talia Springbrook about buying the land on Providence Hill."

"Yeah, that's what she does. Isn't that why you brought her here, because you don't know shit about that?"

219

"Well, yes. But I didn't think she'd use what she learned working for me. At least before the body got buried."

"You put a fish in water, LT, it's going to swim."

"I asked her to keep what she learned confidential."

"Who did she tell about it?"

"No one. But Talia Springbrook thought it was unethical of me, because now Abby has information that a regular buyer wouldn't, and everyone's assuming that we're connected."

"So, she helped you, and you helped her. What the hell is wrong with that? Why do you care what Talia Springbrook thinks? Who the hell is she? From what I heard, Springbrook wasn't exactly Mother Teresa, and his ex probably isn't any better."

"You know I like everything above board. But maybe I got carried away."

"You pick some funny battles to fight. You'll get any half-in-the-bag asshole trying to get in their car at the Dockside or Tavern a ride home. But someone whose business it is to develop shit is interested in developing shit and has taken days out of her life to help your miserable self, and that's where you draw the line. Do you ever think before you speak?"

"Rarely, I guess."

"That business she's in is dog-eat-dog. If you had some geek accountant from Portland look that stuff over, you don't think they'd be telling one of their clients all about it on the golf course? Wouldn't you rather have Abby making money off that parcel than some out-of-town jackass?"

"I guess you're right."

"Of course, I am. It would be one thing if you had threatened the ex-wife and forced her to sell the land to your brand-new girlfriend. But that's not what this is."

"No," I said, sighing. "Will you try to track her down? I'm guessing she went back to Boston. Maybe she'll use her intuition and know it's you calling and pick up the phone."

"That must have been some fight."

"I didn't think it was much of one. Keep trying for her, will you?"

"What do you think happened? She's nearly thirty years old, not some runaway kid. She's probably stuck in Boston traffic. If I were you, I'd figure out how to apologize. Real good. Open up your wallet and get her some flowers. That'd be a start."

"Point taken. But where would I send them?"

"You'll have to use your mighty powers of deduction to figure that out," he said.

Trout's calm, measured response—which was probably spot on—didn't stop me from radioing Ted and Gwyneth and telling them to be on the lookout for Abby's car, a red Mercedes coupe with Mass plates. The feeling in my stomach that I'd had driving past Providence Hill this month, that I foolishly hadn't put any stock in, resurfaced. I spent the night on the couch waiting for the door to open. I was only able to doze because I told myself that she probably went to the Rusty Bullet to get a drink, and when she didn't come home later, that she'd gone to the Compound. I wasn't taking chances now, though I was sure I'd be laughing at myself when Trout got her at home and called to tell me that yes, I had been overreacting, and that, yes, I was hopeless. With my track record with women, it was fairly evident that I didn't know what to think about who. The female that stuck with me was Princess Leia. But she didn't have a choice. She'd been watching me walk in circles as I talked, trying not to tangle myself in the phone cord. She moved to the door, and I assumed that she needed to go out. Without Abby around, she'd be locked up all day. I figured I might as well take her for a walk and wear her out a bit. If I took baby steps, my calf wouldn't hurt much, and I might clear my head in the process.

I'd clearly lost my mind over Abby's actions. I tended to live in black and white. As Trout pointed out, I could handle gray on small items but couldn't manage it on larger issues. That was how I'd navigated and built a life. While I could understand how others thought differently, I believed it was what my job demanded. But that framework didn't translate when it came to my personal life. The times when I was not a police chief—being a boyfriend, husband, or even dog owner, which I wasn't considering as I leashed Princess Leia—disaster seemed to result.

We walked a mile to the beach. It took a half hour, but my calf seemed to be loosening up. We practiced heeling, and I found that she was already a pro, even off the leash. When I told her okay and pointed out in front of us or to the side, she took off in that direction. She ran to the edge of the water and pulled back, eyeing the waves with caution. Then she ran from one mound of seaweed to the next, her nose working to see if there was anything of value under the dark green strands. She went to five of them before she started pawing at one and stuck her head deep into the pile. She came out of it with a dead pollock, which she pranced over and dropped at my feet. I was thinking that Roger had done a remarkable job with her, until she flopped down and gleefully rolled her back, neck, and shoulders over the decaying fish. Now she needed a bath. Great.

But how the dog had worked struck a chord. I'd poked my nose into every place that Adam Springbrook had left his scent in town. All I'd done was run from one mess to the next, directed by the prevailing winds and biases, with no prime suspect. Finally, Blockhead Roger was dropped at my feet. The more I considered it, the more he stank worse than Princess Leia.

Roger had never hurt anyone in his life, even when he'd had reason to, having been mercilessly ridiculed in school. He would have been scared, no doubt, if he'd found Springbrook threatening Jess Consentino. And terrified if he thought Springbrook would fire him from the Sea Squall. He'd never been able to calculate anything other than a recipe. Roger wouldn't have thought: He would have reacted. He wouldn't have gone to get his shotgun from the closet and marched Springbrook out of there. He would have snapped and grabbed him and run him out of the building. Roger wouldn't have taken him at gunpoint to Lost Woods. He had no connection to the place. If he'd killed him somewhere else, he wouldn't have thought to leave his body there. He wouldn't have known what to do. Had he harmed Springbrook, he might have even called us then and confessed. But Roger had someone there to think for him and tell him what to do: Jess Consentino. He was so devoted to Frank and the promise he'd made that he'd have done anything she asked him.

Jess played dumb and trusting. One could almost buy her belief in Roger's innocence, and I had at first. But it just didn't ring true. By the time I'd got

Princess Leia back to the house and washed her with my Johnson's Baby Shampoo, the stink was off of her. But it remained on this case.

There was little I could do but take what I'd learned from the dog and get after it.

Chapter Forty-Five

From across his cell, Roger wouldn't look me in the eye. He sat with his head down and his elbows on his knees, rocking on his feet.

"I've got no choice then, Roger. Princess Leia goes to the pound. Derek didn't want her. She's been at my house, but I can't keep her."

That straightened him up. "You promised you wouldn't."

"That was based on you telling me the truth. Which you haven't done. If you're not being honest with me, I see no reason to keep my word."

"You can't bring her to the pound."

"She's going today. In an hour. I've already called Portland. In case you haven't seen it, it's even more crowded than the one in Milltowne. They pen them all up together. Lots of fights, I've heard."

"I know you. You wouldn't do that to her, LT."

"That dog pissed on my living room rug. I don't give a shit what happens to her, and with you dicking me around here, I don't have time to look for a home for her. It's your choice. You can tell me the truth about Monday, or I'm taking her to the pound."

"She never had an accident in my house."

"Well, that's too bad for her." I shrugged. The dog had been perfect. Roger didn't need to know that, however. "Who knows what she'll be like after that pound?"

His jaw clenched as his lips came together. Concentration stretched his face as he tried to work out whatever was going through his head.

"I promised Frank," he said. He was talking to himself, more than to me.

"What did Jess do, Roger?" Of course, it was her.

224

"Nothing. Like I said."

"Is Jess the one who had you shoot Adam Springbrook?"

He shook his head.

"What happened?"

He heaved his chest and shuddered. But he wouldn't talk.

"Frank didn't want anything to happen to you," I said. "He wanted the best for you. Even if you think you're helping Jess, he wouldn't want you to do it at your own expense."

"What does that mean?"

"He looked out for you. If he were here, he wouldn't let you take the heat for something that wasn't your idea."

His chin quivered.

"You're not responsible for what she may have done or told you to do. She's your boss. The district attorney will be here later. If your confession stands, you're going to go to prison for the rest of your life."

"I shot him, LT. If that's what happens, so be it."

"You're sending your dog to the pound. She'll be ruined. She's such a good girl, too. Didn't Frank teach you responsibility?"

"I am being responsible."

"You can't be responsible for something that you didn't do. I looked at the lab report. I know you didn't shoot Adam Springbrook. Jess was the only other person there. Did she shoot him?"

"How do you know that?"

"There are chemicals left on the gun, Roger. It's science." Technically, I may have been wading into the river of unethicalness, and deep, by making this up. But it was for his own good. I was trying to get him out of a frame, not put him in one. If he had yet to see where I was going with this, he'd catch on soon enough.

"If someone else did this, that's on them, not you. Frank wouldn't want you to pay for a mistake that you didn't make. That's not what he meant by looking out for her, and that's not what you promised him."

"I can't, LT."

"Frank's dead," I said. "You can try to help other people, but you can't hold yourself accountable for what they do. You tried your best to keep Jess safe and that restaurant going. You did great. But this is different. A man died. I need to know the real story. Frank would want you to tell the truth, no matter who it hurt. Isn't that right?"

"I guess I couldn't fix it," Roger said. His body shook.

"It's hard to do things alone, Roger. None of us can."

"Like how you had your girlfriend here helping you, even if she was only looking over some papers?"

"Yes, even me." I wondered how he knew what she was doing here. The only explanation was that Jess had told him, and she'd heard it from Talia. I was going to do whatever I had to, to get the truth out of him. "If you and I help each other, maybe I can get Abby to take Princess Leia. No pound. The dog really liked her. But how it is now, I'm not helping her unless you help me. What happened with Adam Springbrook?"

He looked up and wiped his eyes, then put his head down without saying anything.

"I know you didn't do it," I said.

"Okay."

"Tell me the truth this time."

"I was watching the game like I said. Jess called me at the Post and said there was an emergency at the restaurant and that I needed to come right there. So that's what I did."

"What did you find?"

"That guy Springbrook was there. He was already dead. Jess used my gun. I was worried about leaving it in the car, so I kept it in the kitchen closet. I shouldn't have. Jess said that she wanted to scare him because he kept threatening to take the restaurant from us. That he was going to kick her out and then fire me. She said she couldn't let that happen and that she'd grabbed the gun and just wanted to threaten him back, so he would stop. It went off by accident, she said."

"You didn't think to call us?"

"I didn't think at all, LT. I just did what Jess told me, what she thought was best. She said there were plenty of people who didn't like him. That if we dumped him out where he was building that new place, it wouldn't come back on us. Because if it did, it would hurt the restaurant, too, and we'd probably get closed down if it got out that we killed him, even by accident."

"You left your gun loaded in the restaurant?"

"No," he said, shaking his head. "Of course not. That's one of the ten commandments of hunter safety."

"Where was the ammo?"

"I had my nice LL Bean field jacket in there, too."

"Then how could she have shot him by accident?"

"I didn't think of that. Maybe she loaded it to scare him."

She'd loaded it for something; that much was true.

"What did you do?"

"We put him in the back of my truck, and Jess had me drop him out in the woods. She told me where. Then she took his car and drove it to the house. I followed her, and then we cleaned up the restaurant. There was blood on the floor."

"After that, you went on as if nothing happened?"

"Jess said that it was us or him. I ain't proud of it. I promised Frank. I didn't have a choice, after all he did for me."

"You gave the gun to Derek?"

He nodded. "Then Jess said that we better not do anything different than we had been because it would look bad, so I brought it back Friday. Then I heard what happened that night, so I gave it to Derek again on Saturday. I didn't think it was a good idea to leave it where Jess could get it anymore."

"Did you know it was her who shot me?" It was the only explanation.

"It wasn't hard to figure out."

"You two are the only ones who knew about that?"

"Who else would?"

"Derek, for one."

"No. Jess told me not to say anything to anyone, ever. We made up the story I told you, that she didn't know anything about it. She told me that I should go somewhere for a while, too, so that she could fix everything. But I didn't have anywhere to hide."

"Jesus Christ, Roger. Why'd you go along with this?"

"I didn't want to disappoint her and Frank. She didn't have faith in me the way Frank did. She thought I'd never be able to get away with ditching that guy in the woods, and I guess she was right. When you told her that you were close to figuring it out, she must've got real scared."

"You never thought to come to me?"

"Jess said not to. And her friend told her the same thing."

"What friend?" I nearly jumped.

"The one who was married to the guy. Jess used to babysit her when she was a kid. Her family has been coming here for a long time."

Talia Springbrook.

"She knew what happened, this friend?"

"I don't know. But she and Jess talked a lot at the restaurant."

"When?"

"Last week. She used to come in and see Jess in the summer, too."

"Were they in it together?"

"I don't know."

"Did you ever see Abby Grimes talking to them?"

"Who's that?"

"The girl I was with the other night at the bar. My girlfriend."

"No. I didn't ever see her with them."

That was a break, I guessed. Like having a poor, innocent dog to use as leverage.

Chapter Forty-Six

Quinnie Surrelle's eyes got big when she saw Gwyneth and I barrel through the front door of the Sea Squall. Maybe it was because we didn't look like we were there for mimosas and Lobster Benedict. When I asked her where we could find Jess, she could barely get out that she wasn't there. I sent Gwyneth to the kitchen to clear everyone and told Quinnie that she needed to send what customers they had home and cancel any reservations. A crime lab team from the state police was on its way. She couldn't stop blinking but managed to nod.

"Do you know where she might be?" I said.

Quinnie shook her head. She may have been unable to speak. After several breaths helped her recover from oxygen debt, she managed to say that she hadn't seen Jess since the previous night, when she'd been there with two other women. One was the woman whose ex-husband had been shot, but she didn't know the other. Lily Langford, Mary Queen of Shot's replacement at the bar, was watching with interest.

"Do you know who this other woman was?" I asked, hoping it wasn't Abby.

"Your friend from the other night," Lily said.

"Blond hair or brown?" I asked, that brick again forming in my stomach, as I knew the likelihood of Suzanne running around with Talia and Jess was infinitesimal.

"The brown. Your girlfriend."

"Great," I said and thanked her.

I went into the kitchen. Gwyneth stood in front of the line and sequestered the two cooks to the prep kitchen.

"Any problems?" I asked.

"None," she said. "But I know Rod from the Tavern."

A short cook with black hair looked down. I wondered if he was the one she'd taken down for mouthing off or had just been there to witness it. I told her to send them home and wait for the crime lab team. It looked like Quinnie was in charge, so I took Gwyneth and introduced her. I told her to radio when the state crew showed up, and I'd tell her where to meet me or have her look for the various missing women.

"Where are you going?" she asked.

"Jess Consentino lives on the way to Bishop's Beach. If they're not there, I'll go on to Adam Springbrook's house. That's where Talia's staying. They've got to be somewhere."

"Shouldn't you wait until the lab gets here, so you have backup? I mean, you're still limping and procedure going after a possibly armed suspect, would—"

"I'll be fine. Not my first time out." I couldn't get mad at her questioning my judgment, no matter how annoying. That was how she was, by the book.

"You can't leave Roger alone and take Ted, can you?"

"No. And we have the shotgun."

"We know it's not the only one around." She raised her eyebrows.

I sighed. I'm glad she hadn't heard about "my girlfriend" being involved, or she may have attempted a filibuster.

Chapter Forty-Seven

The Consentinos lived a few miles from the coast in a split-level house that could have been on any street in the country. Compared to Springbrook's place on the beach, one would have never known they'd owned a restaurant as successful as the Sea Squall. The maple trees in their front yard had lost their leaves, which were scattered over the lawn. Some were stuck in the hedges that flanked the windows. Her car wasn't there. I limped to the door, thinking that walking Princess Leia might not have been a great idea, as the calf was barking now that I was moving quickly. I rang the bell. No one answered. I walked the perimeter of the house and looked in the windows. She wasn't there, with or without Talia and Abby.

To get to the Springbrook house, I only had to drive a half mile up the road and take a left to the coast. Talia's car was the only one in the driveway. The shades to the living room were pulled down. I parked on the street and made sure to shut the door quietly. When I got out of the Bronco, I patted the butt of my gun. It was something I hadn't done for years, a nervous tick I'd developed as a rookie. I couldn't explain why I'd been wired to do it now. The vibrations that had started with the trees coming down on Providence Hill were back at gale force. It would have been much less nerve-wracking to be unaware of such things.

I crept to the door and listened. Music played quietly in the background. I rapped the brass knocker three times. There was rustling. I tried the knob. It was locked.

"Who is it?"

"The police, Talia. Chief Nichols."

231

"One second." She opened the door six inches and centered herself in the gap.

"What brings you here today, Chief? Telling me that I've been cleared of Adam's murder because that oaf from the Sea Squall shot him, or have you come to apologize for thinking I may have killed him despite there being no money in it?"

"That is the assumption we're working under," I said, not wanting to spur resistance. "I do have some questions, however. Can I come in?"

"Actually, I was just on my way out." She wasn't smiling.

"Then I'll get right to it. Have you seen Jessica Consentino?"

"No, I haven't," she said. She tugged down on her navy blue sweater.

"That's funny. Because you left the Sea Squall together last night."

She shrugged. "Today isn't yesterday."

"Oh, just let him in." It was Jess Consentino. A dark, seething look crossed Talia's face. She stepped back and opened the door. I walked in. Jess stood in front of the couch. I turned, placing my back to the kitchen, so I could see them both. This was another thing I found myself doing without thinking. The room didn't strike me as being as neat and ordered as the last time I'd been there, but I couldn't determine what was out of place. I noticed three wine glasses on the coffee table. Providence Hill washed over me. Sweat crawled down my back.

"I see the friendship continues," I said.

They looked at each other from opposite sides of the room. Their eyes landed on me. I couldn't help but think that the third glass was Abby's. Where she was or how she fit into what was going on, I didn't have time to consider.

"I didn't know that you two went way back," I said. "Jess, you were Talia's babysitter?"

"Is that important?"

"It's convenient," I said. "Because I have questions for both of you." I paused. "I'd like you to come to the station with me."

"I don't think so, LT." Jess stood with her hands tucked into the back pockets of a new-looking pair of jeans. "I haven't had time to arrange that lawyer yet."

"I don't know that you have a choice," I said.

"Cut the bullshit, Chief," Talia said. "Unless you have a warrant or are arresting her, she doesn't have to go anywhere."

"That's not quite true," I said.

They looked at each other. Talia shook her head at Jess. It was barely perceptible. If I hadn't been so on edge, I might have missed it.

"You're involved in the killing of Adam Springbrook," I said, facing Jess.

"I told you he wasn't so dumb," Jess said.

"Could have fooled me," Talia said. "Chief, can I ask you something?"

"Sure," I said.

"Why do you give a shit who killed Adam?"

"It doesn't matter now," Jess said.

"Don't," Talia said.

I turned and saw the pistol. Jess held it in both hands. It was pointed straight at me.

"He knows, Talia. He can't leave."

"Put that down, Jess," I said. "Don't let this go south."

"South?" She laughed. "We're in the fucking Antarctic, LT. Try to keep up."

"I told you that moron Roger would fuck us," Talia said.

"Look what our men left us with," Jess said. "You got a hollow empire on the brink of collapse, and I got a great restaurant that takes two people to run, and as a bonus, I was left with an albatross called Blockhead Roger."

"Can we take a minute to think things through?" I said.

"Take your hand off the gun, LT," Jess said.

I raised my hands.

"With two fingers, take it out and place it on the coffee table."

Talia took three steps back and watched.

"Jess, stay calm," I said. "Things can get away from you quick in a situation like this."

"Abby will be what's getting away from you if you don't do what I'm asking. Now."

That snapped my head back. As asked, I placed my thirty-eight on the table. She had Talia take it, and holding it as if it was a rattlesnake, she placed it behind them next to an elephant statue on the mantle.

"What's Abby got to do with this?" I asked.

"Little Miss Real Estate is what I'd call flight insurance," Talia said. "I wasn't kidding when I said we were leaving."

"Why did you shoot Adam?" I asked Jess. An obvious way out wasn't presenting itself, but the longer I was able to keep this going, the likelier it was that one would materialize. I needed time. Eventually, Gwyneth would come looking. She'd provide a diversion, one way or another.

"I can answer that," Talia said. "He was a heinous reprobate. If you knew who he was, you'd be throwing a parade for us instead of what we have here."

"If he couldn't get the Sea Squall from you, why shoot him?" I asked Jess.

"I should have burned that place to the ground when Frank died and made it look like an accident. We all would have been better off. There's nothing left now anyway."

"Jess," Talia said, looking at the gun. "Go easy."

"Do you know what Adam said to me that night I slapped him?" Jess asked. "The one you were so concerned about?"

I shook my head. My eyes searched for a weapon. I couldn't move on one leg, which wasn't helping my cause. I could only go in one direction, away from her. That wasn't going to get me her gun, and the door was too far.

"He said, 'When Frank dies in a few weeks, you will sell me this restaurant.' I told him that I wouldn't. Then he said, 'I will have you, too, if you know what I mean, and you will enjoy the hell out of it.'"

"That's no reason to shoot him," I said. "If you could kill someone for being an asshole, the streets would be littered with bodies." That was something I learned this week.

"The truth is, I wish I'd shot him," Talia said, gritting her teeth. "The sick, unimaginable things he made me do when I was younger and didn't know better. I'm still not right. But now that he's gone, I'm becoming myself again, bit by bit."

"You sent Adam to me Monday," Jess said. "You can find satisfaction in that, at least."

"Quiet, Jess," Talia said.

"It's hard to believe that Frank and Adam were of the same species," Jess said. "You'll be okay, Talia, once you get to Mexico."

"Once *we* get to Mexico," Talia said.

"That's the plan?" I asked.

"You look surprised," Jess said.

"I am." I was fairly certain a fugitive could be extradited from there, provided they could be found. That probably wasn't something normal people were aware of.

"Are you a misogynist, Chief?" Talia asked.

"Huh?" It wasn't tourist season. Conversation usually didn't go over my head this time of year.

"He doesn't know what that is," Talia said. "Christ.".

"You believe women are inferior," Jess said, holding the pistol steady. "Your ex-wife was a wannabe prom queen, and your ex-girlfriend is a sandwich maker. Not to mention that she's remarrying the only guy in town as off-putting as Roger, though in an entirely different way. It's no wonder Abby Grimes freaked you out. She knew what she wanted, and she knew how to get it."

"I have great respect for women if they're not holding a gun on me." I was desperate for ways to stall. "Is that a Walther PPK?"

"Frank loved him some James Bond. It was his, and, yes, I know how to use it."

"You missed me with a shotgun. What makes you think you can hit me with that?"

"I was trying not to hit Abby, who I thought might be innocent in all this. Though I don't know where I got that idea. What difference would it have made? Right now, you're close enough. As close as Adam was, that's for sure, and I managed to get a slug into him."

"Speaking of Abby, where is she?"

"Wouldn't you like to know?"

"That's why I asked."

"No one likes a wise-ass, Chief," Talia said.

"Let's just say that Abby wasn't too pleased with us and wound up a step ahead of you," Jess said. "She heard something that she shouldn't have. Now she's out of the way."

"You killed her?"

"Look at him, Jess," Talia said. "He's petrified something's happened to her."

"How did you know, LT?" Jess said. "Tell us, and maybe we'll tell you."

"Roger wouldn't have used a gun to get rid of Adam. And he wouldn't have stored it loaded. Someone put a round in it for a purpose, and it wasn't him. He never would have known to leave Adam in Lost Woods to throw suspicion elsewhere. He didn't know Adam or how many people he'd pissed off. There was too much thought involved for him to be behind it."

"You know what's funny?" Jess said. "I asked Adam to wait while I grabbed something in the office. When I came out with the shotgun, I was going to put that slug into a bag of flour, just to get him to piss himself. But that summer night came back to me. I could smell the salt air, heavy like it gets in July. I thought of the Frank I'd visited that afternoon in the hospital, what was left of him, really. How I kept telling him that he'd beat the cancer when every day it ate away at him and brought him closer to death. We both knew. And there was Adam in front of me, smug grin plastered on his face, a composite of every douchebag I'd ever known. I heard again what he'd said as if his words were still echoing after three months. The look on his face when he saw that shotgun, I didn't even need to shoot him. But I did, and I'm glad."

She laughed so hard she bent over. The pistol remained trained on me. Jess straightened up, the smile replaced by a grimace as if it had taken a lot to right herself. She shook her head and spoke: "'Adam,' I said, 'you're going to enjoy the hell out of this,' and I pulled the trigger."

I sighed, waiting for the gun to move. It didn't. Jess looked into my eyes.

"Do you think I'm wrong for killing someone like that, who deserved it?"

"I do."

"You don't. I can see it on your face."

"And you're wrong for doing what you did to Roger. He's going to jail. All he tried to do was follow through on a promise to Frank to look out for you. He didn't know better. He trusted you, and now he's done."

"Fuck him," Jess said. "He's not the only one."

"Put the gun down, Jess. It doesn't have to be like this."

"Give it a rest, LT," Jess said. "There's no more left of me now than there was of Frank when that fucking cancer finally took him."

Her arm shot up, and she lodged the barrel of the Walther under her chin. I lunged for her, pathetically on one leg, and fell short. Talia's scream was lost in the gun's explosion. My ears rang as a red-soaked wave of flesh and bone splattered the curtained picture window behind her. Talia made for the door. One quick look at what was left of Jess—her head like a smashed red pumpkin—was enough to see that first aid would be useless. I scrambled after Talia. She was not a runner like Jess, but she did have two working legs and was attempting to get into her car. She hadn't noticed I'd boxed it in with the Bronco. She was opening the door as I closed in, half-hopping and trying to sprint. My calf finally gave out, popping like a firecracker. My scream was enough to stop her. As she turned, I tackled her on the driveway. I rolled her onto her stomach and handcuffed her. She started sobbing, the arm she'd landed on raw and bleeding. It was hard to tell what blood was hers and what was Jess's. My eyes watered. I didn't know if it was from what I'd seen or that my calf felt like it had been butterflied like a piece of chicken.

I picked up Talia and leaned her against her car, then dragged her to the Bronco. I opened the door and reached for the radio with the hand I didn't have on her bloody throat. I told Gwyneth to get over here and to send for the state police. I turned back to Talia. A reflection off the window behind her revealed blood leaching from a cut on my forehead. I must have hit the pavement, too, taking her down. I didn't feel it. Talia would not stop crying.

"Where's Abby?" I asked.

She looked up at me with red, bleary eyes but didn't speak. It was as if words couldn't work their way out of the shaking and sobbing. Talia had moved close enough that she could've grabbed Jess's arm when she'd brought the gun to her chin. She'd probably been running more from what she'd seen than from any threat that I or the law posed to her.

"I don't know," she stammered, between shudders.

Gwyneth's siren sounded in the distance.

I slapped Talia hard and asked again. I'd never hit a woman like that. I'd never had reason to. Talia choked on her tears. She tried to breathe.

"Don't make me do that again," I said.

"Something about a meat locker," she spat out, continuing to sob. "I didn't go with them."

Gwyneth pulled up, tires squealing, and jumped out of the car. The blues swirled against the bare, skeletal trees.

She stopped short when she saw us. White vapor puffed from her mouth in the cool air. We must have looked like refugees from a horror movie.

"Chief?" she said.

"What did the lab team find at the restaurant?" I asked, not moving. There were walk-in coolers there, two of them. I was hoping Abby had been safely stashed among the produce and steaks.

"Nothing."

"Did they go through the whole place?"

"Top to bottom."

"Including the coolers?"

"Everything," she said, nodding. "What happened?"

"There's a hostage in a meat locker somewhere."

She nodded. "What happened here, I mean?"

"Jess Consentino shot herself."

"And you're holding that woman by the throat because?"

'She's involved."

Gwyneth tilted her head, trying to understand.

"Take her and lock her in your car. And whatever you do, don't follow me inside."

"Why not? What if—"

"Just don't."

I kept my eyes on my shoes and went past the living room to the phone in the kitchen.

CHAPTER FORTY-SEVEN

I called Trout at the Compound.

"You heard from Abby?" I asked.

"I don't know where she is, LT. Not here, not at work, not at home."

"How well did you know Frank Consentino?"

"Some, but not like we went fishing together."

"Do you know if he had a meat locker anywhere?"

"Uh, did you try the Squall? Why don't you just ask Jess?"

"Because she just put a bullet through her head."

"Christ. What the hell is going on? Don't tell me Abby's mixed up in this?"

"She's what's supposed to be in that meat locker."

"Of course she is," he said.

"If you hear from her, contact me first thing."

"Will do."

I called the station. I had Ted bring Roger to the phone. I was glad I'd left him to hold down the fort. Otherwise, I'd have had to take the time to go there and ask in person.

"Roger, this is Chief Nichols. Did Frank Consentino have a meat locker anywhere?"

"Sure, LT, we had a walk-in at the Squall."

"I know that, Roger," I said. "Anywhere else?"

"You know how the river would flow right into the parking lot on storm tides in the winter when we closed down? Sometimes it would be so bad it would come right into the restaurant. So, Frank put in a cooler at the house, and we'd move whatever we had left over there in December after the Christmas season. You know he liked to eat well and—"

"Where in the house, Roger?"

"The cellar."

I hung up on him.

Chapter Forty-Eight

The Consentino house was quiet and still, as I'd left it. Only it was now covered in shadow from the west. I hadn't thought to rifle Jess's pocketbook for keys. I took out my gun, removed a bullet from the cylinder, held onto the barrel, and punched out the window square on the front door closest to the knob. Then I reached through and unlocked it from the inside. Like a common criminal.

I yelled, "Abby," but didn't wait for an answer. I tried to jog through the living room into the kitchen. I started opening doors. I found a bathroom and a closet before reaching the one that led to the basement. The lights worked, a minor miracle. I called for Abby again. On the far wall, a chest freezer sat next to a workbench. Its cord lay unplugged on the concrete floor. If she'd been placed in there, she could have run out of oxygen hours earlier. It was empty. I turned back to the other side of the room. Under the stairs was a metal door and stainless-steel walls the size of a double refrigerator. It was padlocked. I dragged myself across the room as fast as I could. I pounded on the door.

"Abby, are you in there?"

"LT, get me the fuck out," came reverberating through the walls.

"Hold on and step back."

"Step back? It's not the Boston Garden in here."

I considered shooting the lock, but with my luck assumed the bullet would ricochet into my good leg, if not somewhere worse. I went back to the workbench. I found a hatchet a little larger than a hammer.

I swung at the lock. It rang like a cracked bell but didn't open. I could only balance on one leg and hadn't gotten much behind it. I took a deep breath and tried again. Instead of using the blade, I flipped it and wielded it like a sledge on the bracket itself. I had better luck there. It still took a dozen attempts before I could pry the bracket from the cooler. By then, I was ready to use the blade to amputate my calf, which was screaming. I threw down the ax and heaved open the door.

Abby jumped up into my arms, and we fell backward into a stacked set of luggage. We were lucky to land on a rather large and soft Tourister.

"Jesus Christ, LT," she said, clinging to me and pressing her head to my chest. The scent of her hair in my face put the brakes on a heart rate that had been redlined for hours. "It took you twelve swings to break the fucking lock. Didn't you want to get me out of there?"

"I'm having second thoughts now," I said.

She kissed me.

Then she climbed off me. I couldn't move. She shook her head and pushed her hair back. I was still reclined on the suitcase. She took a long look at me. Blood spray coated my uniform. I could only imagine my face.

"What the hell happened to you?" she said, on the verge of breaking down.

"I really fucked up my calf."

"If that's the worst of it, you're doing better than you look."

She held out her hand and pulled me to my feet.

Epilogue

"Y ou should talk to someone," Abby said, having again watched me jerk awake after nodding off. Princess Leia had noticed, too, and had come over to slide her muzzle under my arm. She nosed me until I scratched behind her ears, her favorite.

"I've talked to a lot of people: Pettibone, the state police forensics and shooting teams, three selectmen, four reporters, two news anchors, Trout, and you." I was sunk into the La-Z-Boy, where I had my calf raised with an ice pack strapped to it.

Abby sat unsmiling on the couch. She put her pen down on the spreadsheets in front of her on the coffee table. We'd bunkered in the house for three days. It was doubling as her office and police headquarters.

"Don't play dumb," she said. "You know what I mean. You're not right."

"I'll get past it." Maybe it had been a mistake to tell her that whenever I slept, at some point, I saw Jess Consentino bring that pistol to her throat. But there was no use hiding it. She'd been lying next to me nearly every time I'd woken with a start.

"I've made an appointment with my shrink for Friday. Getting locked in that cooler hasn't done wonders for me. I can get you in if you want. It might do you good to get out of Laurel for a few days, too. We can do this kind of nothing at my place."

"You're actually leaving?"

She laughed.

"I wasn't staying forever, and you know it. But don't change the subject."

"They won't go on forever, either."

"You saw a woman kill herself. Parts of her were stuck to you when you found me. That's no joke."

I shrugged and got up to grab a beer from the kitchen. My limp was more pronounced. That tearing my calf chasing Talia Springbrook was worse than it getting shot went beyond my understanding of anatomy and physiology.

Abby had started serving as my chauffeur minutes after I broke her out, driving me to the station to make sure Talia had been locked up, then back to the Springbrook house, where I met with Pettibone and the state police teams. When we left there, to her surprise, I didn't resist when she declared that we were going to the hospital. The orthopedic surgeon said that trying to sprint with a gunshot-wounded calf muscle had not been the best of ideas. I didn't bother explaining. I'd changed into a clean uniform at the station, so he hadn't gotten the full picture. He didn't need it. Nor did he need to inform me that I wouldn't be doing any of my own recreational running anytime soon. I just hoped the leg healed before I became a completely out-of-shape slob.

According to Abby, the calf wasn't the real problem. For days, as the television had droned in the background, I'd been replaying the events of the week, trying to understand what I could have done differently to prevent things from playing out as they had.

"I wasn't kidding about the psychologist," Abby said. "You don't have to suffer."

"I'll be fine," I said.

"But it's okay for me to see one?"

"You've been through a lot."

"And you haven't?"

"I'm used to it."

"No, you're not. Or you wouldn't be waking up like someone's sticking you with a cattle prod. Why would you want to go through that when you don't have to, when someone can help you see that you're not responsible for what those people did?"

"That's a little deep for me."

"Stop. You don't have to tough things out all the time."

"I can try," I said.

"Christ," she said, shaking her head. "I give up."

"You know I could have left you in that cooler," I said, laughing.

"That would have been another example of you choosing to suffer because you would have missed out on the best sex of your life."

I could feel myself turning crimson.

"Hmmm," she said, noticing. "You do listen to some of what I say."

I nodded. "I do. If you remember, it was me who asked for your help in the first place."

"I'm glad you did," she said.

"So we could get shot at? Or so you could get kidnapped?"

"So we could get together. Which was another thing that you were afraid would turn into some sort of disaster. You've been proven wrong on that count, too."

"I can't walk. You could be scarred for life."

"But together," she said, waving her index finger between us. "We are fine. It's absurd that tragedy accompanies us as it does."

"If we were to have a real relationship one of these days, I don't know if the state could handle the death toll."

"That's some dark humor, LT."

"Evidence that I'm getting better already."

"It's not like I'm never coming back," she said, motioning to the work in front of her.

"There will be plenty of court dates," I said.

"How fortunate," she said. "And I'm not giving up on that property. If she does wind up with the land, Talia's going to have some hefty legal bills. She'll need to turn it over."

"I have a bad feeling about that parcel," I said.

"I thought you didn't believe in such things."

"Things have changed."

She shrugged.

I hadn't imagined that a singular person like Adam Springbrook could have infected an entire town by doing nothing but going about his self-absorbed business. The damage he'd done remained out of sight for a time, like a crack in a foundation. But eventually, it spread deep and wide, and it came down on all of us. No one had seen it coming, least of all me.

"If you'd like to see me on these return trips," she said, coming over and standing in front of me. The smirk she'd been wearing vanished. "I do have one request. And it is non-negotiable."

"I do not want to see your shrink," I said.

"I know that. Listen."

She paused and took a deep breath.

"You need to keep the dog."

"With my job—"

"LT, shut the fuck up about your job. That's what just got you shot and nearly killed. Your job owes you nothing. Princess Leia is great for you. If you haven't noticed, she follows you around the house, keeping an eye on you. Someone's got to look after you. If you want to bring her to work, you have plenty of room in your office for a rug. While she won't call you on bullshit, she will listen. When you wake up like you've been shocked, you can tell her that you're okay. Even if she doesn't believe you—and she won't—she won't argue about it."

"I don't know," I said. I did like the pup. Roger had trained her well. She'd be able to run with me when I could start doing that again. My only exercise in the last few days had been throwing a tennis ball across the lawn for her to fetch.

"Look," Abby said. "I've been mature about this. I haven't mentioned how Princess Leia is smarter than your old girlfriend. She wouldn't live with that jackass, Derek."

"That's big of you," I said.

"You deserve some companionship, even if it's only a pointer." Abby sat down on the arm of my chair and wrapped herself around me. The flowery scent of her hair would stay with me. "It will be good for you."

"Okay," I said, "I'll keep the dog."

"See," Abby said, smiling again. "You're growing. There may be hope for you yet."

Acknowledgements

I have much gratitude for my wife Kim, daughter Sydney, and son Aaron for their understanding and unlimited patience with me, as well as their continued support. Special thanks go out to my lifelong friend Rob O'Regan, who did some heavy lifting to help me get the original manuscript in shape. I'm also grateful for the time invested by my initial readers Dan Healy and Ray Bartlett. Their feedback is always valuable. I'd also like to thank my former bandmate and marketing guru, Doug Quintal, for his guidance.

THE WRITER IN RUINS NEWSLETTER

Scan below to sign up for Albert Waitt's "Writer in Ruins Newsletter." You'll receive book release and event information; notices for special offers and discounts; bonus content; answers to reader questions; movie, television, and book recommendations; and the occasional cocktail recipe. All usually delivered with humor.

About the Author

Albert Waitt is the author of *Springbrookville, Flood Tide, The Ruins of Woodman's Village*, and *Summer to Fall*. *Springbrookville*, published by Level Best Books in April of 2025, is the third book in a series featuring Laurel, Maine police chief, LT Nichols. Waitt's short fiction has appeared in *The Literary Review, Third Coast, The Beloit Fiction Journal, Words and Images, Stymie: A journal of sport and literature*, and other publications.Waitt is a graduate of Bates College and the Creative Writing Program at Boston University. Experiences ranging from tending bar, teaching creative writing, playing guitar for the Syphlloids, and frying clams can be found bleeding through his work.

AUTHOR WEBSITE:
  Albertwaitt.com

SOCIAL MEDIA HANDLES:
  FaceBook:@Albert Waitt
  Twitter:@albertwaitt
  Instagram:@albertwaitt

Also by Albert Waitt

The Ruins of Woodman's Village

The *Maine Sunday Telegram* on *The Ruins of Woodman's Village*: "Maine writer Waitt reveals a great talent for crafting a provocative, compelling mystery in "The Ruins of Woodman's Village." He exhibits masterful confidence in pacing, taking time to lay out all the pieces, then deeply setting the hook to reel in the ending without a snag. It is a story with social substance, making it all the more engaging."

Flood Tide

The *Kennebec Journal* on *Flood Tide*: "Waitt has a good thing going here—a solid mystery, wholly believable characters, a complex, well-drawn plot, and a 1988 mystery that won't sound like fiction at all."

Summer to Fall

"In this engaging and fulfilling novel, Albert Waitt demonstrates deep empathy for characters we glimpse all too rarely in contemporary fiction: tough guys and girls who are complex in their desires and dreams. We can't help but identify and root for them."—Christopher Castellani, author of *The Saint of Lost Things* and *Leading Men*

www.ingramcontent.com/pod-product-compliance
Lightning Source LLC
Chambersburg PA
CBHW020421110726
47899CB00006B/2079